SWEET TEA & SPELLS

A Southern Charms Cozy Mystery

BELLA FALLS

Evermore Press

Also by Bella Falls

A Southern Charms Cozy Mystery Series

Moonshine & Magic: Book 1

Fried Chicken & Fangs: Book 2

Sweet Tea & Spells: Book 3

Lemonade & Love Potions (a short formerly in the Hexes & Ohs Anthology)

For a FREE exclusive copy of the prequel Chess Pie & Choices, sign up for my newsletter!

https://dl.bookfunnel.com/opbg5ghpyb

Share recipes, talk about Southern Charms and all things cozy mysteries, and connect with me by joining my reader group Southern Charms Cozy Companions!

https://www.facebook.com/groups/southerncharmscozycompanions

CONTENTS

For my mom.

Preface

When I originally wrote *Moonshine & Magic*, I knew Charli's backstory of what made her leave Honeysuckle Hollow. It occurred to me that others might like knowing what spurred her to leave such a wonderful town, so I wrote the prequel *Chess Pie & Choices*. It's available for free if you sign up for my newsletter. https://dl.bookfunnel.com/opbg5ghpyb

You don't have to read the prequel, but doing so will enhance your enjoyment of *Sweet Tea & Spells: Book 3*.

Chapter One

Sweat beaded on my temples and upper lip. I dashed the back of my hand under my nose, wiping away the fine mustache of moisture with guarded embarrassment. Behind the smiles of the *Hey, how're you doin's* and polite nods accompanied by the *You look so nice today, darlin's*, every female tongue in Honeysuckle wagged with my name.

Delicately gloved hands holding tall glasses of sweet tea or waving decorated paper fans failed to hide their interest, and curious eyes followed me like I had a unicorn's horn growing out of the middle of my forehead. To distract myself, I tried to guess which one of the impeccably dressed ladies would stop killing me with Southern kindness and finally ask the burning question on everybody's mind, including mine: *What in the Sam Hill was I doin' attending the bridal shower for the girl about to marry my ex-fiancé?*

Clarice Hawthorne had gone above and beyond her normal natural snobbiness. An enormous white canopy sat in the family's considerable backyard. Held up by some powerful magic, the large structure cooled and shaded everyone from the day's humidity since my almost mother-in-law had paid extra for a heavy-duty air conditioning enchantment.

Everything underneath the tent, from the sprigs of orchids mixed with twinkling fairy lights to the wooden floor beneath our feet, felt over the top and out of place in our tiny town. The whole set up was a preview for the actual wedding and reception right around the corner...something I definitely would *not* be attending.

I did my absolute best to stay out of the way, sipping on a perspiring glass of iced tea and watching. Despite my attempts at hiding, the fates decided to have a little fun, and the crowd parted at just the right moment. Aunt Nora caught me staring as she stood poised next to Clarice, regal as only the mother-of-the-bride could. She shot an icy sneer in my direction and grabbed Clementine by the arm, dragging her daughter to stand next to her like a prize that would buy her way to the very top of the social heap.

My aunt would blow a gasket if she knew that not that long ago, Tucker had made one last declaration of love to me. Of course, at the time, I was dying from a death curse brought on by the circumstances of her trust in a nefarious outsider. Maybe sharing that little nugget of truth about her future son-in-law might wipe that smug smile off her face?

Lavender and Lily spotted me from across the room. Excusing themselves from their current conversation, they weaved through the throng to join me.

Lily scoffed and nodded at my aunt. "She really is a piece of work, isn't she? You know, if Nora were to stop in our flower shop, I'd make her up a beautiful bouquet of yellow carnations, a mix of pink and white petunias, some orange lilies, and some deep purple aconite." The ice cubes tinkled in her glass as she sipped with wicked satisfaction.

Her cousin gasped. "Why, Lily Rose Blackwood, Grandma would fire you on the spot!"

"Why?" I asked. "I suppose those flowers have specific meanings?"

Lavender narrowed her eyes at her cousin, giving her a slight pinch of admonishment on the arm. "Of course. Most flowers and plants do. Yellow carnations symbolize disdain or contempt for the person."

I shrugged. "Sounds about right."

My sarcasm earned my own sharp tweak of the skin from my friend. "Petunias mean anger or resentment," Lavender continued. "Orange lilies can symbolize hatred, and aconite... well, that's just deadly. The purple variety also goes by *Monkshead*, and once was used to poison arrows and spears."

"At least I didn't say oleander," grumbled Lily. "The sap from the stem can be lethal."

I shook my head with widened eyes. "I don't want to kill my aunt."

Lily's left eyebrow crooked up. "So maybe just the carnations and petunias?"

How did I feel about my aunt? Mom had always taught me that the word *hate* was too strong to use on anybody. That it was our duty in life to find the good in everyone, even if the goodness in a person was as small as a speck of fairy dust. About the only nice thing I knew about Aunt Nora was that my mom loved her despite her meanness. And for that, I could spare her a deadly bouquet.

I kissed the cousins on their cheeks. "I love you both for trying to cheer me up, girls."

Lavender stared at the air around me, studying my aura. "Honestly, I can't believe you came today. I think it's really brave of you."

"Or stupid," I snorted. "With Nana off in Charleston for the big meeting thing and TJ feeling a little conspicuous while she's still cookin' Charli Junior in her growing pregnant belly, I was the only Goodwin woman left to represent."

My sensitive friend squeezed my hand. "At least there's not half as big of a crowd as there was for the engagement party. I think you made the right choice not to go."

When I'd originally received the invitation, I thought I might go out of pure spite. Also, I'd have the cover of a date. At the time, I'd had at least two possibilities to choose from to escort me to the dreaded event. Dash would have been a good way to rebel against the Hawthornes and their haughty expectations. They truly distrusted the wolf shifter. But he'd left town on his motorcycle a little over two months ago, and I hadn't heard anything from him since.

Mason would have been the safest pick, but one that came with a couple of minefields around him. Ever since meeting him, our relationship had been very push, pull, and then push away. I loved working cases with him, and he encouraged me to be my best with my strange magical talents. Something about him drew me to him like a magnet, and there had been brief moments of promise. But he always found a reason to throw up a big wall between us.

His latest absence was cloaked in secrecy. Even my own brother and fellow warden couldn't tell me where Mason had run off to. Only Sheriff Big Willie West had the inside scoop, and that sasquatch was keeping his hairy lips tight for once.

Alison Kate bounded toward us, towing a surprised server with her. "Y'all, have you tried the food? These barbecue thingies are incredible." She swiped one off the silver platter and popped it in her mouth.

I shushed her obscene noises she made while chewing. "You better not let Ms. Patty Lou hear you. I feel like it's kind of a betrayal to her husband Steve and the Harvest Moon Cafe." Looking down at the tempting bite, I ignored the hungry rumble of my stomach. "What exactly is it?"

The server brightened at my interest. "This is Duke's signature barbecue bite with shredded pork barbecue, chopped pickled okra and red onion topped with coleslaw in a mini cornbread cup."

Before I could protest again, Lily and Lavender each took a napkin and one of the proffered bites. Alison Kate nabbed one more and flashed her gracious smile at the nervous waiter, letting him go to serve others.

"Here." She held out the small piece of food to me. When I refused, she rolled her eyes. "You won't be doing anything criminal. We all knew that Clarice Hawthorne wasn't going to use any of the services here in Honeysuckle. It's not like my feelings are hurt that they chose someone else to make the cakes for all the wedding events."

My friend did her best to make me believe her, but I knew how sensitive she'd been back when I'd told her that the cake for my almost-engagement party wouldn't be made at Sweet Tooths. Glancing around the groups of people milling about, I spotted Ms. Patty Lou talking up a storm with some of the regulars from the store she used to co-own with my mother. She enjoyed her time with a smile on her face, eating the offered food and asking for more.

My stomach rejoiced. If Ms. Patty wasn't complaining, then I didn't need to starve in protest. "Fine," I conceded, and ate the bite of food. The naughty noises I made in response to the delicious explosion of flavors earned me snickers and a couple of elbows in my ribs. "It's like a tiny barbecue sandwich. But one sprinkled in rainbows and eaten while riding on the back of a unicorn."

"Told ya," bragged Alison Kate. She looked around for another server. "I wish Lee were here."

Hooking my arm around her shoulder, I gave her a light

squeeze. "He's only been gone a few days. Are you missing your Snookie Wookums or Cuddly Wuddly Wigglemunch or whatever you like to call him?"

She pushed me off her. "We've never used the term Wigglemunch before."

"You sure?" I asked. "I'll admit, the sweeter the nicknames get, the more we tune you both out, Ali Kat."

Wiggling her eyebrows, she beamed. "Exactly."

"Speaking of Lee," I leaned in closer to her and lowered my voice. "I don't suppose he's told you whether he's heard anything from you-know-who?" My heart rate kicked up another notch despite my unwillingness to say his name.

"No, he's heard nothing from Dash, and he's not happy about it." Alison Kate flagged down a nearby server and took two of what they had to comfort her. "There are deals being made for his spell phones, and not having his business partner there is making things difficult for Lee. He may have to sign things and then be honorable in bringing Dash back in financially."

The way she said the wolf shifter's name matched my own annoyance with him. I snagged another finger food off the platter of a nearby waiter before she sped away. "I can't lie, I'm a bit worried about him."

Alison Kate licked her fingers clean. "Oh, Lee has Ben with him to make sure he gets the best deal possible."

"Not Lee. Dash." Saying the shifter's name out loud stirred up more emotions I couldn't deal with. To shove them down, I concentrated on the appetizer. "What's so special about a deviled egg?" The spicy tang of it caught me off guard.

Ever the lover of food, Alison Kate explained. "If I had to guess, the chef crisped up some chorizo sausage. Maybe even used some of the oil to mix with the yolk instead of just mayonnaise to make it creamy and seasoned."

I finished off the egg, carefully considering its flavorful merits. "It's good, but I still prefer the good ol'-fashioned ones Nana makes. If you get too fancy, then I think it changes things too much. I say simplicity beats out overdone every time." My personal view had been a bone of contention that wedged the distance between me and Tucker's family, which in the end couldn't be bridged.

While licking my fingers clean, I spotted Blythe standing with Lady Eveline. A tiny pang sparked in my chest. Ever since that night with Damien, my best friend had become increasingly distant from me and our group in general. Catching her eye, I smiled and waved at her. She replied with a polite nod and leaned in to say something to her constant vampire companion. Anger and disappointment squeezed my chest.

My other friends circled around me. Alison Kate offered me a second deviled egg in comfort. "I'm sorry."

I didn't have words to say. And if I found any, they wouldn't be of the nice variety.

"We have to give her more time," Lavender said, leaning her head on my shoulder. "She went through a lot."

"So did I," I countered.

Lily furrowed her brow. "But what she went through...I don't know, Charli. I think she'll come around, and then we'll get back to normal again. You know things were tougher than we thought when she quit her job at the cafe."

I sighed. "I know." I just missed the girl who stood by me through everything. I didn't understand the one who avoided me all together.

We fell silent, unable to come up with any words of explanation or comfort. My eyes scanned the tent for the quickest way out. I'd made an appearance and been seen. Perhaps slipping away undetected would be far better than waiting until the end when I'd have to actually speak to Aunt Nora.

"Well, well, my eyes must be sore from the beautiful sight in front of them," a deep voice with a strong Southern accent rumbled behind us.

All four of us turned our attention to a man wearing a white chef's coat sauntering over. He stopped and spoke to a couple of the older women, saying something in a low voice and winking.

His white teeth about blinded me when he flashed his cocky grin. "Ladies, I trust you are enjoying the event and having a piece of me inside of you."

It took a considerable amount of effort to keep my upper lip from curling in disgust. "I beg your pardon?"

He chose to sidle up beside me, slipping his arm around my waist. "My food. I hope you've been eating my food and findin' it to your liking." The man pointed at the logo embroidered on his pristine jacket that read *Duke's Delicious Dishes*. "I'm Duke, and I assure you that everything about me is delicious."

Chills slithered down my back, and I attempted to take a step away from him. He tightened his grip and pulled me closer.

Not wanting to make a scene or draw more unwanted attention to myself, I gritted my teeth and forced the closest thing to a smile I could muster. "The few things we've had have been good," I admitted.

Duke pressed his hip against mine. "Today's just the foreplay. The wedding reception will be even more explosive."

With my fingers, I tore his away from my body, bending them in my grasp until they jammed and he hissed in pain. "Thank you, but I'm pretty sure we've had enough."

Instead of getting the clue and walking away, his eyes glinted with determination. "I like a challenge. I'll make sure to do my best to convince you that once you sample what Duke has to offer, you'll be forever changed."

Clarice tapped a piece of silverware against her crystal glass with light dings. "Ladies, if I may have your attention."

"Oh, thank goodness," breathed out Lily.

Duke leaned into me and whispered in my ear, "That's my cue to take my leave, but I hope to be seein' you sometime soon, Charli." He patted my behind and walked to the center of the room to join Clarice.

My fingers curled into fists, and I debated how much

trouble a little retribution might get me into. The tsk of a tiny tongue interrupted my thoughts of revenge.

"Charli Goodwin, you are a horrible tease. First the wolf shifter, then the detective, and now the chef?" Sassy flicked her green hair off her shoulders. "Is every single man within a hundred mile radius supposed to belong to you?"

I wiped a little of her dust out of my eyes. "I don't have a clue what you're talkin' about, Sass. But you clearly weren't payin' close attention."

The annoying fairy stuck her nose in the air. "Just leave some of the men to the rest of us girls, won't you?" In a jealous huff, she zipped off to no doubt gossip about me to a willing ear.

Between Sassy with her smart mouth and an arrogant chef who dared to blow a kiss at me when he caught me scowling, I couldn't decide who annoyed me more. My fingers tingled to take care of those who were just beggin' for a hexin'.

Chapter Two

Duke enjoyed my disgusted stare and waved after he blew the kiss. I shuddered and choked on my repulsion. "I feel like I need to take ten showers. And even that might not be enough."

Alison Kate joined me in my contempt. "He came into Sweet Tooths earlier this week with another woman, asking us all kinds of questions about our recipes. Even during that short time, he gave me the creeps."

Clarice spoke up so everyone could hear her, interrupting our discussion. "I would like to thank you all for comin' today to celebrate our dear Clementine's upcoming nuptials to my son, Tucker."

Polite clapping filled the air, and my cousin blushed. Her mother pushed her forward to accept all the attention.

Mrs. Hawthorne took Clementine by the arm and

presented her to the attentive crowd. "We are honored that through our children's union, two of Honeysuckle's founding families will be joined forever, creating a powerful bond. My son's choice in the *right* partner for his life will secure a better future for our town." While her gaze focused on those around her, the words Clarice chose hit their intended target. The number of eyes that turned in my direction confirmed her aim.

My cheeks blazed hot as a poker in a fire. The woman never let go of her anger and frustration that I turned down her precious prince. After all, Tucker had lowered himself to want to marry me in the first place. It didn't take a psychic to know that Clarice and Aunt Nora shared the same disdain for me and belief that my status as a Goodwin was shaky at best.

"Poor Clementine," lamented Alison Kate.

My cousin looked down at the ground, her own cheeks stained pink with embarrassment. She might not have been the intended mark, but she sure was a victim of Clarice's point.

I pushed a stray strand of hair out of my face. "I guess it doesn't feel great to have your upcoming marriage treated like a business transaction."

My sympathy stretched only so far. The girl knew what she was doing. If Clementine had wanted to leave, she'd had multiple chances, yet she stayed standing in silent suffering despite being a pawn in whatever game the two mothers played.

Unaware or uncaring, Clarice continued to hold court.

"Today would not be possible without the wonderful catering from a new friend of my husband's. Duke Aikens, come join us, please."

The smarmy chef stepped into the limelight of attention, smiling and winking. "Thank you, Mrs. Hawthorne, for the opportunity to share in this event." He snaked a hand around Clementine's waist. "It will be an honor to be a part of this beautiful bride's special day."

I shuddered for my cousin, knowing how it felt to have Duke so close. The chef waited for Clarice to offer more words of praise for her son and the upcoming wedding. When she and Clementine's mother became engrossed in the talk about the future and the attention of the room, he pulled my cousin closer and whispered something into her ear. When she tried to pull back, he hugged her tighter.

I'd never been a huge fan of my cousin, but I couldn't stand by and let that man say something only she could hear that made her flush deep red from her collarbone to her forehead. Because Clarice referenced her throughout her speech, Clementine was stuck in her predicament until her mother remembered she was the focus of the entire event and took my cousin's hand to pull her out of the chef's grasp and pose for a few photos.

Duke stared at Clementine for an extra moment, and broke away with a wave to everyone else. He left the tent, but my cousin's clear discomfort remained. When the two mothers thanked everyone for coming and invited them to stay for the cake, Clementine excused herself and scurried away.

"I'll be right back." Without waiting for a response from my friends, I found a loose flap on the side of the tent. Ducking out, I walked toward the Hawthorne house, trying to spot my cousin.

Clementine scampered away from the tent, and I followed behind her to the side door of the Hawthorne house, avoiding the chaotic entrance and exit of the waiters at the back. She rushed up the stairs before I could catch her, and I took the first couple of steps to follow.

Now that I was inside the house, I didn't have a plan for what came next. Entering further into the domicile of my ex-fiancé's family made me uneasy. Once Clarice or Aunt Nora finally became aware of Clementine's absence and came looking for her, they might trap me in a small area where they could attack me without repercussions. I felt sorry for my cousin, but I didn't care so much that I was willing to risk my own safety and sanity. Reversing my position, I decided to stay downstairs in the parlor to wait to check on her.

A crash followed by loud yelling echoed down the hallway from the kitchen. The sound of Duke's displeasure filled the air. Curiosity won out over my sympathy, and I tiptoed toward the noise to listen in.

Duke confronted a woman dressed in a chef's jacket covered in stains. "What did I tell you about messing stuff up today?" he shouted.

The target for his venom cringed. "That wasn't my fault.

The server dropped the tray when you barged into the kitchen," she defended.

He tightened his grip on her. "Shelby, I hope you're not trying to shift the blame of what goes on in that kitchen on me?"

"No, Duke. I—"

"Because nothing goes on around here that ain't in my best interest. That waiter could have gotten pizza all over my jacket." He wiped his hands down his pristine coat, examining it.

Shelby glanced at the stains covering hers. "It's not pizza. They're tomato tartlets, mini versions of the regional take on tomato pie."

How did the supposed chef misidentify one of his delicious dishes? I loved tomato pie, but it didn't take a genius to know that it looked nothing like a pizza.

The female cook held up her hand to stop Duke from chastising her more. She helped a server place a bunch of food on a platter, paying attention to each piece and finishing them off with a spoonful of something green.

With serious intent, she explained the dish to the waiter. "These are Rockabilly Oysters, my take on Oysters Rockefeller. They've got a celery root béchamel, pickled ham hock meat, and braised collards on them."

Duke checked out the second batch of oysters and lifted it to his nose to sniff it. "Don't you mean *my* take? You seem to think that you're in charge here and forget that it's my name on the catering service."

Shelby ignored the man's ego and plated more food. Insulted at her hard working attitude and her lack of response, he batted a poor pixie waiting for the next serving tray out of his way and leaned on the counter next to her.

Crowding her space, he held her wrist in his. "Did you hear me? I don't think you did."

Shelby winced, dropping the spoon she held. "I heard you," she whispered, her eyes darting around to see who watched her humiliation.

"Then what are you supposed to say when I allow you to work in my kitchen?" Duke pressed.

The girl mumbled something and then covered a moan of pain while glancing at her wrist. "Yes, chef," she replied with a shaky voice.

Duke let her go, and she cradled her hand. "That's better. I'm really disappointed in you, Shelby. You need to make sure you keep me happy because when I am, then you get to do what you love and you don't get hurt. It's a simple concept."

Anger rose in my chest at his treatment of the girl. If it were me, I'd dump the nearest pot of boiling hot food over his head and quit. Nobody deserved the abuse he gave her.

Without looking up at him, Shelby continued working. She whispered instructions to the next server instead of giving them with authority.

Duke backed off a step to let her finish the job, but he refused to shut up. "You know what keeps me happy? Food that makes the client want more. I don't care how you make it or what goes into it. It just has to be good enough for it to have my stamp and name on it."

"Yes, chef," mumbled Shelby.

Duke snagged food off the middle of a serving dish, messing up its presentation so that Shelby had to fix it. "It's too bad your sister doesn't have your talents in the kitchen. She knows how to keep me satisfied." He sneered and popped the bite in his mouth.

Shelby glanced up at him. "Half-sister."

Duke scoffed. "The better half. At least she doesn't waste her considerable talents and provides me with the juicy stuff. All you bring to the table is legitimacy. And I find that less and less necessary the more treasures your sister gathers."

With a couple of elaborate flourishes of his hands, a black notebook appeared out of nowhere, and he gripped it in his fingers. Opening it, he flipped the pages until he found what he wanted. "Look at everything your sister's given me." He shoved the book in Shelby's face. "She's worth double to me, and yet I'm stuck with you. Can't you for once just do what is expected and get it right?"

Shelby hung her head in frustration. "Yes, Duke."

The young woman gripped the handle of the knife she held a little tighter and my stomach clenched. But I took no action to stop what I thought might be coming.

Closing her eyes, Shelby pulled her arm back, loading it to spring. With a grunt, she thrust the pointed end at Duke's stomach, but he knocked the knife out of her hand before it touched him with a cruel snicker.

"I don't have time for one of your tantrums, Shel. Even if you had succeeded in cutting me, you know the consequences wouldn't be what you wanted anyway." He caught her by the throat and slammed her against the nearby wall. "You are mine, and there is nothing in this world that will change it except my death, and that won't be happening any time soon with all the protection I have."

Shelby clutched at his hands, trying to breathe. I prepped a spell to help her, but he let go first. The young woman clutched at her reddened skin, coughing and catching her breath.

Duke waved the black book in front of her face and chuckled. "But I do like it when you try. It means that I have more to do to kill your spirit, and you know how much I enjoy a challenge." With a wave of his hands, the notebook disappeared. "It should be time for the cake soon. Is it prepared?"

Shelby nodded. "It's ready, but I still don't think it's a good idea." She pulled a piece of paper out of her pocket.

Duke snatched it from her hands and read it over. "We just went over this. Your job isn't to think. Your job is to do what I say, and I'm telling you to make sure that cake is ready and then bring it to the tent. Wait until I'm there so that I can take the credit."

The young woman frowned but nodded in acceptance. She bent down to pick the knife off the floor. Duke sneered behind her back and lifted his foot as if to kick her, but thought better of it at the last second.

When she stood, he grabbed her chin, squeezing her cheeks hard. "And Shelby?" He leaned his face into hers. "The spell better work right or you will receive the consequences I deem necessary tonight. Got that?"

He didn't wait for her reply, and exited through the kitchen, barely missing another collision with a server and smacking another poor unsuspecting pixie out of his way.

Dainty footsteps approached from behind me. "Cousin Charlotte? What are you doing here?" Clementine asked.

Caught in the act of eavesdropping, I smoothed out my dress and shifted on my feet. "I came to check on you, Clem. I wanted to make sure you were okay after Clarice's speech." I didn't add on the extra horror of her dealing with Duke as well.

My cousin cocked her head to the side in surprise, her eyes widening. "I...that's so..." She took a deep breath and regained her composure. Taking on an almost perfect imitation of my aunt, she lifted her nose in the air. "I am perfectly fine, thank you. We should both be getting back to the party."

She made her way to the side door. Before she cleared the frame, she paused and turned her head to the side. "Thanks, Charli," she called out and disappeared.

To anyone who didn't know our family dynamics, they would have registered a polite interaction. But Clementine calling me by my nickname meant more, and I was glad I had followed my instincts to check on her.

With Duke gone, Shelby's voice rang clear and true in the

kitchen. She barked out orders like a good leader, and prepared her team to get the cake ready for the grand presentation. Maybe I could talk to the woman later and commiserate. Then again, she might not be pleased to know someone else had witnessed the humiliating altercation.

I hustled back to the tent, and snuck through the side flap to rejoin my friends. Although they gave me the third degree over my absence, I dodged their questions about where I'd been, keeping my moment with Clementine between us cousins. With the commotion of the arrival of the day's special cake, I held onto the rest of the information about the fake chef for gossip fodder after the event.

Duke allowed the servers to set up the cake and pulled out the piece of paper he'd snatched from Shelby from his pocket. He addressed the waiting crowd with a toothy smile. "And for the finale, my team and I bring you a masterpiece fit for a princess's celebration. Our confection for the day is a three-tiered cake of vanilla with honeysuckle buttercream icing."

Alison Kate stiffened next to me. "Those are flavors that I put together for my cupcakes."

"It could be just a coincidence, Ali Kat." I grasped my friend's hand.

She shook her head. "No, I don't think so. He raved about the frosting and made me identify the flavors in front of the woman he was with. I got the feeling that she was the one who understood baking. Not him."

My friend's observation confirmed my suspicions from the conversation I'd overheard. While Duke took credit for the food, he didn't put in the work for it. For all I knew, he couldn't, relying solely on others. A man like that deserved to have his plans thwarted.

Duke held up his hands to quiet the crowd. "And now, here's a little something extra from Duke's Delicious Dishes." He made dramatic gestures with his fingers over the cake, and the surface came to life with unusual motion.

"Oh, no," exclaimed Alison Kate. "He wouldn't."

With a grin, Duke spoke the words of intent he read from the paper. "May your love take flight with wings."

Tiny frosted wings exploded off of the cake and fluttered around the room in pale pastels, lighting on people like butterflies. Much like my devastated friend's flying frosting spell she used on her own cupcakes.

A few eyes turned in Alison Kate's direction. A gentle murmur rustled across the room. Duke stood baffled, unsure why his trick didn't earn him loud applause.

Anger for the betrayal of my friend, for the man's ill-treatment of women, and for the look on his face boiled inside me. The man earned the hex coming his way, and I had no doubt he deserved more.

Lavender held me back by my shoulders. "Charli, no."

I yanked out of my friend's grasp and raised my hand at the ready. *"For the man who stands in the center of the room, hex his hiney with a—"*

Before I could finish, the beautiful cake and all of the flying frosting exploded into a million pieces.

Chapter Three

Aunt Nora paced in front of me in the parlor. "She did it. I know it was her," she accused.

The stiff settee underneath my accused behind creaked. I opened my mouth to protest, but my aunt cut me off.

"She's always had it out to embarrass our family. It's not enough that she has her weird magic and flaunts it all over town. Now she has to ruin my darling Clementine's bridal shower by blowing up the cake. It's too much." Aunt Nora waved a lace handkerchief in front of her.

Clarice tried to console the hysterical woman. "Now, now, Leonora. Charlotte is a bit unconventional, I'll grant you. But she can't think that disrupting a wedding event for our children would bring her anything but scorn." Tucker's mother patted my aunt on the shoulder.

"I love it when you two talk like I'm not in the room." My comment earned me icy glares, and the two women consoled each other with murmurs, no doubt planning my ultimate demise.

Big Willie arrived and crashed his way into the house. "Here now, what's this I heard about an exploding cake? It better not be one of those spell pranks that's happening all over Honeysuckle." He took off his hat and scratched his shaggy head. "Some kid blasted me with a humid hair hex, and, dagnabbit, I looked like a hairy pom pom for a whole day."

Aunt Nora dragged him further into the room. She held him by his arm and pointed a finger at me. "Willie, I want you to arrest her."

My eyes widened. "Arrest? All that happened was a little bit of cake got on those nearest to the incident. I hardly think frosting stains are a reason to incarcerate someone. Besides, if you let me talk, I could tell you that I. Didn't. Do. It."

My aunt narrowed her eyes at me. "Is there anyone else in attendance at the shower who would have wanted to ruin the day other than you?" She didn't wait for me to answer. "Exactly. Arrest her," she demanded with an added petulant stomp of her foot.

Duke entered from the hallway and stood with my upset kin. "I don't know if the law needs to be brought into it, but a measure of compensation wouldn't go amiss. Maybe y'all can put your heads together and come up with a figure that would appease the two of you," he indicated at Aunt Nora and

Clarice, "and I'm sure that Charli and I can come up with the way that she can pay me back." He raised his eyebrow at me and licked his lips.

"I changed my mind," I said. "You can arrest me, Big Willie."

"That's Sheriff to you," the Sasquatch replied. "And I'm not doing nothin' till someone tells me what in the unicorn horn has gone on."

All three of us women jumped in at the same time, giving our own accounts of the entire event. Clementine stood to the side with her hands crossed, looking between her mother and her future mother-in-law without saying a word. Once in a while, her gaze flitted to me, but she kept her mouth sealed tight.

Duke kept a watchful eye on me while the two older women clucked in the sheriff's face. If I could flip him off and get away with it, I would. But I didn't think I needed to escalate the situation.

Big Willie waived his hairy hands and arms in front of him. "Now, wait a hot minute. If I'm understanding correctly, once the cake was brought to the tent and the chef presented it to you, it just exploded? I can understand why that would be disturbing, but unless you've got proof, I don't see how Miss Charli is involved."

I reiterated my innocence, but kept my lingering doubt to myself. Last I remembered, I was getting ready to blast Duke with a hex, but never finished my intent. And my anger was directed at him, not the cake. However, not one ounce of power had sparked inside of me when the cake went boom. Even after my confrontation with Damien where I absorbed some of the founders' tree magic, the little extra that stayed within me didn't act on its own or on a whim. Did it?

I examined my hands, flipping them over and wondering if my magic did have a mind of its own. If it did, it missed its target. Also, Duke would be cussin' up a storm because I still wanted to hex his haughty hiney. Yet he stood there, enjoying the drama and stirring the pot, unaffected and unhexed.

Shelby shuffled into the parlor unnoticed and tapped Clarice on the shoulder. "I'm sorry, ma'am. But I think I know what may have caused the trouble."

"Charlotte did," spit Aunt Nora. "Wherever there's trouble, there she is." She looked down her narrow nose at me.

Duke uncrossed his arms and frowned. "Shelby, now's not the time."

The young woman shook her head once at him and stood her ground. "You see, we visited the bakery you have here in town earlier this week when we came to prepare for today. They had the most interesting baked goods, but I was really fascinated by their cupcakes. I'm afraid that we may have taken a little too much inspiration from them, and perhaps someone associated with the bakery took issue with that." She shot a meaningful glance in Duke's direction.

The supposed chef stuttered in shock and swallowed hard. He cleared his throat and ran his fingers through his hair, regaining his composure. "It's not uncommon for chefs to find inspiration in many places. I think Shelby overstates that we took our cue from the quaint bakery you have here in town."

"There is nothing quaint about Sweet Tooths," I protested. "It rocks. And you might get away with your explanation if you were talking solely about flavors. But everyone in town knows about my friend's amazing talents and her frosting spells, especially for the popular butterfly cupcakes she sells out of every time she makes them," I accused.

The corner of Duke's mouth crooked up. "Sounds to me like you're suggesting that I copied her. Pretty strong words unless you have proof."

"In this room, it seems you don't need proof in order to try and get someone arrested for something they didn't do." I stood up from the settee and faced off with Duke.

Shelby raised her hand. "I-I think this is all my fault. I tried to warn him that it wasn't a good idea, but I made the cake and did my best to enchant the frosting."

Duke cut her off. "Shelby, you get back to the kitchen and let me handle this."

"Why don't you let the girl speak?" I asked with a raised voice.

"All of this it is irrelevant," Aunt Nora sputtered.

Clementine uttered something so low that I couldn't understand her. "What did you say, Clem?"

Her mother jumped to respond first. "She has nothing to say to *you*."

Clementine blinked and curled her fingers into fists.

"Mother, I said that I didn't think Charli had anything to do with it." She held her ground for less than a minute before her mother's withering glare wilted her.

The room erupted. Clarice talked to Big Willie, and Aunt Nora went to her daughter to fuss at her. Duke held Shelby by her wrists, whispering something in her ear that made the poor girl tremble. I didn't know which fire to put out first.

Fed up, I eyed the side door and wondered if they would come after me if I left now. The sight of Alison Kate entering the chaotic scene surprised me. My friend kept her eyes on the floor until she reached the middle of the room.

"Excuse me," she uttered in a low voice.

Everyone ignored her, locked in their own verbal battles.

I approached my friend. "Ali Kat, what are you doing here?"

"I can't let you get in trouble for what happened. Especially since you didn't do anything," she replied.

I furrowed my brow. "I'm pretty sure I didn't. I mean, things have been a little different for me after that one night with Damien. But nothing out of control has happened." Okay, a few glasses had shattered in the first days after the incident. But that hadn't occurred in a while.

Alison Kate took my hand in hers and squeezed. "But I know your aunt. And if Big Willie's here, then you must be in trouble."

I shrugged. "What's new? Still, I can't completely vouch that I didn't do it. I definitely wanted to blow something up."

I glared over my friend's shoulder at Duke, who still berated Shelby.

"I'll take care of this." Alison Kate cleared her throat and shouted to garner everyone's attention.

Clarice turned to address my friend. "Is there something the matter, dear?"

Alison Kate took a deep breath. "I first wanted to say how sorry I am. I didn't mean to ruin the end of your bridal shower. I'm especially sorry to you, Clementine." She gestured at my cousin who nodded once.

"What are you apologizing for?" asked Big Willie.

Blowing out a breath, Alison Kate steadied herself. "Charli didn't blow up the cake. I did."

Shelby tore herself out of Duke's grasp and rushed to my friend. "I am so sorry. You were incredibly nice to talk to me about your baking and share with me what you were doing with your recipes, and it must've been a shock for you to see the cake today."

Clarice clutched the pearls around her neck. "Are you telling me that you stole Alison Kate's recipe?" Her eyes darted to Duke's.

"If you had visited Sweet Tooths before, you might have seen some of Ali Kat's incredible skills on display," I explained to Tucker's mother. "Instead, you gave the job to outsiders who didn't think twice about plagiarizing."

Duke put on his slickest smile. "The better word is *inspired*. And it seems as if I'm the one who owes the apology for my worker who took it upon herself to steal this girl's ideas. I can assure you, I will deal with her with the firmest of hands."

Shelby cringed, and I hated that she'd gotten caught in the crossfire of this whole thing. Whatever Duke had planned for her would be far worse than arresting her. We needed to shut the whole problem down as soon as possible.

I addressed the sasquatch, who scratched his bewildered head. "Sheriff, am I under arrest?"

Big Willie ignored Aunt Nora's pleading eyes. "No, not this time, Charli."

Hooking my arm around my friend's shoulders, I pressed, "What about Alison Kate?" I turned my attention to Clarice. "Are you intending to press charges against her?"

I knew that Tucker's mother valued reputation above anything else. If she insisted on arresting my friend, then the news would spread throughout town and everyone would know why Alison Kate blew up the cake. She would do better to let the whole thing become something of legend rather than gossip fodder.

Clarice's eyes softened. "I can see how it might affect you if you thought that something you created was copied. Although I cannot endorse whether or not this woman is guilty," she nodded at Shelby, "I don't think there is any reason to arrest you for hurt feelings."

Alison's Kate's shoulders slumped in relief. "I'll stay and help clean up," she promised.

Clarice agreed and mollified an annoyed Aunt Nora.

Big Willie tipped his hat to take his leave, but I stopped

everyone from moving. "What about Duke? I don't think he's as innocent as he's claiming to be."

The sheriff blew out a breath. "Like he said, without clear evidence, there's not much I can do."

"And I said that I would deal with it on my own." Duke shot daggers with his eyes in my direction. "Let's go, Shelby." He grabbed the girl by the arm and forced her away from us.

I squeezed Alison Kate around her shoulders. "Come on, I'll help you clean up." When we got to the bottom of the porch stairs, the sound of feet following us made me stop. I turned around and found Clementine hot on her heels.

"Clem, what's wrong?" I asked.

"Nothing," she said. "I thought I might help, too."

"But it's your shower, and it was me who ruined it," protested Alison Kate.

My cousin pondered the truth of my friend's words. "They'll be talking about this for years to come. It will be unforgettable, even though most of the time nobody notices me. And not too long after today, I get to marry the man I love. So I don't think anything was ruined except my chance to taste the cake. I thought maybe if I helped, you might let me try one of your cupcakes sometime." She walked ahead of us toward the tent.

Frosted fairy wings, my cousin surprised the heck out of me. Who knew that underneath her shy exterior beat the heart of a girl who wasn't a total loss?

Alison Kate gave me an impressed look and hooked her

arm through mine. We practically skipped, following Clementine back to the tent.

"Did you see that?" I asked my friend.

"What?"

I pointed at the sky. "I swear I saw a pig flyin'."

Chapter Four

After a couple of days passed, I ventured back into polite society, answering a text from my brother and meeting him on Main Street. Other than a few odd glances and a couple of whispers behind hands, for the most part, the citizens of Honeysuckle went about their business.

Maybe I should be embarrassed by the incident, even though it wasn't my fault. But I couldn't help the swell of pride knowing that my usually nicer friend got so angry that she blew up an entire cake. The fact that Clementine didn't seem one bit angry and maybe was warming up to me after all these years made me smile at the gossipers instead of flipping them off.

I approached my brother and his wife standing on the sidewalk. "Hey, Matty D. And Traci Jo, whadda ya know?"

My very pregnant sister-in-law rubbed her swollen belly. "I'll tell you what I know. Your niece likes to tap dance on my bladder ten thousand times a day. If she keeps this up, I should just move into our bathroom and never come out again." She patted my brother's arm. "I'm gonna go across the street to the cafe. Come and get me when you're done." With a walk that resembled more of a waddle, TJ crossed the street.

My brother groaned. "I'll bet you ten dollars that she's gonna order food after she uses the bathroom." He shook his head. "Either my daughter is a black hole phenomenon or my wife's stomach is a bottomless pit. I can't keep up with her or her crazy cravings. Who wraps melon slices up in ham?"

I chuckled. "I'm pretty sure the Italians do. That's not all that weird."

Matt shook his head. "What about peanut butter on pickles," he challenged, scrunching up his face. "Or pineapple on *everything*. I'm not sure there's even enough of that fruit in our entire town to satisfy her."

"I like pineapple, especially on pizza." I elbowed him. "And it's pretty good with ham, too."

Matt threw his hands up in the air. "You're just going to take her side, aren't you?"

"Yep. Female solidarity, man." I patted him on the shoulder, watching our reflection in the vacant storefront window. "Now, why did you ask me to meet you here? Don't tell me you found someone to rent the tiny space? Wasn't this the old Spell-A-Gram office?"

Matt turned his attention to it and walked to the dirty

window. He traced the worn lettering on the glass. "It hasn't been open in over fifty years. The space is so small that it would take a very special business to rent it. Probably why Uncle Tipper left it closed all this time." He took out some keys from his pocket and unlocked the door.

Sunlight streamed inside and lit up the darkened room covered in decades of dust and grime. The musty smell of the stirred stagnant air tickled my nose. Remnants of objects from days gone by remained on the walls, but other than that, the old store gave off a lonely and abandoned vibe.

"So who's running this special business you say can fit in here?" I asked. I ran a finger down the wooden counter left over from the Spell-A-Gram days. Finding a rusted bell, I hit the top of it with my palm. It dinged clear and true despite its age, and I pictured some witch with a beehive rushing to help me send a message.

Matt cleared his throat behind me. "I know the perfect business for this place."

"Oh, yeah?"

"Yeah. Yours, Birdy."

I whipped around to catch him snickering at his own joke. He stood his ground with an intensely serious expression on his face.

Panic and denial filled my chest. "Last I checked, I don't have a business to speak of. So, I don't know what's gotten into your head. Maybe you're high on goblin fruit or something."

Matt took a steady step toward me. "Think about it,

Charli. You can use your talents to make money. You've been helping everyone from Honeysuckle for free all these years. They can afford to pay you back."

I waved my hands in front of me. "No way. Nobody's gonna pay me for my magic."

He leaned against the counter. "That's a load of unicorn manure, and you know it, Bird. You can't do anything in this small town of ours without word getting around, and I know that a few people have approached you for your lost and found services. Frosted fairy wings, you carry a card around with you, don't you?" He pointed at my pocket.

I didn't know how he knew, but I shoved my hand inside the fabric and touched the corner of the card that Horatio had made for me. The thick paper was wrinkled from sitting in my pocket all the time, and the corners were curled from me touching it, toying with the idea of setting myself up and placing a monetary value on my talents.

I pulled out the worn card and flipped it in my fingers. "For the life of me, I can't seem to charge people. How do you determine what helping someone is worth?"

Matt's lips curled up in victory. "You can sit down with your friends and family and have them help you come up with rates for starters. Come on, it'll be good for you to have something to do. Some place to go outside of your house and Nana's. I know that Tipper left you some money to live off of, but aren't you getting bored?"

The judgmental tone in his voice ruffled my feathers. "You

put me in charge of managing the rental spaces on this side of Main Street," I countered. "That's not nothing."

Matt pushed off the counter. "And I appreciate your help. With everything I've got going on between my pregnant wife and my warden duties, you're doing me a huge favor."

"And making a little bit of money." My brother had worked with Ben to add my name as the property manager for the stores he now owned after inheriting them from Tipper's will. For a small percentage of the rents I collected, I would work as the point person for the tenants.

He grasped me by both shoulders, holding me still so I couldn't ignore him. "It's about time you valued yourself. And this space is perfect since you don't have any goods here to sell. You could take down this counter and maybe paint the walls. A desk would go great here."

Matt let me go and walked about the small room, pointing and explaining with excitement. His enthusiasm was catching, and I began believing in the idea sooner than I thought I would.

About the time I wanted to say yes, the thought of a former client popped in my head. "It's an interesting concept, Matt. But what am I supposed to do when someone like Timmy Belford wants me to find his lost puppy? How am I supposed to charge a little kid like him?"

My brother flashed a wide grin. "I love your heart, Charli. That's the beauty of owning your own business. You get to set the rules. What did he give you in return for finding his dog?"

I thought back at how serious the little boy had been,

handing me his payment. "An old tin full of buttons, a few rocks he'd found in the creek, and a treasured tin soldier. I gave him back the toy and made sure to return the container of buttons to his mom." I threw up my hands. "So, you see? I can't run a business like that."

"Sure you can. Read me what that card in your hand says," my brother demanded.

My thumb brushed over the careful calligraphy. "Charli Goodwin. Lost & Found Services. *For there is nothing lost, that may be found, if sought.* Fees to be determined on case basis."

Matt sniffed with satisfaction. "See? You determine what each case is worth. And that particular one was worth a handful of rocks. Maybe the next job would be worth a few dollars."

I wanted to grab onto the thrill of maybe something good coming out of all my years of frustration with being different, but the fear of failure stirred inside me. "I don't know," I stalled.

My brother mumbled something about the stubbornness of Goodwin women. "Will you at least consider the idea?"

I replaced the handwritten card into my pocket and pondered things. My brother wasn't wrong that I had time on my hands, especially with Dash and Mason gone. The rest of my friends had steady employment. Maybe if I kept myself busy, I could stay out of trouble.

"I'll think about it," I acquiesced.

Matt checked his watch. "Good." Taking out his keys, he

slipped one off and handed it to me. "Keep this for now. Maybe you can come back and think about it some more."

He ushered me out the door and locked the space. I pressed my nose to the dirty window and peered in, picturing what it would look like with me inside.

"Come on, Charli. We have one more appointment to keep." My brother waited for me to follow him.

On our way down the sidewalk, a few teenagers ran past us, almost knocking me over. "Hey, watch where you're—"

In a split second, my feet flew out from underneath me, and I fell on my behind. Another young man ran up to me and held out his hand. "I'm so sorry, Miss Charli. That slipping spell was meant for my brother."

I accepted the help to get back up on my feet and rubbed my sore bottom. Facing down the culprit, I recognized the taller Mosely brother. "Try to have better aim next time," I warned.

The embarrassed boy backed away from me. "Yes, ma'am." He ran off after his friends.

"I'm not old enough to be *ma'am*-ed," I grumbled under my breath.

"That's nothing," Matt chimed in. "It seems that there are a lot of spell pranks going on. It's that time of year."

My hand rubbed the spot that would bruise on my behind. "I guess. But they better not do anything when I'm teaching the spell permit course."

"Ha! I knew Nana would convince you," my brother

teased. He strolled down the sidewalk until he stood in front of another abandoned business space. A faded painted sign declared it the last location of Mr. Steve's very first restaurant, the Honeysuckle Diner. Wooden boards blocked the windows.

"It's on a trial basis. If her dear friend hadn't had a family emergency and needed to leave right away, I would've had more time to tell Nana no." I tried my best to peek through a small crack between the boards.

Matt lifted his eyebrows. "Would you have?"

I hung my head and sighed. "Probably not. What are we doing here?"

"There's something I didn't tell you because I haven't really told anyone. I wasn't sure how you would take it." He rubbed the back of his neck in awkward discomfort.

"Did you already find a new tenant for this space? Isn't this the old diner Mr. Steve started before he moved into the bigger place across the street? It would be an odd space to renovate for anything other than a restaurant of some sort."

"Exactly," Matt responded.

I waited for him to say more, still trying to find a way to look inside. When he didn't elaborate, the full truth dawned on me. "Is someone trying to open another restaurant here in Honeysuckle?" I shot a glance at the busy cafe on the corner. Who would want to compete against Mr. Steve?

Matt approached the door. "I think it would be better if you came in here and saw for yourself." He gripped the metal handle and pulled. Walking inside felt like a betrayal to our friends and our town.

"Hurry up and get in," hissed Matt. He reached for my wrist and yanked me inside, letting the door close behind him.

Our entry stirred the musty air. Dust covered most of the surfaces in a grimy gray. There were few signs of the former diner except a couple of broken tables and chairs stacked on the edges. The pass-through window to the kitchen resembled the one in the cafe. Dark stains outlined blank spaces on the wall where pictures used to hang.

"Remember the story Mom told us about her first date with Dad here?" I asked in a reverent tone.

Matt nodded. "He took her out for their first meal."

"And Mom knocked the cup over, spilling vanilla milkshake all over her. In her panic to spellcast the ice cream off her blouse, she knocked over Dad's shake into his lap," I finished.

My brother reached out and held onto my hand. "He told me that was the first time he knew he loved her."

We fell into a comfortable silence, sharing our memories of our parents. I tried to imagine them younger and sitting at a table in this room. The love from my brother helped ease the ache in my chest.

The door opened and sunlight streamed in. Hollis Hawthorne entered followed by a smiling Duke. My stomach turned when the fake chef spotted me and grinned like a lion who'd spotted its prey.

"What are they doing here?" I asked.

Hollis sniffed and stood up straighter in his impeccable

suit. "We are here to sign the contract I trust your brother has had drawn up. Since you're such a champion of change and acceptance in our fair town, Miss Charlotte, I would think you would welcome a new business."

Matt took out some folded papers from his back pocket and handed them to the banker. Tucker's father ignored my presence and focused on the contract, skimming it and analyzing its terms. "This all seems standard and acceptable. Do you have a pen?"

The possibility of Hollis backing the sham of a chef to help open a restaurant of all things slammed into me all at once. My brother held out the instrument to seal the deal, and I panicked.

Grabbing Matt by his arm, I yanked him away from the two men. "What do you think you're doing?"

"I'm renting an empty business."

I shot a look of death at the other two. "But he's going to open a restaurant in direct competition with the cafe. You can't do that."

"Do you think I like it anymore than you do?" My brother demanded. "Trust me, I went over every possible way to deny Mr. Hawthorne and Mr. Aikens. But Ben informed me that I might have legal problems if I turned them down as long as their financials checked out. Which they did."

Why hadn't Ben told me before he left out of town with Lee? Instead, he left it up to my brother to reveal our big betrayal. "How long have you and Ben been working on this?"

Matt sighed and ran a hand through his hair. "Listen, Birdy—"

I held up a finger in front of me. "Don't call me that. Don't you dare call me that in this moment. If you let them sign a lease, then we'll be branded as traitors."

"And if I don't, then I'm making a decision based on how I feel rather than on rational business terms. I can't turn them down simply because you dislike them." He acknowledged the awkward cough from Hollis and asked for one more moment.

I tugged on his sleeve. "Then why did you bring me here? You can't think I'm going to work with either one of them on any level."

My brother quieted me with a heated gaze. "You signed on to manage the storefronts that I own. You can't pick and choose which ones you want to work with." He blew out a long breath. "Seriously, Charli. I need you with me on this."

It took me a hot minute to cool down, but I managed to force a smile on my lips. Snatching the pen from my brother's hand, I extended it out to Hollis. "Here you go," I said with syrupy sweetness. He needed to sign fast before I changed my mind. Bless his heart. My fingers tingled to hex his arrogant hiney.

"I am cosigning this lease," Hollis said. "But it will be Mr. Aikens and his employees that will be working on refurbishing the space and getting it ready for its new operation." He handed the pen to Duke who signed underneath Hollis in all the right places.

Matt took a set of keys off of his own ring and handed

them to the newcomer. "Good luck in your new venture." His tone suggested that he wished the chef the exact opposite, but he'd finished the deal.

My brother's spell phone chimed, and he checked the incoming text. "I need to go. TJ's wanting me to pick up some baked goods at Sweet Tooths and bring them over to the Harvest Moon."

Normal politeness dictated for Hollis to ask Matt how his pregnant wife was doing. Tucker's father ignored propriety. "I'll follow you out, Deputy Goodwin."

I needed to get out of the space, all good feelings from the memories of my parents' first date fading with the presence of the man who made my skin crawl. "I'm coming, too."

"Hold on there. I'd like to talk to someone about my plans for the space," requested Duke.

Matt turned around and stopped me from walking out. "Come on, Charli. Please," he pleaded.

I poked him in his chest. "I will stay one minute alone with him. That's it unless you come back. The guy bothers me."

My brother kissed my cheek. "I'll do my best to return as quick as possible. If you don't make it that long, I'll meet you at the cafe." He mouthed a final *thank you* and left me standing alone in the same space as the fake chef.

Gripping my hands in fists, I swallowed my disgust and settled a mask of indifferent business on my face. "How may I help you?"

Duke sauntered toward me. "That's a good question to

start with. I've been told that you have extraordinary talents that can be very...useful." His eyes slithered up and down my body with slow deliberation.

I shuddered at the thoughts that must be slithering around in his head. "I don't know what you're talking about."

His creepy grin matched his leering gaze. "I heard from some associates I work with that there was a tracker in our area. An untrained one hidden somewhere in a small town. Imagine my utter delight to find you so close."

Shock and awe outweighed my anger. I'd never taken any steps to hide my magic from the general population, but it sent cold shivers down my spine that he knew about me. Or that somebody he knew had also heard. I thought back to Damien's words and wondered if the vampire had gotten word out after all.

If he wanted to press my buttons, I could do the same and see if he would reveal his secret. "Is that the kind of information you write down in a book somewhere?" I batted my eyelashes in mock flirtation.

Duke lifted his eyebrows. "I do keep a record of things that will pay off in the future. As of right now, I've only heard tales of your talents. I have to see them in action in order to place a value on them." He closed the distance between us, and I backed away until the wall pressed up against my back. He trapped me between his long arms.

Alarm bells blared in my head. I thrust my hands against his chest. "Back off," I demanded.

He leaned his body closer, letting me know he had no

intentions of obeying. "Not until I get what I want. And I always find ways to get what I want."

"Last chance," I warned. "Step away from me or else."

The bold man scoffed. "I've heard that many times from girls like you. There is very little you can do to stop me."

"Then you've never met a girl like me." Power surged and sparked inside me, and I almost willed it to my fingertips. Instead, I grabbed him by the shoulders and held him while I lifted my knee with great force.

He wasn't worth expending any effort with my magic, and I stepped over his crumpled form on the floor, heading to the cafe to reward myself with a tall cool glass of sweet tea.

Chapter Five

Restless sleep wrestled with me all night, and I drifted in and out of stressful dreams. When the dawn's first light glowed behind my bedroom curtains, I gave up. I needed to clear my head of empty business spaces filled with new possibilities or threats from annoying men.

Peaches stretched at the foot of the bed and yawned. She turned three times and settled back into a tiny ball, keeping one eye on me as I changed out of my pajamas.

I scratched her little orange head. "Wanna go for a ride?"

She curled her tail around her body and buried her head in her paws.

Giving her one more nudge between her ears, I sighed. "Fine. Be that way." I opened my bedroom door and headed downstairs to go for an early morning bike ride.

The sound of giggles stopped me at the bottom step. Low murmuring voices caught my attention, and I snuck around the corner to take a peek. My vampire roommate rested his open mouth on the nape of the neck of one of his favorite dalliances.

"Beau," I called out in horror.

Startled, the vampire poofed into his bat form and fluttered about the parlor. Ms. Flossy clutched the ivory skin of her neck and attempted to say something to me.

Beau changed back to his regular form and placed a hand over his undead heart. "Charli, you scared me half to death."

"Hard to do to a vampire. What were you doing to her?" I pointed a finger at his female friend.

She smoothed out her blouse. "Don't worry, Miss Charli. He was just whispering sweet nothings in my ear." The elderly woman fanned herself with her hand.

"Uh-huh." I made no attempt to hide my disbelief. "Beau?"

The vampire gathered his wits about him and held a finger up to me. He addressed his date. "Flossy, darlin', I'll be just one moment." With a sigh of annoyance, he ushered me out of the doorway and into the foyer. "Charli," he hissed. "You're ruinin' my mojo."

I placed my hands on my hips and squared off with him. "What did I tell you about bringing your dates here to the house?" Staring the vampire down, I gave him no room to wiggle out of my one steadfast rule.

"I know, I know," he admitted. "But we couldn't go back to her place because she lives with her sister."

"And?" I pushed.

My roommate tilted his head and scratched the bald spot on top. "And it would be awkward for me to woo her since not more than two nights ago, I was there. With her sister. I had no choice but to come back here."

I pointed at the door and raised my voice. "You have lots of choices. The whole wide world was available to you. Anywhere else but here." Poking him in the chest, I didn't hold back. "I can't say this enough. There's gonna be no hankyin' or pankyin' in this household. And definitely no neck bitin'."

Beau's cheeks turned almost a regular flesh color with embarrassment. "I only act like I'm biting her. I don't actually break the skin. The effects it has on her is—"

"No!" I interrupted. "I don't need to hear any more." I covered his fanged mouth with my hand.

He attempted a muffled reply underneath my palm, and I removed the obstacle in his way and asked him to repeat himself.

"Does she have to go home *now?*" he asked, his lip jutting out like a pouting schoolgirl.

He didn't fool me for a second. "She shouldn't even be up right now. We witches don't typically keep the same hours as you vampires."

"Unless she has reasons to stay awake." Beau waved at Ms. Flossy, who giggled.

Unable to take anymore, I headed to the door and opened it. "Be a gentleman and escort your lady friend home. When I get back, I don't want to stumble on any more uncomfortable scenes." I stepped out onto the porch and let the screen door slam shut. Thinking of how else my roommate might break the rules, I yelled at him from outside. "And absolutely positively *no* dates in your room."

I hustled to get my bike, but Beau came out on the porch. "Hey, did you hear that really loud screeching last night?"

Cringing, I shook my head no. "Please tell me that it wasn't coming from the two of you and...whatever you were doing together." I filled my head with thoughts of butterflies and unicorns farting rainbows not to think about what activity that might be.

Beau rolled his eyes. "It wasn't us. It sounded more like a loud shrieking of some sort. You really didn't hear it?"

I remembered a loud noise in my dream lingering far longer than it should, but couldn't place what might have made it. "Maybe it was an owl or something."

"If an owl made that noise, then it was screaming before it died. Perhaps it was your wolf shifter friend finally home and howlin' for you." He smiled like his words would make me happy.

I swallowed hard. "Doubt it." Dash would have texted me on my spell phone at least, right?

My roommate paused and dragged his feet on the creaking wood. "You sure I can't let Flossy stay? It is morning, and the trip to her house would be so long. We can eat breakfast together."

"You don't eat regular food most of the time," I accused.

He pouted again. "Then I'll watch her eat. But she can stay?"

I wanted to get going and not be having the same conversation again. "Make sure you take her home eventually, please. One annoying roommate may be too many."

Ignoring the clapping and cheering from Beau, I walked my bicycle across the field to the road. Summoning up a little of my energy, I flipped the switch that connected my magic. Placing my feet on the pedals, I let the wind dance with my hair as I took off.

A wilder part of me that I buried deep down inside yearned for the freedom of hopping on Dad's broken down motorcycle Old Joe. Or riding behind Dash on his rumbling bike. My thoughts drifted to the wolf shifter, and I indulged in memories mixed with emotions, allowing them to bubble to the surface.

Ever since Dashiel Channing entered my life at my grandmother's house, he'd become a major distraction. When he was around, my emotions changed like riding a roller coaster, building slowly up and up until I thought things were good between us. And then, bam, the bottom would drop out, and I would free fall into an abyss of confusion and hurt feelings. When things were good, they were really really good. When things got tough, the man disappeared. It had happened more than once, although he usually managed to return.

It didn't surprise me that my ride of freedom around town brought me to a house that I'd been to before. The lawn was covered with overgrown grass, and stacks of old *Honeysuckle Hollers* rested against the front door.

Dash's house sat still and quiet with no signs of life. It stood in defiant silence much like the man who didn't answer any calls or send any word about how he was doing. For all I knew, he could be hurt from his fight with his old Red Ridge pack. Or maybe even worse.

I touched my stomach and willed the fear in my gut to ignore that last possibility. Wouldn't I know if something had happened to him? At least, I thought we had forged a strong connection between us. He told me before he left that my scent would call him back home. Closing my eyes, I lifted my hands in the air and waited for a breeze to blow.

When a cool one picked up the tendrils of my hair, I made a quick wish. "Come home, Dash." I willed the wind to carry it as far as it needed to go. Turning my bike around, I left his house in a mix of sadness and hope.

Not too far of a ride away, I found Mason's house just as empty. But the detective had made arrangements with somebody to take care of his lawn, his mail, and the newspaper deliveries while he was gone.

The modest home fit the organized detective to a *T*. Everything was neat and tidy. Nothing too fancy stood out, but it looked like it could weather any storm. Unlike with Dash, I didn't need to make a wish for Mason to return. I had no doubt he would come back. Even when things got tough, he always found a way to show up and be there for me, although sometimes I had to endure his disapproving scowls. I'd give anything to be the recipient of one right now.

A sharp caw from the sky above snapped me out of my fog of loneliness. A dark feathered figure hovered in the air high above me, and I waved my hand at the crow. "Hey, you old Biddy."

The bird croaked her reply, flapping her wings and circling above for a moment. I watched her float on the wind, envying her winged liberation. She squawked another time and flew away. I guess she'd served her purpose, and I smiled, peddling again and focusing on moving forward in my life.

I patted the slight bulge in my pocket, reminding myself where I'd slipped the key to the small store on Main Street. Maybe the early morning light would offer me some fresh new insight to whether or not I should open up my own business.

A tiny spark of excitement bounced around inside me, and I pointed my wheels in that direction. I could explore the space and maybe make some plans. And when my stomach rumbled with hunger, I could head to the Harvest Moon for an early morning breakfast.

Pleased with my plan, I almost rode right past a stumbling figure on the side of the road. Pulling over, I let my bike drop and ran to assist the poor person. Lifting them up by an arm, I got them to a standing position again. The figure smelled like a distillery, and I held my breath until I saw the face of the drunken fool.

"Tucker," I exclaimed, almost dropping him in surprise.

He squinted his eyes and studied me for a brief second. "Is

that you, Charli?" He blinked until he recognized me and smiled. "I thought you might be the angel of death coming to get me."

He lurched forward, and I steadied him. "It's only me. Tuck, what happened?"

My ex-fiancé waved a hand in front of his face, trying to either fan away his putrid breath or cool himself off. "Been drinking. Need to stay numb and forget."

I knew about Tucker's enthusiasm to party once in a while when he was younger. But most of the time, he kept his dalliances to his trips down to Charleston. I'd never seen him drunk as a skunk in Honeysuckle. I gave him a once over and noticed a bruise underneath his left eye and scuff marks on his right hand.

Gripping his wrist, I studied his knuckles. "Why is there blood here?"

He brought his hand right in front of his eyes. "Don't know. Must have hit something."

Or someone, I thought. I touched the puffy skin underneath his eye, and he winced. "Do you remember where you've been?"

He tapped the side of his nose in a dramatic fashion, missing the mark a few times. "Don't know. Last I remember, I was at Lucky's." He giggled.

"What's so funny?"

"Lucky's name is Lucky. And at Lucky's bar, I wasn't so lucky." Tucker cracked up at his own joke and wobbled off-balance. He stopped laughing and frowned. "I think I'm going to—"

He never finished his statement, bending over and purging himself on the side of the road. I rubbed his back and uttered words of sympathy, debating internally whether or not to knock on a nearby door to get some help. But if I could save him the public embarrassment of others knowing about his debauched state, that might be the bigger help. With a groan, I chose to shoulder the burden alone.

When he finished retching, he wiped his mouth with the back of his hand. "I feel better now." He threw his arm around my shoulder and leaned on me. "Charli, Charli, Charli. You know, it's all your fault."

"What is?" I asked.

He gestured his hand up and down his body. "I wouldn't be like this if you hadn't gone away."

My emotional guard went up with immediacy. Surely the man couldn't blame his night of overindulgence on my actions from over a year ago. "I haven't been anywhere, Tucker. And I think you need to go home and sleep this off."

He shook his head. "But I don't sleep. I can't anymore. Too many things to worry about." He tapped the side of his head. "But I figured a way out so that I won't ever have to worry again."

His drunken ramblings grated my nerves. I struggled against his dead weight against me. "Figured what out?"

"I made a plan, and the world liked my plan. It screamed and screamed its delight." Tucker turned his head and focused on my face, his eyes widening in instant recognition. "Charli, where did you come from?"

We weren't getting anywhere. Either I needed to leave him to his own devices or escort him home. "Never mind," I said.

He surprised me and pulled me into a tight hug, rocking me back and forth, almost losing his balance more than once. The motion turned into an awkward stumbling dance. "If you had just married me, then everything would be fine. Why didn't you marry me? Maybe if you did right now, things would turn out okay."

I pushed away from Tucker. "What are you talking about? You're about to marry Clementine, and you love her, don't you?"

At the mention of her name, he warbled the old song off key at the top of his lungs. I shushed him and tried to cover his mouth, but he drunkenly danced away from me, singing about his Darlin' Clementine.

"Tucker," I hissed. "It's too early."

He stopped singing and shook his head. "No. It's too late. Too late for me." He stumbled away, mumbling and humming to himself.

If he was determined to blame me for the state he found himself in, then he could find his way home on his own. The town limits were small, so the chances of him doing more harm to himself were low. I vacillated between hoping he would make it and wanting him to get a little more hurt in the process.

I rode my bike onto the empty Main Street. At this time of morning, at least I wouldn't be the victim of a stray spell prank. I parked and walked the length of the sidewalk across the street from the old Spell-A-Gram store. I envisioned the letters of my business etched in gold on a clean front window: Lost & Found.

Something strange and out of place caught my attention. The door to the old diner stood wide open. Although I hadn't stayed to make sure the day before, I couldn't believe that the new tenant would have left his new place so vulnerable.

Maybe Duke was an early riser, getting a jumpstart on refurbishing the insides. The lack of noise coming out of the space fed my growing doubt. With slow steps, I made my way to the storefront. The familiar gnawing of my gut raised my suspicions, and I approached with caution. Inching through the doorway and glancing inside, I prepared to bolt if Duke saw me.

I spotted him first. Or rather, I saw his body lying in a lifeless heap on the floor of the old diner. Checking my surroundings, I entered and approached the body. With the toe of my shoe, I nudged Duke's arm. No response. I held my breath and watched to see if his back rose up and down with breathing. No movement.

Pixie poop. I took out my spell phone and dialed my brother. "Matt, we have a problem." I didn't wait for his inevitable question. "I think I found another dead body."

Chapter Six

I didn't know who missed Mason more between me and Big Willie. When he showed up to the crime scene, he couldn't manage to snap out of his confusion to lead the chaos.

"Holy unicorn horn, Charli Goodwin. Will there ever be a day where I don't find you and a dead body together?" The sasquatch pushed hair out of his line of sight. "You know, I should have my people tail you on a regular basis. Nobody would have to call us wardens because you'd lead us right to the problem."

A few wardens on the scene attempted to record and scrutinize the environment, but with no clear leadership, they fumbled the investigation, crashing into each other and duplicating the same jobs. Matt did his best to call out the plays, but the sheriff kept getting in the way.

"Deputy Goodwin, get your tail over here." Big Willie waited for my brother to stop bossing Zeke and another warden around. "Now, correct me if I'm wrong, but you own this place, right?"

"I do, sir," my brother answered.

The sheriff pointed at the door. "Then you need to get your behind out of here."

"But, sir—"

The sheriff shut Matt down. "No but's. You bein' the owner and all, it's a conflict of interest."

My brother contemplated the order for a second but stood his ground. Without Mason here, the investigation's best shot rested with him.

I pleaded with the flustered sasquatch. "Big Willie, come on. You need Matt."

His furry head turned to face me. "Don't you go sassin' me, young lady. I ought to throw your behind in jail. At least then I'd know where you were and that you couldn't get into any more trouble."

Matt and I both exploded in protest. Zeke came over and asked the sheriff a question about the body. A bright flash from a camera went off, and Big Willie rubbed his temples. "Everybody pipe down for one bloomin' second. I gotta think," he roared.

All movement in the room stilled. I started to say something, but Matt touched my arm and shook his head. He cocked his head toward the sheriff, and I observed a professional overwhelmed by his surroundings. When was the last time the head of the wardens had worked an actual case? Ever since Mason's arrival, I'd bet dollars to demons that he was more than a little bit rusty.

Big Willie wiped his massive paw-like hands down his long face. "All right, y'all. Here's what's going to happen. Deputy Goodwin, as the owner of this space, you really can't work the scene. I need you to step outside and wait for me. Zeke, I want you to stand here next to Charli and make sure she doesn't do anything, say anything, or get in the way."

The young deputy nodded. "Yes, sir."

Annoyed with the limitations set by the sheriff, I couldn't help myself. "Can I sit down?"

"What did I just say?" Big Willie waved his hands around him. "Do you see any chairs for you to rest your nosy behind in? You can stand and wait, preferably while keepin' your trap shut, and let me get to work."

Zeke sidled up to me and stood close enough that his arm brushed against mine. "Mason's gonna kill me," he muttered.

"Why?" I asked, tickled that the young deputy was already breaking the sheriff's orders.

As if realizing his transgression, Zeke winced, but continued to talk. "He told me to watch out for you and keep you—"

"Out of trouble?" I finished. "Yeah, I'm sorry, Zeke, but that was his mistake, not yours. Nana could've told him my entire family's been tryin' to do that for decades and it hasn't worked yet. Don't blame yourself." I patted the young man on his shoulder.

Zeke shrugged. "Still, he really might kill me."

"Then we'll know who committed the murder and lock him up straight away." We shared in a hearty chuckle until I couldn't take anymore of the ineptitude of the investigative procedures. "What in the heck is Big Willie doing?"

"Miss Charli, please don't move," Zeke begged. I ignored the slight twinge of guilt as I made my way to the sheriff.

The sasquatch stepped all over the area immediately around the body, possibly contaminating any small pieces of evidence. He didn't even put on a glove before he picked up the dead man's left hand to look at it. "Nothing there," he dismissed all too fast.

"Are you sure?" I inquired, looking over his shoulder.

Big Willie jumped, dropping the hand. "Charli, you're gonna give me a heart attack. I should've told you to come join in the fun and maybe you would have stayed put since you're so determined to do the opposite of what I asked."

I ignored his tantrum and concentrated on the body. "Zeke, do you happen to have a handkerchief I could use?"

The deputy approach me with caution and held up a folded white square he took out of his pocket. "And now, the sheriff's gonna kill me," he mumbled.

I winked at him. "Don't worry about it so much. If anyone's at risk, it's me, and how much more trouble can I get into?"

"Could the two of you stop actin' like I'm not right beside you waitin' to find out what's so important that a civilian is doin' my job?" whined Big Willie.

I crouched down next to the body and carefully plucked the hand from the floor, using the handkerchief to protect the skin from my fingerprints. With careful scrutiny, I confirmed that the sheriff was actually right. "Nothing underneath these nails."

"I could have told you that," Big Willie stated. "Same thing with the other one."

"So no clear evidence of a physical altercation." My mind drifted to finding Mrs. Kettlefields' lifeless form at the library and the evidence underneath her fingernails.

"Not necessarily," the sheriff said. He took the hanky from me and lifted up the right hand. "See? He has scratches and blood on his knuckles."

My stomach dropped. I knew someone else with similar injuries. If I were working with Mason, I might tell him what I saw with Tucker, but with the sheriff, I couldn't be sure that he would handle it the right way. Making a quick and possibly risky decision, I kept my suspicions to myself.

"The man hit something," I proposed.

"Or maybe someone," added Big Willie. I'll have to check his face to see if he has any contusions. That would at least prove he was fighting another person." He reached out a hand to lift the head.

I tugged on the sheriff's arm and stopped him. "Look." I pointed at a spot on his hair matted with blood. "He must have gotten hit with something."

Big Willie pondered the suggestion. "He could have banged it against some sort of surface when he fell."

I examined the location of the blood. "Maybe," I conceded. "If he fell backward. Have your people found any evidence of blood around?" I asked.

With a sigh, Big Willie barked orders at his minions to search for blood evidence.

"You might want them to look for anything that might have been used to strike him as well," I added, pressing my luck.

The sheriff stood up in a huff. "I don't know who you think you are, but I know you're not on my payroll. We're doin' the best we can." The concern in the sasquatch's eyes conveyed the doubt in his own words.

When the other wardens came up empty for other marks of blood, he breathed out a sigh of relief. "Then maybe this isn't a murder. Maybe the man had some bad luck, slipped, and fell." He addressed the wardens, "Let's tag and bag the body, please, and get it back for the doc to examine it and close this case."

The sheriff's hasty conclusion bothered me. The short investigation turned up nothing at this point. Rusty or not, Big Willie was falling down on the job.

"You can't move the body," I protested. "You haven't made enough discoveries yet."

Fed up with my interference, the sasquatch closed the distance between us. "In case you were confused, I'm pretty sure that I wear the badge of the sheriff in this town, missy. If you keep buggin' me, I will arrest you for harassment, being a hindrance at a crime scene, and being an all around a pain in my—"

"But Sheriff," I interrupted, "you haven't taken the time to look at the wound. How big is it? How much blood is there? Is there any blood around him to suggest how long he might have been laying there? Have you really scoured the entire area around him for any evidence of others being here? The place is covered in dust. So how many sets of footprints can be seen? What about any fingerprints?"

The red in the sasquatch's cheeks underneath his hair deepened until they looked like lava about to explode. He squeezed his eyes shut and bellowed, "Enough!"

Rooting around in his pocket, he pulled out a spell phone. He flipped it open and punched in a bunch of numbers. After a few seconds, his shoulders sagged in relief. "Detective, I'm glad I caught you."

A new batch of adrenaline coursed through my veins. The sheriff was talking to Mason, and I longed to snatch the phone out of his hands. Without thinking, I reached out to take it.

Big Willie smacked my hand away. "Yeah, I'm glad it's finished. You need to come back down here. You are? How did you know?" He paused to listen and shook his head. "Yeah, I know, I owe you money. Of course she found another body. When? Good. As fast as you can. Break the speed limit if you have to." He ended the call and closed his phone, stuffing it back in his pocket.

"Was that Mason?" I asked, trying not to give away my excitement.

"It was none of your beeswax, young lady." He shook his head. "I don't know how your grandmother puts up with you."

I shrugged. "Me neither, but she knows when to listen to me."

All activity in the space stopped. Every single warden watched the two of us, and I saw the proverbial line I'd stepped over in the distance behind me.

Big Willie pinched the bridge of his nose. "Okay, Miss Sassy Pants, what else do we need to do."

"You're actually going to listen?" I asked.

He nodded. "Against my better judgment, I'm gonna let you say a few words and then decide afterwards whether or not they're worth anything. You got sixty seconds startin' now." He looked at the watch on his hairy wrist.

Unwilling to let the opportunity pass me by, I spoke as fast as possible. "First, I would collect any anything that looks like it could have been used to hit him. Small pieces of wood, any kitchen utensils still lying about anywhere in the entire building including the kitchen and the storeroom. You can easily test things and rule them out quicker than making a fast judgment here and leaving something important behind. Before you move the body, make sure to document everything on it from the clothes to any other injuries. Once you secure the scene, you have to consider your best suspects." I paused to take a breath.

The sheriff raised his eyebrows. "I suppose you already have one cookin' in that noggin' of yours?"

I thought about it, feeling the last seconds of my chance ticking by. "Well, it has to be someone who had a reason to want to hurt him. Someone that maybe he had upset or made mad." I stopped talking, realizing how many people could fit that description.

Big Willie's eyes sparked with understanding. "You mean someone he might have stolen something from?" he asked.

I didn't like the lightbulb look on his face. "I suppose."

"Like someone who got so upset that she made an entire cake explode?"

I definitely didn't like where the sheriff was going with his train of thought. "No, no, not necessarily." I tried to wave him off.

Renewed with purpose, the sheriff cleared his throat and gave orders. "Y'all do what she said and investigate the scene here." He stomped toward the door, and I rushed to catch up with him.

"Sheriff, where are you going?"

He turned to face me and grinned. "Goin' to interrogate the first likely suspect." Pushing open the door, he disappeared.

Chapter Seven

I tried to stop Big Willie from breaking down the door to Sweet Tooths, but the sheriff rebuffed my efforts. Although it was still early morning, enough Honeysuckle residents noticed the commotion and stopped to check it out.

"Why do I get the feeling you said something you shouldn't have?" my brother asked, eyeing the few people watching with caution.

The sasquatch pounded on the bakery's door. "Where are those blasted tooth fairies," he demanded.

Noticing a few onlookers standing a bit too close, I leaned in and whispered to my brother. "It's not like he was handling things all that well. Y'all really need to get Mason back here."

Matt nodded. "I called him while Big Willie made me wait outside. He was already headed this way."

"Yeah, Willie called him, too." My heart rate kicked up another notch, and I bit my lip to stop myself from smiling.

The sheriff stopped knocking on the glass when Twinkle bobbed up and down at the door with a distinctive frown on his lips, unlocking it. Big Willie pushed inside, and Matt and I followed close behind.

The retired tooth fairy glared at the sheriff. "What in tarnation seems to be the problem? I've got baked goods in the oven."

Puffing out his chest, the sasquatch spoke with authority. "I need to see Alison Kate."

"She's in the middle of making her honeysuckle buns. Can it wait?" challenged the tiny but fierce tooth fairy.

"Listen, Twinkle. You and me are gonna go a few rounds if you don't rustle her behind out here. Now."

I nudged Matt and pointed at the crowd gathering in front of the store gazing through the windows. My brother cleared his throat. "Sheriff, maybe you want to speak with her in the back instead." He jerked his head at the numerous eyes watching the scene unfold.

The sheriff shifted on his feet and stroked his scraggly beard. "Yeah, maybe," he acquiesced, a little less sure of himself.

Twinkle zipped into the kitchen ahead of us. Unwilling for my friend to be interrogated alone, I followed behind against the protests of my brother. Giving up fighting me, Matt caught up to join everyone in the back room that was hot from hard-working ovens.

Sprinkle stopped dusting sugar on top of a batch of jelly doughnuts and stared at the sasquatch. Alison Kate pulled out a tray of freshly baked honeysuckle buns and sniffed them. When the sheriff called out her name, she squeaked in surprise and dropped the entire tray on the floor, scattering the sweet buns everywhere.

"You want to talk to me?" my friend asked, pointing at her chest.

"Is it true that you were angry with Duke the other day?" Big Willie asked.

I rolled my eyes. All three of us had been in the Hawthorne's parlor and already knew the answer to the pointless question. "You know she was, Sheriff."

The sasquatch held up his long finger at me. "You stay quiet," he warned. Turning back to Alison Kate, he prompted, "Answer the question, please."

"Yes, I was a bit miffed," my friend admitted.

The sheriff scoffed. "Miffed? Is that what you call being so upset that you shot a hex at the cake and blew it up?"

Twinkle fluttered to Alison's Kate side and crossed his tiny arms. "If I'd been there, it might not have been the cake that exploded. The nerve of an outsider trying to steal from our bakery. I've been waiting to cool off before confronting Hollis and Clarice, but now you've got me all riled up again." His wings quivered in frustration, and a little bit of his dust floated down on Alison Kate's shoulders.

"So I should add you to the list of suspects?" Big Willie asked.

Sprinkle joined the group. "For what?" she asked in her high-pitched voice.

The sheriff winced at his mistake. "I'm the one asking questions." He turned his attention back to Alison Kate. "Where were you all last night?"

My friend's eyes widened. "At Meemaw's house. We had dinner together, and then I helped her set her hair in curlers. She has bridge today with her friends."

"What time did y'all go to bed?" pressed the sheriff.

Alison Kate squinted her eyes while thinking. "I guess Meemaw went to her room at around nine, and I stayed up for a while."

"Did you stay at her place all night long?" Big Willie asked.

My friend nodded. "After she was asleep, I called Lee and talked to him for a few hours until I got sleepy. I stayed over all night and left early this morning so I could change clothes and come to work. Why are you asking me all these questions?" She glanced at me with a worried expression. "Charli?"

Unable to withstand my friend's predicament, I broke every single protocol that would have gotten a warden fired. Good thing I wasn't one. "That chef, Duke Aikins, who stole your frosting spell. He's lying dead on the floor of the old diner," I blurted out.

My brother smacked my arm and Big Willie whipped around and glared at me.

Heat rose in my cheeks, but I didn't feel a bit sorry about what I'd said. "What? It's a small town. The news is gonna spread like wildfire anyway. It's better for you to be upfront."

Alison Kate's lower lip trembled. "Are you askin' me these questions because you think I did something to him?" Tears welled in her eyes. "I didn't like what he did, and I know it was wrong to make a scene at Clementine's bridal shower, but I would never take a person's life for any reason." Her voice grew higher in pitch until she squeaked out the last part, breaking down into sobbing tears.

The sheriff grimaced and backed away from the crying young woman. He turned away and focused on me. "Come over here." Dragging me by the arm, he pulled me into a far corner of the kitchen. My brother stood behind him.

"Now, listen here. I'm tired of your shenanigans. Unless you want to go to a wardens' academy and become one of us, you gotta stop interferin'. I really should arrest you." Big Willie ran a hand through his beard.

"But you're jumping the gun, Big Wi—, I mean, Sheriff. You can't go asking questions of anybody for any reason. Sure, Alison Kate might make it on the suspect list, but I'd bet there are others that should be interrogated first. Heck, even I had issues with the jerk." I clasped my hand over my mouth, silently cursing my own stupidity and slip of the tongue.

Big Willie grinned like he'd caught me. "Don't stop talkin' now. Why did you have issues with Duke?"

I thought as fast as possible. Any observation I told him about what I'd seen at the Hawthorne house would be considered hearsay. I stuck with my own experience. "When

Matt brought the contract for Hollis and Duke to sign to rent out the old diner, I stayed behind to listen to some of the chef's ideas. Except the only ideas he had were to threaten me verbally and physically."

Matt clenched his fists. "What did he do to you?" he growled.

I waved him off. "He didn't actually do anything other than mention that he knew about my tracking powers. Said he'd heard about them from someone, whoever that may be. And when he backed me up against the wall and trapped me between his arms, I gave him two chances to back off."

"And did he?" asked the sheriff.

"Nope. I know how to take care of myself because I had a big brother who taught me what to do with boys who don't listen."

Relief and pride replaced the anger in my brother's eyes. "Knee?" he asked.

"One blow," I confirmed with a nod.

"So if Doc finds any injury in that particular area, I guess we know who to talk to." Big Willie blew out a breath. "It's all a big mess, and we need more experienced hands. But you gotta stay out of this, Charli. I mean it. If you can't help yourself, then I'll throw you in the tank myself."

Matt stepped in front of his boss. "You can't arrest her."

"Did I say arrest?" He ignored the fact he'd said it a few times already. "I said I would put her in the tank to think about whether or not it's smart for her to stick her nose where it's not needed. At least then, we'd know she wouldn't get in the way."

Matt challenged the sheriff. "My grandmother wouldn't stand for it."

Big Willie closed the distance between the two of them. "Well, Vivi isn't here right now, and you are my subordinate. And if you don't like it, then you can run for sheriff the next time around, Deputy. Until then, don't challenge my decisions."

I opened my mouth to ask the question but my brother beat me to it. "Are you arresting Charli or not?"

The sasquatch looked between the two of us and closed his eyes. "No, I guess not. At least not right now." He walked back over to my upset friend being consoled by the two tooth fairies. "I guess that's all I need from you right now. I'll be talkin' to your grandmother to confirm your whereabouts. For now, make sure you don't leave town without notification. I'm going to go see if I can make heads or tails out of this mess."

"Sheriff, you might want to use the back entrance to avoid attention." I pointed at the back door.

The sasquatch smacked his head. "You really can't help yourself, but I guess it's a good idea. You know that directive I just gave your friend? The same goes for you, Charli. Deputy Goodwin, come with me and maybe you can help out until our detective's return."

With the sheriff gone, my adrenaline evaporated and the weight of the whole morning crashed down on me. I went over to my friend and threw my arms around her, consoling her and letting her snot onto my shoulder.

After a few shared tears, I looked up and asked Sprinkle, "Do you guys mind if she takes the day off?"

Twinkle spoke first. "She can have as long as she wants off. I don't know where that bumbling fool thinks he gets the right to treat her like that. Thinkin' our sweet girl could be responsible for anyone's death."

I patted my friend on her back. "Chances are the sheriff would have sent someone to question her eventually."

Mason never would have treated her with such disrespect and immediate suspicion. At some point, maybe I needed to talk to Nana about Big Willie and suggest that retirement needed to be in the sasquatch's future.

Once she calmed down, Alison Kate sniffed and wiped her eyes. "What am I supposed to do now?"

I rocked her back and forth. "Oh, Ali Kat. Here's what you're gonna do. You're going to go home with me today, and I'll send out the bat signal and call the girls to come over. We'll make a morning of it and do all kinds of girly things until you feel better."

My friend looked at me with hope in her eyes. "You'll let me paint your nails?"

"Sure thing, Ali Kat."

"And curl your hair?"

"Okay," I agreed with some hesitation.

"And put makeup on you?" she pushed with twinkling eyes.

My protest hovered at the tip of my tongue, but I noticed

the slight quiver of her bottom lip and gave in. "If treating me like your own personal doll will make you feel better, you can give me the works."

Sprinkle and Twinkle sent us out into the world with a couple of boxes of free baked goods. We stopped off at Alison Kate's place, and she packed a small suitcase worth of stuff to take to my house. What had I gotten myself into?

Chapter Eight

I parked my bike under the sprawling magnolia tree in front of the school. Students filed out of the doors at the end of the day. The younger ones met up with parents or older siblings to go home. Most of the older kids walked away in groups, busy talking and having more fun than sitting in a stuffy classroom. I remembered not liking attending a school with every single grade level, but in our small town, we never had enough children to justify separate schools for the different class levels.

Striding toward the front door, I attempted not to throw up from my nerves. Nana had promised me that her friend had left detailed lesson plans that even a monkey could follow. The screams and squeals of the young ones running around didn't help. I needed a distraction, but thinking about the murder case probably wasn't a good idea before walking in to mentor a bunch of students.

Something hard whacked me on the top of my head. I rubbed the spot where it hurt and found Timmy Belford standing on top of a picnic table, waving a stick in his hand about to hit me with it again.

"Stop," I commanded.

He halted mid-swing and held it behind his back. "Hey, Miss Chawi."

His little speech impediment wouldn't make me smile this time. "Timmy, what are you doing?"

The little imp dared to giggle. "I put a spell on you with my wand. Just like the movies."

I'd forgotten that Honeysuckle had finally gotten around to viewing the series of movies based on a bunch of popular books about witches and wizards with a magical academy set in Great Britain. I watched all the films while traveling during my year away, and wasn't so sure how good of an idea it was to show them here with young impressionable actual magic wielders.

Distracted with my thoughts, I missed Timmy's swing and got hit again. "Expelliwhompus," he exclaimed.

"Expelli-whatus?" I grabbed him under his arms and lifted him down, taking away his weapon of choice. "That's not even a real spell. What are you trying to do anyway?"

His big brown eyes gazed up at me. "I heard my mommy say that there was something wong with you."

My eyebrows rose to the top of my head. "Really? Did she happen to mention what she thought was wrong?"

He shook his head and stared at the stick in my possession. "No, but she said something had to be 'cause you keep finding the bodies. What did she mean by that, Miss Chawi?"

How could I explain the truth of his mother's overheard gossip without scaring the poor boy? I stammered to find a response but failed to come up with a good explanation. "I think she means that I'm really good at playing Hide and Seek and finding people." Great, I was starting off my career as a substitute teacher lying to a little kid.

"Can I have my wand back?" he demanded, blowing right past my flimsy explanation.

I gathered up all of my futile babysitting skills and replied, "Only if you promise not to hit anyone with it. That's not how we cast spells in the real world anyway, and you're gonna hurt someone. You promise not to use this to hit?" I held out his treasured stick.

With great earnestness, Timmy nodded. "I pwomise."

Against my better judgment, I let the little boy with big eyes have his pretend wand back. He immediately ran off and chased a little girl, coming awfully close to hitting her over the head. So much for my ability to teach. Thankfully, his older brother intervened and grabbed him, giving him a little whack on his behind that only a sibling could get away with.

The good news was that I had been indeed distracted, letting my nausea subside. The bad news was that I still had to get inside to teach. I walked up the small set of stairs to the front doors, catching my reflection in the glass.

Despite the bike ride over, my hair still held the curls Alison Kate gave me, and the makeup she'd applied made me look like myself, only better. I smiled at the pretty me staring back, enjoying my berry lip-stained grin, and pulled open the door.

New layers of paint brightened the walls and different banners hung from the ceiling, but the familiarity of it all transported me back in time. I knew all the hallways and staircases, the best way to get to where my last locker was, and where I'd enchanted a permanent mark under the bleachers in the gym, stating *Charli wuz here*. But I didn't know in which classroom the spell prep class was being held. I wandered the empty halls, listening for clues.

An enormous figure popped his head out of one of the rooms. "Miss Charli, what brings you forth to our hallowed halls of education?" Horatio smiled a toothy grin.

"Horatio, I didn't know they had you here teaching." I hugged the troll, stretching my arms as far as I could to reach around his wide body.

He released me and pointed to the poster taped to the door with the Shakespeare quote, *There is no darkness but ignorance*. "I'm filling in for Kelly Miller while she takes care of her newborn babe. However, I strive to impart knowledge to the young minds with such alacrity that I may procure the opportunity to continue on a more permanent basis."

I chuckled. "Sometimes I feel like I need to carry a

dictionary around with me to speak to you. I'm guessing you hope you're doing a good enough job that if the former teacher chooses not to come back, you can stay on?"

"Your ability to detect the truth from the clues of my words remains at the highest level, Holmes." He tipped an invisible hat to me.

Glancing inside his new domain, I spotted a poster of a famous Shakespeare play. "Horatio, did you teach *A Midsummer Night's Dream* this semester?"

His eyes brightened. "Why, of course. In fact, I obtained permission for a field trip to view a production in Charleston. They were quite taken in by seeing the venerable Bard's words performed live. They especially enjoyed the thespian who played Robin Goodfellow."

"You mean Puck?" I asked. "The trickster character?"

Horatio pondered my question. "Yes, he went by the moniker of Puck as well as Robin. I believe that Will did a fine job of characterizing young Goodfellow, but maybe wrote in a bit more mischief than the actual Puck in real life."

My jaw dropped. "He's real?"

The troll guffawed, his scraggly hair shaking. "Oh, very much so. And a merry fellow he is. I do not think he would be so bold as to go against King Oberon nor Queen Titania's wishes, but I do recall he found great amusement in tricking humans."

I tried to imagine the fantasy world of the fairies and humans, forgetting where I lived for a second. "So

Shakespeare's play is based on reality? I thought he made it all up."

"My gracious, no." Horatio stroked his chin. "In fact, it was my meeting with the great Bard that brought about his awareness to those of our kind. I must admit that it ruffled many feathers of the fae that I exposed a mortal to our world. But Will's gift of words and a quick-witted tongue charmed them all. They fell in love with him as much as I had. Members of the royal fairy court were the first to view his finished work. King Oberon particularly enjoyed the transformation of a man's head into that of a donkey."

"So your students enjoyed watching the play with Puck and his pranks." Perhaps the little class trip had encouraged the current atmosphere of walking through the Wild West on Main Street with hexes and spells being shot at each other. "You might want to impress upon your students that it was just a play. I could have cracked my tailbone when one of the Mosley boys missed his target for a slipping spell and hit me instead."

Horatio winced. "I confess, the thought did occur to me, although they could also be taking their cue from the twin red-headed brothers in the films being shown at the theater in the town hall. They are most amusing in their hijinks. I can attempt to curtail their shenanigans, but with me not having any magic of my own, I am not sure how effective a scolding from a humble troll such as myself would be."

"Perhaps that's a job for the substitute spell permit class

teacher," I said. I asked Horatio to help me find the classroom, and he walked me to the door.

The noise emanating from the room should have alerted me to its location. I peeked inside with trepidation. Kids sat on top of desks and talked fast and loud. Some of them possessed spell phones and texted each other, laughing at whatever they wrote with their thumbs.

Horatio gave my back a slight push. "I wish you luck in your new endeavor, Charli. For this and the other challenge."

I paused in confusion. "What challenge?"

He winked at me. "Honeysuckle is indeed a small township, and someone considering taking up residence in an empty storefront does get noticed. However, that is a conversation for a later time. Your students await."

Taking a deep breath, I centered myself and forced my nerves to stop producing butterflies. I plastered on a wide grin that hurt my cheeks and faced the daunting task with as much bravery as I could muster.

The second I entered the room, all the students stopped talking and stared at me. My cheeks lit up like fireballs, and I rushed over to the desk at the front of the room, knocking over the chair behind it. So much for a smooth entry. I searched the table for the promised lesson plans and found a folder with detailed notes and worksheets for the students to fill out while I lectured.

Figuring out my lack of confidence in a matter of seconds, the students went back to talking and ignoring me. All except the Mosley boy who'd shot the spell at me, sitting in the back row and trying to be invisible.

I coughed. "Um, hey, y'all." My voice came out barely louder than a mumble. Clearing my throat, I tried again. "Excuse me, but I'll be your teacher for this session of the spell permit course. You may call me Miss Goodwin. No, that's too formal. Maybe you should call me Charli since I'm not that much older than you. Except that makes it sound like I wanna be your friend, and it's not that I don't, but I'm really supposed to be your teacher..."

I trailed off, aware that maybe only one or two of the students were paying me any attention. One of the girls in the front row popped a bubble of gum and focused on her spell phone. Irritated, I snatched it out of her grip.

"Hey," she called out.

"You can have it back after class." Now I sounded like an old unicorn's fart of a teacher. The phone dinged, and I checked the message out of sheer habit, reading the words, *I hope this hex doesn't miss its mark. Tag, you're it with this zapping spark.*

A jolt of energy burst out of the phone and stung my hand, and I almost dropped the phone. "Ow! What was that?"

The noise in the room stopped, and all the students stared at me. Yet none of them volunteered any insight as to what in tarnation happened.

I held up the device and waved it around. "I want to know why this phone just zapped me."

The kids looked at each other, and a couple shook their

heads in warning to the others to maintain silence in solidarity.

If they wanted to play dirty, they were messing with the wrong witch. I flipped the phone open again and checked to see who sent the last message. "Eric Mosley."

The tall kid who'd accidentally hexed me on Main Street groaned and raised his hand. "Yes, ma'am."

I stifled a smirk, knowing he owed me. "Explain what your text means. Or what it did."

Murmurs of concern erupted, and the poor boy defended himself. He reassured the others and quieted them down. "I sent a spell through the phone with a text. There's something about how they operate off the magic of our town that makes it possible. I told my cousin about it down near Atlanta, but their phones work differently."

Holding the device in the palm of my hand, I stared at it. "How did you send a spell through a text?"

Eric's cheeks reddened, and he succumbed to the pressure of the other kids not to say anything more.

"Listen," I said in a louder voice. "This class is meant to prep you to take your spell permit tests. We can do this the hard way or the easy way. The hard way is for me to hand out worksheets for you to fill in and take notes while I drone on and on for an entire hour. Or someone can show me how you send a spell through the phone, and we'll come up with a better way to study."

One of the Tiller twins rolled her eyes and raised her hand. "I can show you."

I had a fifty-fifty shot at guessing which identical twin she was. "Thanks, Anna."

"I'm Emily," she retorted.

Her very-similar-looking sister pointed at herself. "I'm Anna."

"It's my phone," piped up the girl in the front, who I remembered was their cousin Helen.

Emily shrugged her shoulders. "Then you show Miss Charli."

Helen took the phone back. "Who do you want me to text?"

I didn't even hesitate. "Why don't you send one right back to Eric." Today might be my first and last day I was allowed to teach, but I'd make it worth my while.

The girl hesitated, thinking about how to explain the process. "First, you think up the spell you want to send. So far, we've found you can't do anything really big or expect too much. About all that's reliable is to hit someone with a tiny spell."

"And how do you do that?" I asked.

Helen paused with her fingers hovering over the keys. "You come up with what you want the end results to be. Then you think about how to create a spell to make that happen. Type in what you want and will it to happen with intent. Then press Send." She thought for a moment, snickered, and typed something in. Showing me her phone, she hit the green button.

A buzz from the back of the room alerted us to Eric's

phone receiving the text. He raised his hand. "Do I have to read it?"

"I think since you sent one to her, it's only fair," I challenged. "And while you're at it, as long as Helen's okay with it, you can read it out loud."

"Oh, I'm okay with it." Helen turned around in her seat to watch him with the rest of the class.

Eric flipped open his phone. "*You think I can't spellcast something big. Let's try it out, oink like a pig.*" When he finished the last word, he opened his mouth to talk and only oinking noises came out. The effect lasted a couple of seconds before it wore off, and the boy laughed along with everyone else.

I took my own spell phone out of my pocket, wondering who I might try this new skill out on. Lee would want to know about the students' ingenious use of spell phones immediately if only because he enjoyed a good prank. I'd send something through to Mason, but if he was on his way back to Honeysuckle, I didn't want to cause him to have an accident or anything.

"We've been calling it *hexting*. You know, a combo of hex and texting?" explained Eric. "You're not going to get us in trouble, are you?"

Having the fate of the students in my hand was an awesome power. At the same time, I couldn't help but put myself in their positions. "No, as long as nobody is really getting hurt. Zapping someone or sending a small transformation spell isn't a big deal. The second any of your pranks get out of hand, you have to stop them. They won't let you even apply for your spell permit."

One of the kids sitting in the middle blurted out, "I don't know why we have to take the test anyway. We've been using magic here since we were little."

I really should take attendance so I could know everyone's name. "Yes, but you want your permit so that you have your first license and so you have the ability to use magic if you're ever not in our special town. Just because we're a little more isolated and free to be ourselves doesn't mean we don't need to learn control."

Anna raised her hand. "What if we don't plan on ever leaving Honeysuckle, miss?"

At one point in my life, I'd thought the same thing. I liked my hometown and couldn't think of any reason why I would want to leave it. Due to my disastrous engagement to Tucker, I changed my mind so fast that I left without telling anyone. "Even if you stay here all your life, you need to follow the rules. That goes for just living here or to make sure that your magic never hurts you or anybody else."

"But why?" pressed her twin, Emily.

I hoisted myself on top of the teacher's desk and swung my legs. "The best answer I can give you is that magic has consequences. Y'all know that if you use more than a little at a time that you get hungry or really thirsty. That's because we can't use an infinite amount of it. Also, spells themselves have consequences. It's why we have different categories you get tested in, including defensive spells."

"But there are bad spells, too, like in the wizard movie, right?" Eric chimed in. "I mean, there are ones that are forbidden but the villains use them all the same."

I had to give his question a lot of consideration. Furrowing my brow, I blew out a big breath. "Yes and no. Even a simple spell can be used against someone for a bad purpose. I think it comes down to intent. And if the intent is a really evil one, then I think once the spell is cast that it takes a bigger toll on you."

Helen mumbled, "Like that guy who died in your uncle's house?" She avoided my surprised gaze, but I couldn't fault her for stating the truth.

"Yes, kind of like the guy who died at my house." It was a simplistic answer for a very complicated explanation.

Ashton Sharpe had died by his own hand, ingesting his own poison rather than dying by the death curse my great-Uncle Tipper had accidentally placed on me and that had finally found its correct victim. But the truth existed in my answer. The evil he'd done through spells and potions had eaten away at him.

Helen looked up at me. "Were you scared?"

"Yes." Better to be truthful than to lie in this case. "But I think I did the best I could in that situation. And maybe the take away from all of it was that in the long run, I needed to be true to who I was and trust myself and my magic. Which is something I hope you'll learn from our short time together."

I clapped my hands to break us out of such dark thoughts. "I think we have the beginnings of a good discussion, which is how spells work. We've seen how *hexting* works once we broke it down. Why don't we try some other simple pranks and see if we as a class can come up with a good explanation to the test question, 'How does spellcasting work?'"

I pushed the detailed instructions and worksheets out of the way and scooted further onto the desk, crossing my legs and waiting for the students to clear their seats to the side of the room to give them space to work. Their enthusiastic faces and participation were my reward, and when they told me at the end of our time that they couldn't wait for the next class, my heart almost burst with pride.

Eric stayed behind for a brief moment. "I wanted to say that this is the most fun I've ever had. But also I learned a lot about how to think my way through a spell before casting it."

"Good." I patted his arm. "Maybe next time, you won't be the literal pain in my behind." We both laughed and walked out of the classroom. He ran off to join his friends, and I sent my very first *hext* to Ben, the self-proclaimed king of spell pranks.

Chapter Nine

Filled with energy to burn and a pinch of self-satisfaction, I directed my bike to Main Street. I didn't count on the fact that while I was teaching the kids, I was also learning a whole lot at the same time. It had been ages since I thought about the basics of spellcasting, and there were a couple of techniques that the students had come up with I wanted to try with my tracking talents.

Although my time with the class refreshed me, it also renewed my determination to get the investigation of Duke's murder under better control. If Big Willie couldn't do it and Mason wasn't here, then someone needed to figure things out. Taking my own advice, I remained true to myself and parked my bike at the back of the old diner, prepared to do whatever it took to do a thorough investigation.

Raising my hands in front of the back door, I tested to see

if a wardens' protection blocked the entrance. Nothing repelled my reach, and I gripped the door handle. Feeling lucky, I turned it to the right and found it unlocked. With caution, I entered the storeroom and made my way into the galley kitchen. A general hush and lack of lights in the space suggested I was alone. Finding a switch on the wall, I flicked it once. Light illuminated the remnants of the crime scene through the kitchen's pass-through window.

I'd tried myself to redirect my thoughts from the murder, forcing myself to ignore the compunction to follow the rabbit down the hole of too many ideas. But now that my mind had permission, theories broke through the dam one after another. Based on what I knew about Duke, the problem wasn't who wanted to kill the chef. The question I needed to ask was, who didn't?

From what I'd watched at the Hawthorne's house, any number of people could have issues with him. If he stole with ease from others to pad his business, how many people had been victimized? His rudeness warranted irritation, but maybe he took it too far with one of the servers or pixies? Or Shelby? Perhaps other choices Duke had made caught up to him in the end.

I entered the main room and scoured the area to find any evidence. Dark red stained the wood floor, marking the faint outline of where Duke's head had rested. It frustrated me not to have a direct line into the investigation because of Big Willie's stubbornness. If Duke was hit on the head, had the wardens found the weapon used? Did they determine that the head injury was the cause of death? There were too many questions and nobody to help me find the answers.

I crouched down to investigate a bit of dust around where I'd found the body. I swiped my fingers through it, and studied the smut up close. Green flecks floated in the air when I wiped my thumb against my skin. I knew one Honeysuckle Hollow citizen who that might belong to.

"I've already got Sassy on the suspect list," a deep male voice cut through the silence. "And one of these days, you'll learn not to break into a crime scene."

All thoughts about the murder evaporated, and I leapt to my feet, running toward the voice. Throwing my arms around Mason, I hugged him close. "You're home."

His stiffened body melted into mine, and he embraced me long and hard, rocking me back and forth and rubbing my back in slow circles. "It's good to see you, too, Charli."

"Where have you been?" I muffled into his shoulder, hiding my face so he wouldn't see the sudden tears leaking out of my eyes. It caught me off guard how his mere presence punctuated how much I'd missed him. I sniffed and tried to compose myself, pulling back.

He smiled down at me. "Remember the phoenix feather I obtained to help solve your Uncle Tipper's demise?"

Matt had hinted back then that the cost was more than Mason let on. "But I thought you said it was payment for favors you had already granted?"

The detective shrugged. "I may have left out a detail or

two. Something that rare required more favors on their end than mine. They called in their chips and I had to go."

I waited for him to elaborate on who *they* were. He shook his head in refusal and continued.

"When the sheriff called me back, I was already on my way. Something in my gut told me that you couldn't stay out of trouble, despite my orders to Zeke to watch out for you and Sheriff West's promise to me you would be staying out of things this time. What changed?"

Missing you and what we do together, I thought. "Hey, I almost made it a whole twenty-four hours."

"I'm surprised you survived that long. Big Willie said under no circumstances were you supposed to help me." Mason lifted his eyebrow.

My excitement waned. "Does that mean you're sending me home?"

I waited for him to erect the inevitable wall to keep me out. But Mason stepped forward and brushed a strand of my hair behind my ear with such gentleness that a single shiver danced down my spine. "The last few days, I've been pushing against authority and breaking a few rules." He paused and flashed me a devilish grin. "It feels good to be a little bad."

I took a better look at the man in front of me. His clean-shaven appearance gave way to stubble. It broke the mold of his *by-the-book* image, looking less like a detective and more like the criminal. The hot gleam in his eyes melted my insides into jelly.

"Who are you and what have you done with Mason?" I swallowed hard and licked my lips.

His eyes dropped to them and lingered. "Let's just say I took advantage of my time away to think some things over."

What things? I wanted to scream at him, but grabbed onto any shred of control to stay cool. "Okay," I managed in a breathy voice.

He brushed another strand of hair away from my face. "You look...different," he murmured, studying me.

I swallowed hard, ignoring the flaming heat in my cheeks. "I let Ali Kat give me a makeover." His attentive gaze made me squirm. "Is *different* a good or bad thing?"

Mason studied my appearance like an experienced detective. "Good. Definitely good."

The air around us crackled with tension, and my knees shook. I grabbed onto his arms to stay upright, pulling our bodies closer. His breath hitched, and he cupped the back of my neck. Leaning in, the hot air of his breath caressed the line of my jaw, on my neck, and up to my ear.

"Not yet and not here," he whispered, his lips brushing the sensitive lobe. With a sigh, he pushed my shivering body away.

He was right, a crime scene was no place for unexpected flirtatious banter. The new distance cooled the heat between us, and I cleared my throat. "So which is it? Am I staying or going?"

Mason relaxed. "I'm beginning to wonder which was more dangerous, you or my last job? I guess you can stay on the case as long as you work with me and not on your own. And I hope you'll say yes to my next question."

"Yes," I joked, reveling in the detective's return.

With unusual patience, he waited for me to take him seriously. Once I quieted, he made his request. "Have dinner with me tonight."

For a person used to throwing up barriers between us, his offer confused me. There were so many things we needed to say. I wanted to tell him all about the bridal shower, what I'd witnessed in the Hawthorne's kitchen, and my first experience teaching. He needed to tell me where he'd been and why it changed who he was now that he was back.

"At the Harvest Moon?" I asked.

"No, my place."

The last time I witnessed the product of the man's cooking, I told him to throw it into the trash. "So you're telling me I need to cook some food and bring it over?"

"A gentleman would never invite you to a meal at his home without providing the food himself," Mason teased. "Are you saying yes?"

I nodded my head in affirmation and pointed to his scruff. "I think a gentleman would shave."

He scratched the whiskers on his chin. "It's something I'm trying. I needed it while I was gone, and I want to see if it's too hot to keep."

Oh, it was definitely hot and he needed to keep it. "You have to let me at least bring the dessert. A lady doesn't show up empty-handed."

"But she shows up at crime scenes?" Mason teased.

"Fair point," I conceded.

He bumped me with his hip. "Bring whatever sweet thing you want, but just you would be enough. For now, walk me through your take of the situation."

I filled him in on all of my observations, and he shared with me the facts from the wardens' side. Duke did sustain a head injury, resulting in some blood loss. However, the doc ruled it out as the cause of death since the chef had died from asphyxiation.

"A lack of oxygen?" I asked. "Was there bruising around his throat?"

Mason approved my inquiry with a slight nod of his head. "Good line of thinking, but no. No bruising as if someone tried to choke him with their hands or by pulling something tight around his neck. The whole thing is really bothering Doc because there's no physical evidence on the body that suggests how he basically choked to death."

I crouched down next to where the body had lain, sorting through the little bit of facts I'd gleaned during Big Willie's confusion. "There was no blood or skin underneath his fingernails, which suggests that he didn't fight someone off."

Mason joined me in my thinking position. "He was hit over the head, so maybe he was knocked out. It's possible that someone restricted his flow of air in a way that wouldn't leave behind obvious clues."

"True," I sighed. Eric's question from the spell class popped in my head at that second. "Unless the unthinkable happened, and someone found another way to limit Duke's respiratory system." An all-too-familiar instinct gnawed on my gut.

The detective frowned. "I'm not following."

"Someone could have cast a spell to somehow remove the oxygen around him," I offered, wanting the idea not to be true. "But that's a crazy theory, right? Who would risk their own life casting something like that?"

Mason ran his hand over his stubble, making a scratchy sound. "I've seen people do worse in bigger cities. There are lots of witches willing to risk their souls by using magic to do bad things. If we had a spellweaver on hand, maybe there'd be enough magic residue left over on Duke's body to figure out if a spell was used and who cast it."

I gaped at him. "There are people who can do that?"

He closed my mouth with a nudge of his finger. "They're even rarer than a tracker, and can be pretty unreliable since magic is tricky even at its simplest. The one we used in my last department cost too much for the consultation and gave us little results. I was pretty sure he was putting us on to begin with to con us out of money, but I couldn't prove it. And the case we used him for was bad enough that my captain was willing to chance it."

We both stood and pondered everything in silence. I walked around, inspecting the entire area free from Big Willie's complaints. Mason let me examine the scene with care and take my time until I was satisfied.

"You say you've got Sassy on the list. I can see her maybe

interacting with Duke, but killing a man?" The fairy annoyed me, but I didn't believe she could do anything so reckless and evil.

"You've got your own list, I'm sure. Sheriff West shared some of the insights you forced upon him in my absence." The detective took out his notebook from his pocket. "If you were in charge, what would be your next step?"

I almost exploded from the spark of excitement of Mason inviting my input for the first time. Not willing to let the opportunity pass, I dove in head first. "Sassy wouldn't be the first person I'd interview. Duke's partner, Shelby, should be at the top. Also, I know that Lucky was running a late-night game of cards. Maybe he saw or heard something."

The detective ushered me to the back door. "Since he's just a few doors down, we can start there. How did you know about the game?"

Visions of Tucker in his drunken state appeared before my eyes. Bringing him up would change the focus of the investigation. I had questions I wanted to ask him first to see if there was a reason to maybe interrupt his life and ruin his impending wedding...again.

"Lucky's secret card games aren't exactly classified. Everyone knows about them." I bit my lip, ashamed of the second lie uttered from my mouth today.

"Okay, go get your bike and meet me around front," Mason instructed.

"How did you know I parked my bicycle nearby? Or that I had it with me?"

The detective leaned against the door frame, and the afternoon sun hit him at the right moment, highlighting the intriguing changes in his outward appearance. "You riding around on your magic-powered bike is not a big secret either. Meet you out front." Letting the door close with a metal clang, he left me with too many emotions about him swirling inside and perplexing me.

With no walls up between us, what kind of trouble would the two of us get into?

Chapter Ten

Mason and I knocked on the door to Lucky's bar, The Rainbow's End. In the light of day, I admired the thick wood carved with elaborate Celtic symbology and a large tree. After three loud tries, the leprechaun answered with a frown.

He glanced back and forth between the detective and me, glinting out of a swollen black eye. "And what may I be doin' for ya this fine afternoon?" he asked in his Irish accent with a less than friendly tone.

"How'd you get the shiner?" Mason gestured at the leprechaun's eye.

Lucky showed us inside and busied himself behind the bar. Only the top of his red hair showed above the dark wood. "Ran into a wall. What have ye come here to ask me?" He stepped onto a platform of some sort, elevating him to our eye level.

Clearly, the leprechaun wasn't in a sharing mood, but neither Mason nor I had the time to try and wrangle the truth out of him. I spoke up, "Let's not get bogged down in unicorn manure. I know you know about Duke's death, and we need to ask you about your card game last night."

Lucky opened his mouth and closed it. He reached for a pint glass and filled it with a dark, thick beer with a hint of foam on top. "Guinness?" he asked both of us.

"We're on the job," explained Mason.

The leprechaun shrugged, gripping the pint in his hand and holding it up. "Suit yourselves. *Sláinte mhaith*." In huge gulps, he finished the entire thing. He slammed the glass down and wiped the foam from his lips with the back of his hand.

"Who was here in the bar last night?" Mason asked, taking out his notebook.

"It was a slow night, and where you want me to start is to tell you that the dead man was here." Lucky took a nearby rag and wiped down the bar. "So was Steve, Henry, Raif, Tucker, and me. That's who stayed to play poker." The leprechaun shot a wary eye at the detective.

Mason shook his head. "I'm not here to bust you over illegal gambling. But I do need to have details about everything. What time did the bar empty of other patrons? What time did the game start? What happened during the game? How'd you get the black eye?"

Leaning forward with both hands on the bar, Lucky looked like he wanted to fight the detective. His shoulders slumped and he sighed. "You better come with me."

Lucky hopped down and led us to the back of the bar. Taking out some keys from his pocket, he unlocked a door I'd never noticed before and opened it. The secret room lay in complete destruction with cards and chips scattered about, chairs knocked over or broken, and a couple of holes in the wall.

"What happened?" I marveled, taking a careful step inside.

"Tucker Hawthorne," exploded Lucky. "He's what happened. I've never had any trouble with him before, but he's been comin' to The End more and more frequently. A couple of times, I even escorted him back to his place after I closed down to keep the rest of the town from knowin', especially that sweet lass of his." The more the leprechaun got excited, the thicker his accent grew.

"Start from the beginning," insisted Mason.

Lucky righted an overturned chair and ran a hand down a tear in the table's green felt. "I shut the bar down early around eleven and we came back here. We played a few rounds, and the vampire quit, leaving early. He thinks he's a cards man, but he was way out of his league. It only took losin' a few *bobs* as he called his money for him to figure that out."

"So Raif's not responsible for the damage," I clarified.

The leprechaun picked up a piece of a broken chair. "No, we had an hour at least of good gamblin'. That fella Duke is a right bast—um, backside of a unicorn. He did his best to rile up Steve with the prospect of opening up a competing restaurant."

I watched Mason write down the cafe owner's name underneath the fairy's. "Was Sassy here at any point?" Waiting for Mason to scold me for jumping in, he surprised me with supporting silence.

Lucky nodded. "She was in earlier before I closed things down out front, hoverin' and buzzin' around Duke like he was pecan pie and she was the fork. But I shooed her away before the game started."

I leaned into the detective. "Maybe he got some of her dust on him then and transferred it to the old diner when he was there."

Mason made some notes and paused. "When and how did the fighting start?"

Lucky stroked his red beard. "It must have been some time after midnight. Henry and Steve left with their meager winnings at the same time, leaving just Duke, Tucker, and myself. I suggested to young Hawthorne, who was several sheets to the wind by that point, that perhaps him takin' his leave would be best. Like an ignorant untrained pup, he ignored me."

"So he hit you?" I asked.

"Not at first." Lucky stopped cleaning up the room and faced us. "Duke started in on Tucker, something about how he should hand over all his money right then and there and make it easier on himself. The way those two spoke, it seemed as if they knew each other."

"Well, Duke's company did cater the bridal shower," I explained. "Although I'm pretty sure he's not the actual chef doing the cooking."

Lucky pointed at me. "That's what young Tucker said. Told Duke that he would expose him if he didn't stop."

"Stop what?" both Mason and I asked at the same time.

The leprechaun pointed at the table. "He didn't say much else. Tucker launched himself across the table at the other man, and the fight started. I did my best to stop it and earned this from one of them." He pointed at his black eye. "I think you people forget that though we leprechauns are not tall, we harbor a considerable amount of magic. We're not all rainbows, pots of gold, and cereal with fake marshmallows in it."

Having known Lucky most of my life, it surprised me he brought up his personal powers. "What did you do?"

He pointed at the holes in the wall. "That's where I tossed them. Told them they better leave unless they wanted me to do worse."

"Did they leave?" I catalogued the injuries I'd noticed on Tucker, trying to match them with the leprechaun's story.

"I shoved them out the side door into the alley there and wiped my hands of what happened after. It'll be a while before I let Tucker back in." Lucky picked up a broken tumbler, inspected it, and tossed it on the floor to shatter.

Mason checked the timeline he wrote down. "At some

point after midnight, those two fighting men left your bar and one of them had their life taken."

The leprechaun blinked. "I can tell you exactly when. At precisely eight minutes past one in the morning."

"How can you know that?" challenged the detective. "That's pretty specific."

"Because of the wail of the banshee." Lucky waved his hands for us to leave the room. He locked the door behind us. "I heard her cry long and loud at exactly eight past one."

A loud cry. Or maybe it was heard as a howl like the one Beau asked me about. "A banshee," I muttered.

"Surely you've heard of them, *a chara*." He patted me on the back. "They are not stuff of legend, being one of the fae folk attached to a family and magic bound to mourn their passing. It was a banshee's keening I heard, and no doubt about it. I recognized the shriek from my days in the Old World."

"I think my roommate heard it, too," I said.

"Chances are many in the town did. It is a sound not easily ignored nor forgotten. I was happy that none of my glasses shattered. Are ye sure you don't want a pint? You look a bit peaky." He gestured at the bar.

I shook my head, the gears inside of it turning fast. "Are all banshees women?"

The leprechaun nodded. "In my recollection, they are."

"And they are connected to a family, you said?" I pressed.

"Aye." Lucky scratched the bald spot in the middle of his

head. "They come back again and again for generations of deaths."

A line of connection formed between Duke and a likely suspect. "And if a person was the last of the family, once they were mourned, perhaps the banshee would be free."

Mason stepped up next to me. "You've got an idea who it is." He took out his spell phone and flipped it open.

"Yeah, I think I know someone who might fit the description of being stuck with Duke and wanting something bad to happen to him." I watched Mason check the text.

The detective closed his phone. "That was Zeke. Flint alerted the wardens that someone on the watch list was trying to leave Honeysuckle."

"And I'll bet her name is Shelby," I exclaimed.

Mason thanked Lucky and pulled me out of the dark bar and into the warm light of the afternoon. "I think you'd better accompany me. It seems you know more than I do, and I could use your help."

❧

MASON TOOK me to the guard house at our border. When we approached, we both noticed a large wooden gate blocking the road. I imagined the invisible magical barriers were at their maximum strength as well.

Flint came out to meet us once we parked on the side of the road. "We've been monitoring who comes in and out since this morning. She's just a slip of a thing and could have made it past us. Except I was on duty." He pointed at the small structure.

Mason thanked the gnome and checked on the car she'd driven, calling in the license plate to the warden station.

"How's Goss doin'?" I asked.

Flint smiled. "My wife is doin' fine, although she's not so hot on the enforced bed rest."

"When's she due?" I'd learned a while back that the gestation period for fairies was way shorter than humans from TJ in an outburst of jealousy.

The gnome's face went pale. "Soon. And I'm not quite done with the cradle yet."

One of the traditions of his people Flint wanted to bring to his family was the hand carving of the baby's cradle. The task took the length of a pregnancy, resulting in beautiful handiwork and elaborate designs. The finished product would be presented to everyone who attended the naming ceremony to show how dedicated he was as a father to taking care of his family.

"I'll bet what you have right now is more than enough," I promised my friend.

He shook his head. "Nothing will ever be good enough for my Gossy and my baby."

Mason got off his spell phone and approached us. "Yeah, the car she's driving is registered to Duke Aikens. Looks like she was trying to flee. Where is she now?"

Flint pointed at the guard house and walked the two of us over. He asked the other gate guard to take a break, leaving Mason and me to question a shaking Shelby.

"I know what you're thinking. You think I did it. That I killed Duke." She looked up at the two of us from her seat with tears falling down her face. "But I didn't, I swear."

"But you did see his body lying there in the old diner, didn't you?" I asked, testing out my theory of who...or what... Shelby was to the chef.

"Oh," she uttered, hanging her head. "You think you know what I am."

I crouched down in the small space to meet her at eye level and touched her hand. "A lot of people heard a loud scream or shriek late last night. I can't say for sure, but I think that what they heard was the wail of a banshee."

Shelby shut her eyes and squeezed them tight. "That was me," she whispered. "I made that noise. My father was a witch and my mother was a banshee. She bonded herself and me to Duke's family long ago in order to ensure that we were taken care of when my father left us. You see, he wasn't exactly a nice man."

I squeezed her hand. "From what I saw, neither was Duke. Why'd you stay with him?"

She looked at me with watery eyes. "I wanted to leave so I wouldn't end up like Mom, dying for a family that barely wanted her to begin with. I begged Duke to let me go. He was the last of his family line, and he had the power to say the right words and release me from my bond." Her bottom lip trembled.

"I'm guessing he wouldn't let you go. Especially when you were so useful to him." I sat down on the wooden floor, hoping that Mason didn't mind me taking the lead and not really caring if he did.

She sniffed and wiped under her eyes. "I was always a good cook, like my mom. I think my dad's side of the family had some kitchen witches in it because I took to cooking and baking from an early age. Duke saw an opportunity and forced me to work for the company he created. You'd never guess how many places a caterer can get into and be ignored. It was his free pass into many houses or to be around important people."

Mason coughed, and Shelby jumped, remembering the detective's presence. "Is there a reason he needed to be around important people?"

The frightened young woman kept her eyes trained on the floor in front of her. "Yes, sir. You see, Duke liked information. Any kind or variety from anybody. He would use what he collected to gain what he wanted. Sometimes, he wanted money and would blackmail people. Sometimes, he wanted access. There's no record of any speeding tickets even though he never drove slow."

The pieces clicked together and I understood the importance of Duke's words to her in the Hawthorne's kitchen. It also alerted me to the magnitude of what I saw and how much worse the situation might be.

I placed both my hands on top of hers. "Where's the book, Shelby?"

Her eyes widened. "You know about it?"

"What book?" Mason asked.

I spoke to the detective but kept my gaze steady on Shelby. "Duke could produce a black book out of nowhere, and I'm guessing he kept the secrets he collected inside of it."

Shelby's hands quivered underneath mine. "Early this morning while it was still dark, something snatched me out of my sleep. It took me a few moments to gather my bearings and figure out that Duke's moment of death had called to me and brought me to him. It about ripped me into pieces having to mourn his passing with an instinctive uncontrolled cry while my heart rejoiced that he was gone."

Mason wrote down details with hurried purpose. "After the mourning stopped, what did you do?"

"I figured that the book must appear out of the ether. If he was dead, then the spell he used to keep it hidden wouldn't work anymore. I waited and searched, but never found it." The talented cook sobbed, and I let go of her hands to let her bury her face in them.

I stood up and pulled Mason outside of the guard house. "Whoever has that book has the biggest motive. Whatever's inside it, I'm betting it was worth killing over."

"How do you know she doesn't have it and is lying?" Mason looked over his notes. "If she was trapped into serving the man, then she all but said that his death set her free. If anyone has a huge motive to take Duke's life, it's her. Especially if he was half as bad as he sounds."

My heart ached for the girl, but the detective had a point.

"I know it's not admissible as real evidence, but my gut doesn't scream that she did it. More like she was one of his victims. Plus, there's something that he said to her..." I returned to the small structure. "Shelby, I have to tell you that I was eavesdropping on you and Duke during the bridal shower."

"You were? So that's how you knew about the book. I thought maybe something about you was in it." Relief eased the tension in her face.

Despite her fast becoming the main suspect, I couldn't help but like her a tiny bit. "There was something that happened, and Duke told you that the consequences wouldn't have the outcome you wanted." I kept the specifics of her attempt to stab the chef to myself. "What did he mean by that?"

Understanding replaced the fear in Shelby's eyes. "Oh, that. He meant that if I wanted to kill him, I couldn't. A banshee cannot bring harm to the family she is bonded to."

I pulled Mason out of the guard house again. "See. She couldn't have done it."

The detective tapped my hand to get me to release him. "I'll have to double check on the rules for banshees, but let's say she's right and she couldn't be the one to kill him. That doesn't mean she didn't arrange for his death."

My hope in the tiny kernel of the girl's magical nature deflated. "You're right."

Mason tipped my bent head up. "Don't look so defeated. While your gut instincts may not hold up with the law, I have high regards for them. I'm not saying I'm arresting her right now. We need to go through the car, search where she was staying, and check what evidence was found at the scene."

"I wouldn't count on anything being logged right. Big Willie kinda fumbled the play from the start. Speaking of." I tipped my head in the direction of the car heading our way. The sasquatch's hairy arm hung out the window.

Mason left my side to greet his boss, and Flint joined me at my elbow. "Think she's the killer?" the gnome asked.

Keeping my eyes on the sheriff gesticulating wildly at the detective, I leaned down to give my quiet answer. "I don't know for sure yet, but no alarm bells are goin' off with this one." I jerked my thumb at the wooden structure by the gate. "I think she has more questions to answer and could give valuable insight to help us find who might have had it out for Duke. Problem is, I think that list might be very, very long."

I straightened up as Big Willie stomped his way over. "Charli Goodwin, didn't I tell you to leave things to us wardens?"

"Yes, sir, but I—"

"No, that's not how this goes. I tell you to stay out of it and you just do what I say." He placed his hands on his hips. "Now, Charli, go home."

I was not a fan of anyone treating me like a child or telling me what not to do, especially a man. Looking to Mason for help, I pleaded with my eyes for him to stick up for me. After all, he'd asked me to come with him.

"I can take her back to town," he said without glancing my way.

Disappointment welled in my chest. "I can walk," I grumbled.

"No, Zeke'll take ya." Big Willie tossed the young deputy the keys, not caring that his aim sucked and he missed his target by a hot mile. "Then he can check on his mama and start going through the stuff there since the girl and the dead man were staying there."

"I can go with him and help," I volunteered, wanting to get my hands on the infamous black book sooner rather than later.

"Bye, Charli. Now, where's that girl?" The sheriff marched toward the guard house.

Mason stalled the young deputy for a second. "Listen, I'll do my best to convince him that having you help will be a good thing. I'll finish here and then get started on that dinner."

"We're still on for that?" I asked, unsure if now was the time to stop investigating.

"You gotta eat plus...you said yes. And there are things to say. Don't give Zeke too hard a time, and I'll try to arrange for you to work on the case as much as possible." Mason backed away to answer Big Willie's barking call for him. "I'll see you tonight."

"What time should I bring the food over?" I called out.

He checked his watch and calculated. "Would seven be too late?"

That would give me enough time to bake dessert. "Seven's perfect."

The smile that spread on his face warmed my insides again. "See you at seven. And, Charli?"

"What?"

"Have a little faith in me." He winked and walked away.

When I walked over to Zeke waiting by the sheriff's car, his last sentence echoed for me. Did I have faith in the man or trust him?

"Zeke, we need to make one stop before you take me home. And if you do me this one favor, I'll repay you in two baked goods of your choice."

Finding out that I wanted to stop off at Sweet Tooths was enough of a bribe. Zeke drove me back to Main Street and let me buy his two treats along with the plethora I planned to ingest to mull over my answer.

It took one red velvet cupcake, two snickerdoodle cookies, a honeysuckle and lavender scone, and one moon pie for me to accept my answer. Yes. I absolutely trusted Mason.

Chapter Eleven

I showed up on Mason's doorstep five minutes early, carrying a picnic basket with a red-and-white checkered towel covering the top. Rubbing my glossy lips together one more time, I smoothed out my favorite dress with sunflowers on it.

Mom loved sunflowers, and I needed a piece of her with me tonight to keep my nerves from getting the better of me. I might have been a little overdressed, but it felt good to have a reason to fuss. If I'd read his reactions right, there was a pretty good reason for me to be all gussied up.

With a deep breath, I knocked and waited. In the short time it took for him to answer, doubt worked its way through the cracks. What if he didn't mean this as a date? What if he was just being nice? What if all he sees me as was a person with specific talents that could help him with his job?

The door opened and ended my cycle of incessant questions. Mason held it wide in invitation. He wore a dark blue button-down shirt with the sleeves rolled up to his elbows, showing off the strength of his forearms. I was afraid he'd decide to shave his face but admired his willingness to keep the stubble.

He ran a hand across his whiskers. "I thought about it, but ran out of time working in the kitchen."

I stepped past him and into his home, impressed and not surprised by its neatness. "You're a mind reader now?"

"My job requires me to be observant, and your gaze lingered on my chin. I'm not sure anyone is strong enough to survive what's in there." He tapped my head playfully.

I sniffed the air. "I don't smell any smoke. I thought I might run into a cute fireman or two with you doin' the cooking," I teased, giving back as hard as I got.

"Is that why you packed a dinner?" Mason collected the basket from my hand. "I thought you trusted me." He peeked inside and smiled.

I shrugged, suddenly embarrassed by my choice. "Only chess pie."

"Your favorite," he commented.

Frosted fairy wings, the detective had done his research on me. "I'd ask how you knew, but you'd tell me it was your job."

He walked through the living room. "No, I asked your grandmother once."

I stopped moving. "Why?"

He cocked an eyebrow. "Because I wanted the recipe to try and make it for you."

The man wanted to bake for me. And not just anything—my favorite dessert. Something warm settled in my heart, and the air around us shifted. It didn't matter if tonight was an official date or not. I didn't need special magic to know things would be different between us from here on out.

I cleared my throat. "It's just a simple pie. Few ingredients but big on taste."

"Nothing wrong with simplicity. And I hope you don't mind that our dinner won't be complicated either." He directed me to his dining room where he'd set a small table with two place settings, two wine glasses, and a single candle. Doubts about what to call this occasion banished with a flicker of the flame.

"Pour us some wine, and I'll bring out the food," he said, disappearing into his kitchen.

We feasted on a mountain of spaghetti with the most delicious sauce I'd ever tasted. It beat Nana's hands down, which I would never tell her, and it was a far cry from the burnt mass of carbon that was supposed to be lasagne he'd attempted before. More unexplained changes in a short amount of time.

"Did you get enough?" Mason asked, eyeing my plate.

Still hungry from the late afternoon time spent mulling over what was or wasn't happening between us, I must have eaten at least two full helpings. I covered my mouth in embarrassment with my napkin. "I'm so sorry. I don't normally wolf my food down like that."

Mason's body stiffened at my bad choice of words, but he shook it off. "No, you have no idea how nice it is to eat with someone who's enjoying the food you've prepared for them. If you want, I'll send you home with the recipe so you can make it."

I finished the last drops of wine. "Or you can make that your signature dish you take to potlucks. People will love it and will always ask you to bring it. Besides, if you give me the recipe, then you might not invite me back for more."

"Oh, you will be getting more invitations from me." His flirty tone returned and warmed my insides.

I struggled to come up with a witty response, and an awkward silence grew between us. "Has there been any progress finding the book?" I asked.

The light in his eyes dimmed. "If you don't mind, I'd rather not talk about the case tonight."

"Oh." I dropped my gaze, fiddling with the napkin in my lap.

Mason continued. "Sorry, I don't mean to cut you off. But I want tonight to be about something other than solving a murder. Would that be okay? There are things I want to share with you."

My head snapped back up. "Of course," I gushed.

Mason had been closed off from the first time we met. He let me into his world inch by inch, but had a habit of shutting me out when I got close, erecting walls and tearing them back down with maddening regularity. If he wanted to give me an opportunity to slip past his defenses and get to know him better, I couldn't say no.

He pushed himself away from the table and blew out the candle. "I think we should have dessert outside."

I took his offered hand, letting him lead me to the patio in his backyard. With a strike of a match, he got the fire pit going and went inside to fetch the pie. When he joined me, the flames glowed and danced. I was grateful for the cool night breeze, although I would have sweat bullets to endure the ambience.

He handed me a plate with a slice of my pie and a fork on it, but the folder he carried in his other hand caught my attention.

"Not yet." He placed it down on the table between us. Leaning back in his chair, he took a bite of the pie. "Mmm. So good."

Mason was right. The pleasure he took in the dessert I made for us warmed me from the inside out. I felt a little guilty that I hadn't expended more effort, making a pecan pie or a fruit one with elaborate latticework.

He stopped chewing. "Charli, stop worrying about what kind of pie you brought me. It's absolutely delicious, and I'm glad you wanted to share something that you love with me. Let that brain stop working overtime and relax or I'll eat your slice, too."

The night setting offered a symphony of comforting noises. Cicadas chirped and the fire spit and crackled, its embers floating like beacons into the night sky. The Spanish moss hanging from a tree on the edge of his yard rustled in the cool night breeze.

When he finished with his dessert, he placed his plate down and picked up the folder. "I know you have questions for me, but there's some stuff I can't tell you no matter what. If you can accept that, I'll be as open as I can."

I almost regretted the calmness of the night being broken by my chance to interview the detective. But the desire to find out more tempted me. "If I ask something you can't answer, you'll tell me."

"Yes."

"And what if I ask you something you don't want to answer?" I pushed.

Mason situated his seat to face me. "Tonight, there are no walls. Nothing stands between us. If you ask, I'll answer. But make sure you want to hear what I have to say."

I filed some of the more personal questions away, starting with an easier one. "Where were you?"

"I can't tell you the specifics, but somewhere up north close to where I used to live." He gripped the folder a little tighter.

Not so easy a beginning. I watched for his response to my next inquiry. "Were you in danger?"

He nodded. "Yes, a couple of times. But I can't tell you what kind, only that I knew how to take care of myself and that I've returned."

"This is going well," I joked. "It's going to take me forever to find questions you can answer, so what if we switched it up and you told me whatever's safe?"

The detective pondered my suggestion and agreed. He handed me the folder and nodded for me to open it. Inside, I found a bunch of pictures of different sizes taken from different eras. I studied the first few but didn't recognize the subject.

"That's me," admitted Mason.

I picked up the smallest snapshot, a proof photo from a school picture packet. He couldn't have been more than seven or eight years old. His grin was missing a tooth, but his smile shined bright and happy.

"That was me after the social worker found me and placed me with a proper witch family. I didn't have a hard life before that, but being around people who could show me how to harness my powers freed me to live like a normal kid who was no longer scared he might cause something bad to happen." He frowned, remembering something.

Mason had never spoken so freely about his past. My heart raced with the excitement of knowing him better.

He continued. "Trying to contain magic can be dangerous, which is something you know very well. It's like voluntarily locking yourself away in a cell and throwing away the key. But a sweet woman found me and set me free."

I bit my lip, trying not to get too choked up. As a kid, I'd wished someone would come and take away my talents because they made me different. Now, I wanted to find out more so I could understand them. I shuffled through more childhood pictures, listening to his stories. "When did you know you wanted to become a warden?"

A sadness shadowed his eyes. "Marian, the social worker, kept in touch with me all of my life. She was the closest thing to a mother I had. She watched me play sports and was there for me when I graduated from school. I got a full ride to college because of her. I knew that I wanted to help others in her honor so they could have better lives."

"She sounds like an amazing woman. Do you still talk with her?" I asked.

He cleared his throat. "I didn't have to go up there when I did. I took an assignment with greater risk, but it let me be there for Marian when she passed away. These are the photos that she kept of me over the years. They're the only ones I have to mark my history."

My heart dropped, and I yearned to give him comfort. He waved me off and pointed at the folder. I looked at photo after photo taken by someone who cared very much about him, making sure to catch every smile of his. When I flipped to the next one, my heart stopped.

"From the look on your face, you found Jessica," Mason said.

My fingertip drew an outline around the girl with the light brown curls and full lips smiling back at me. "She's pretty," I uttered in a hushed voice.

"Took after her mother. Jessica is Marian's daughter, and we grew up together." He reached out to take the picture from me.

"So she was like your sister?" I proposed.

Mason's response shattered my hope. "No, we were childhood sweethearts. You have to imagine what it was like growing up without a lot of affection. Marian placed me in a solid home, and they took good care of me. But when I turned eighteen, it was my duty to leave and let them care for someone else. I didn't really attach to any of my foster siblings either. The only person who connected with me was Jess."

At the mention of her name, an ugly emotion rooted itself in my heart. I found another photo of them together. Mason had his arm around her shoulder, staring at her while she posed for the camera. This beautiful girl had possessed Mason's heart, and I didn't like how it made me feel. It didn't take long to figure out the pinnacle of their story. "Was she your fiancée?"

"Yes," he replied. "I asked her after I graduated from college and before I went into the warden academy. The problem with falling in love when you're a child is that it's hard to sustain when you're not done changing. Only a lucky few who choose to change with each other make it.

"She said yes when I asked, but I think by the time I made the force, her love for me had cooled. I got busy with the job and didn't notice, or didn't want to notice, how much she pulled away from me. I thought in order for our relationship to be perfect, I couldn't stain it with my job, so I kept that part of myself out of our lives. It drove a wedge between us."

The next picture I turned to featured the two of them. It looked like one that had sat on someone's mantle, faded by the sun. Jessica didn't know Mason at all if she gave up on him so easily. At the same time, if the walls he built around his career were as tall and tough as the ones he'd constructed to keep me out, she might have had her reasons.

He pointed at the wrinkle in my forehead. "Don't judge her. She's not a bad person, but she broke my heart when she called off the engagement. And I'll admit that I didn't handle it very well. I was in my twenties when I had to deal with my first heartbreak. I hadn't even experienced crushes when I was younger, so it was like all that love that I needed from childhood got ripped out of me. I volunteered for special assignments that put me in touch with a less than savory crowd. It took me years to stop intentionally putting myself in harm's way."

The person he described sounded nothing like the stoic detective I'd met. "Did danger mend your broken heart?"

Mason shook his head. "It took Marian and her insistence to interfere with my life to dislodge my head from my behind. Even though Jessica was her daughter, Marian still took care of me. To fix myself, I swung to the opposite extreme, becoming a rule follower rather than a breaker, and found solace in order. And that worked for a while until I found out that Jess was engaged to someone else."

"What did you do then?" I asked.

"I moved here."

I searched through the pictures and found one of the two of them together. They both seemed happy, and my jealousy lessened. If they had not had the history they did, I might not be sitting here tonight with Mason.

Putting the picture back in its place, I closed the folder. "Thank you for sharing that part of your life with me."

"The story doesn't end there," he exclaimed. "I told Marian all about life here in Honeysuckle, including you. She loved my story about our first meeting and scolded me for being so rude at your grandmother's house.

"But you know what she liked best of all? She said that it sounded like I'd found the family I'd been wanting all the way down in a small Southern supernatural town. She asked what I was willing to do to keep it, and I told her anything. And then I gave her back her ring." He watched me close for my reaction.

I frowned. "I'm confused. That was *her* ring?"

"It belonged to her, but she gave it to me to give to her daughter. When Jess broke things off, I couldn't bear to part with it, and it's been in my wallet ever since. I don't know why I wanted it. I suppose it was a reminder of the pain for a while and then a tether to my old life. But when I saw it sitting in your hand that day, I knew it didn't belong in my life anymore." He paused. "I'm glad I got a chance to give it back to Marian before she passed."

I didn't know what else to say. He wasn't the kind of person who needed platitudes of sympathy. I chose to remain quiet and swallow the desire to know if it was Marian's passing or the fact that he put his life on the line again that caused him to change.

Mason chuckled. "I know I seem different to you, but that's because you didn't know me before. I feel more myself than I have in years, and finally accept my life as it is. I guess it took a funeral and a threat to my life to get me to break past my barriers."

I shivered at his ability to know what to say at just the right time. He shared a lot of information, and it would take a while for me to digest it.

He stood and offered his hand. "I know it's getting late, and we have a lot of work to do tomorrow. If after hearing all of that we're still a *we*."

I allowed him to pull me up, and I fell into his body. If ever there was a time to give him a hug, it was now. But I let the moment linger too long and it passed.

Mason picked up the empty plates and folder, escorting me inside. I offered to wash the dishes, but he told me to leave them.

He'd promised me more and delivered, leaving me with so much to process. But I couldn't shake the disappointment of not making the *more* take a different direction.

He walked me to the door and handed me the empty basket. Unwilling to leave without hugging him, I put it down and wrapped my arms around him tight so he couldn't escape. I squeezed my eyes shut and tried to convey everything I felt into the embrace. My sympathy for his loss. My gratefulness for him opening up. My hope for whatever our futures held.

Trying to avoid the awkward moment of the *will we, won't we kiss*, I picked up the basket and rushed out the door and down his front steps. The interior light bathed the night in a soft glow, and I used its gleam to find my bike.

Mason called to me from the doorway, his shadow extending across his lawn. "Tonight's been about ending old chapters and beginning new ones. I hope after everything I shared, you understood that."

I tethered the basket on the rack behind my seat. "I did, but I'm not sure what that means for us."

He stepped into the light for me to see his face. "I'm saying that all the walls that I built between us before? I've torn them down, and they're not going back up."

Even with all the clarity from before, his cryptic statement still confused me. "I'm glad," I replied, straddling the frame of my ride.

"I'll pick you up in the morning."

The light on the front of my bike lit my pathway home but did nothing to illuminate whether Mason meant there would be no barriers between us professionally or personally. A small seed of guilt planted itself, nagging me that after all he'd shared, I chose to keep my suspicions of my ex-fiancé locked away.

Justifying that he'd asked not to bring the case into our time together, I did my best to ignore my regret and focus on the moments of our night that made my heart skip.

Chapter Twelve

The morning humidity clung to my skin, and dark clouds circled overhead. A storm was coming in more ways than one. It took me six times riding past the house and at least three trips back and forth from where I dropped my bicycle to the front door before I found my courage. Time was running out if I wanted to talk to Tucker and make it back to my place before Mason arrived.

I knocked on the front door with a light rap of my knuckles, not wanting to make a whole lot of noise that the neighbors might hear in the early hour. My heart thumped loud enough I mistook it for footsteps from inside. When nobody answered, I increased the strength of my banging until my palm pounded on the wood.

"I'm coming," Tucker's voice grumbled from inside. With a click of a lock, he pulled the door open.

In all the time when we were together, I couldn't remember him not looking put together and well-groomed. The disheveled man standing in front of me wore a stained undershirt over loose fitting shorts and sported a deep purple black eye.

"Charli, to what do I owe the honor?" Tucker lifted a thick crystal tumbler in his left hand to his lips and gulped down the amber liquid inside it. "Wanna drink?"

"It's after six in the morning, Tuck. What're you doing?" I scolded.

He sloshed the liquid around. "I'm taking my medicine. What do you care? I'm not your concern anymore." Finishing the last drops of liquor, he waved me in. With unsteady steps, he left the door to his house open, so I stepped inside.

The neatness of his place contrasted with his personal appearance. Tucker walked me into his living room, stopping by the fully stocked bar and pouring more alcohol from a fancy crystal decanter into his glass.

When he filled it almost to the top, he lifted it in the air in my direction. "Breakfast of champions." He smirked and took a long sip, smacking his lips with dramatic effect.

"We need to talk," I insisted.

"I tried to do that with you not too long ago and you ran away," he slurred. "I don't see what we have to discuss now that's so important."

A big part of me wanted to correct him and argue I hadn't run away from him. That I had stopped his former business partner before he did any more damage. But I didn't want a futile verbal match that went nowhere. I needed to stay focused, even if he couldn't.

"How about we discuss how I found you yesterday morning, blind drunk and stumbling down the road? Or you can tell me how you got that shiner. Or how your knuckles on your right hand got messed up. Start with any of those." I crossed my arms and waited.

Pain and regret cast shadows across his face. He opened his mouth to answer but managed no words. Unable to handle my inquiry, he dropped his head. It plucked at my sympathies to wonder if the once strong man was on the verge of tears.

Tucker glanced up and held my gaze, silently pleading with me...except I didn't know what he wanted.

I sighed. "Talk to me, Tuck. We've got to figure this out before things get worse."

As if someone flipped a switch, his countenance changed in an instant. He wiped a hand down his unshaven face. "It's morning, right? Breakfast time. You want some breakfast?" He stumbled out of the living room, leaving me standing in the middle of it, bewildered.

Without a plan in place, I made my way to his kitchen. "We don't have time for food."

He stood in front of the open refrigerator. "I can rustle you up some eggs. Do you still like them scrambled with a little onion and cheese in them? I don't think I have any bacon."

"I don't want breakfast. I want you to answer my questions," I pushed. "What happened to you?"

Tucker slammed the fridge door closed with a rattle. "See, what I don't understand is where you get off comin' to my house and actin' like I'm your problem to solve. You left me, Charli, and I moved on."

"That's not how you put it to me when you came to my grandmother's house that night." I didn't know what possessed me to bring up the subject of his professed feelings, but his boozy indignation rubbed me the wrong way.

"So are you here to try and win me back? Because I'm a real prize. I am the most successful guy in town. The one with the most promise to go the farthest in life." He snorted and gulped down more alcohol. Holding out his arms, he presented himself. "If you want me, take me as I am. Because it don't get any better than this." Pain radiated off of him, and I knew I needed to change tactics.

Walking with careful steps to close the distance between us, I took the drink out of his hand and led him to the eat-in table. Pulling out a chair, I waited for him to sit. He reached for the drink but I moved it away and took the seat next to him.

"Not yet," I said. "I think what's wrong with you started before last night. You can talk to me. I'm still your friend."

Tucker's body crumpled in on itself, and he placed his elbows on the table and held his head in his hands. "It's all gone so wrong so fast. I've been tryin' to handle it on my own, but things just got worse and worse. I wanted a clean slate when I married Clementine, you know."

"I know." I didn't want to say too much to stop him from talking.

He tilted his head to look at me sideways. "She thinks I'm the hero. The way she looks at me makes me think I could do anything. And I used to think I could. That I could get away with murder." He flinched. "Bad choice of words."

"Are they?" I asked. "Do you know about Duke?"

He nodded. "I assume that's why you're here. You think I might have something to do with his death."

"Do you?" My voice came out as a barely audible whisper.

Tucker paused. He straightened in his chair and reached out a finger to push a strand of my hair behind my ear. "You know, you used to look at me like I could hang the moon. I miss that, too."

"Tucker—"

"I don't remember," he interrupted. He slumped against the back of his seat. "I'm serious. It's all gone so wrong."

"You keep saying that, but I don't know what you mean."

He eyed the glass of what I guessed was scotch I kept out of his reach. "You do and you don't. I'm pretty sure you knew or at least suspected what went on when I went down to Charleston sometimes when we were together."

I thought hard about our shared past. "You had scheduled meetings. You were young and ambitious, and you were trying to make business connections."

His eyes widened. "You mean, you really didn't know? That wasn't the reason why you left me?"

"What reason, Tuck?"

He paused, giving me a wary glance. With a sigh, he continued. "I said that I thought I could get away with anything. One of those things was visiting a gentlemen's club outside the city. It's a place where a lot of the Charleston magical elite went for after-hours entertainment."

Something that Ashton had said on his last night bubbled to the surface. "That's where you met your former business partner."

Tucker nodded. "I met Ashton at Hex Kittens as well as a few influential high rollers."

My mouth dropped. "Hex kittens? Really? What, is it a gentlemen's club with supernatural strippers?" I mocked.

"Yes," replied Tucker without missing a beat. "But that's not what's important. Who I met there and what happened is where the trouble began."

It didn't take me long to connect the dots. "You met Duke there, didn't you?"

"Once or twice. Nothing happened when I did, but that doesn't mean that catching his attention didn't screw me in the long run." With a grunt, he reached past me and grabbed the tumbler of scotch. "They have the most beautiful women there. And I'm not so sure, but I think some of them are part succubi."

My nose wrinkled in disgust. "Maybe I don't need to hear the specifics."

Tucker glanced up after taking a long sip. "Maybe not. But you get the picture. Girls plus booze plus influential people equals a whole lot of potential money in the wrong hands."

I groaned. "Tell me Duke didn't have anything on you. Tell me I won't find your name written down in his black book."

He reached out and grasped my wrist. "Did you find it? Tell me you have it."

I shook my head. "No, we don't know where it is." Fear gripped my heart and I grabbed his hand. "Tucker, if he had something on you and was doing damage, then you had a whole lot of motive to do something to him. You need to talk to the wardens and tell them everything. Get ahead of this before—"

"Before a detective comes to your house, asks the right questions, and arrests you," finished Mason.

Tucker and I jumped in our seats. Heat burned in my cheeks, and I swiveled to catch Mason's unhappy glare. "What are you doing here?" I asked.

"That's my question for you," he replied with a sharp curtness.

Clementine stepped out from behind the detective. "I let him in. I was coming over to check on you, Tucker, and make you breakfast." She set a paper bag of groceries on the kitchen counter. "Imagine my surprise to run into Detective Clairmont and see your bike sitting out front, Charli."

Realizing how the scene might look to someone walking in on us, I yanked my hand away from Tucker's. "It's not what it looks like."

My ex shot out of his chair and rushed over to my cousin. "She was only trying to help me, Clem. I promise."

Mason ignored the couple's murmuring discussion and beckoned me out of the room with the crook of his finger.

Hanging my head in shame, I shuffled into the living room. "I was trying to get him to tell me what happened."

Mason kept his back to me, and I watched his muscles flex and tighten. When he turned around, the hurt expression on his face made me regret my mistake.

"After everything I told you last night," he hissed. "Sitting around the fire, showing you those pictures. I let go of my past for a reason. And I find you here at an unreasonable hour in your former fiancé's house alone with him, coaching him on how he shouldn't be at the top of our suspect list."

I held up my hands in surrender. "I know it looks bad. I get that. And I really am so appreciative of how much you shared with me."

"Are you?" Mason stepped close enough I could feel the heat from his body. "Because I told you that I didn't want any more walls between us. You could have told me your suspicions about Tucker but you chose not to say anything and cut me out of your own personal investigation."

"That's not what I was doing," I defended. "And you said you didn't want to talk about the case."

The detective held up his finger. "Do not think you're getting off so easily by throwing in a technicality. You had plenty of time yesterday when we were together and could have told me what you thought about Tucker." He glanced out the window. "When we went to Lucky's, did you already suspect him?"

I dropped my eyes to the floor. "Yes."

"And you kept that to yourself?"

I wanted to defend myself. I wanted him not to look with me with crushing disappointment in his eyes. But I had no defense, and needed to take the consequences of my choices. "You're right. I should have told you."

Mason blew out a hot breath. "What were you thinking, Charli?"

Unable to take the guilt, I blurted everything out. "I was thinking that even though we are no longer together and I am not in love with him that I still care about Tucker's future. And I care about my cousin's happiness. I guess I wanted to clear him of any part in all of this before I said anything to a warden. And I was wrong. I'm sorry," I ended on a whisper.

Closing my eyes, I waited for him to continue yelling or to walk away. The light stroke of the back of his fingers on my cheek startled me.

He spoke in a low voice. "If we have any chance, we have got to start trusting each other."

My breath caught in my throat. When he pulled away, I felt the acute absence of his touch. "Do you mean personally or professionally?"

Hollis barged into his son's house with a loud bang. "What in tarnation is goin' on here?" he bellowed.

Tucker emerged from the kitchen with Clementine hot on his heels. "Father, what are you doing here so early?"

"When you have a number of people crashing your house at once in the early mornin', it tends to get noticed by your neighbors. My question is, what are they doing here?" Hollis pointed to Mason and me.

The detective took a step away, allowing his professionalism to take command of the situation. "We're here to question your son. It seems he has some connection to the murder victim."

Hollis narrowed his eyes and furrowed his brow. "My son won't be answering anything right now. In fact, I suggest you leave the premises immediately."

Tucker took a step toward his father. "Dad, I think—"

"You need to stop thinkin' and stop talkin'." He reached into his back pocket and plucked out his wallet. Opening it, he pulled out a card. "You may contact Jed if you want to talk to Tucker. Without an advocate present, he has nothing to say to you. Please leave."

"I think this is your son's house," I challenged.

Hollis cocked an eyebrow at Tucker, and his son bent his head in submission. "Please, go."

Mason placed a hand at the small of my back, urging me to the door. "Until you hear otherwise, do not leave Honeysuckle," he directed at Tucker. We both walked down the steps outside.

Hollis watched from the doorway, his eyes sunken with dark circles beneath them. "My son will be getting married shortly. He will not be going anywhere. If you need people to interrogate, perhaps you should be lookin' at who would be upset about a new restaurant openin' up in town. Rivalry can be a big motivator, don't you think?" He let the storm door close with a click and stared at us through the glass pane.

I grabbed my bike from where I'd dropped it in the bushes. "I suppose you want me to go home now?" I asked Mason.

The corner of his lip curled up. "Are you trying to read my mind now?"

"No, I just assumed." I shrugged.

"Well, don't do that." He opened his car door. "That'll get you into hot water, too. I was going to tell you to meet me at the Harvest Moon. I'll buy you some breakfast, and then we can question a couple of people who work there."

My embarrassment and shame evaporated. "You still want me to work the case with you?"

"Remember, I said we needed to trust each other. This is me trusting you."

He was offering me a second chance, and I grabbed onto it with both hands. "I might even beat you there because I can take some shortcuts," I teased, ringing the little bell on my handlebars.

"You're on." He winked and got into his vehicle.

I threw my legs over my bike and almost took off, but Clementine called out my name, running down the front steps toward me and holding onto my arm once she made it. "You need to continue helping Tucker," she said in a breathless voice.

I patted her hand. "I swear to you, Clem, what you saw in there wasn't what it looked like."

"I know. I overheard what you said to the detective, and I believe you. He needs you to solve the murder. If you do, then he'll be free." Her big eyes glanced at me with so much hope.

"You realize we might discover that he did it?" I cringed at my question.

She nodded. "My heart says he didn't, but I think you need to prove whether or not that's true. I'll help him face it one way or another. I love him, Charli," she gushed.

Hopping off the bike and letting it drop to the ground, I wrapped my cousin in a tight hug. "I know you do. I'll do what I can," I promised.

Her stiff body relaxed for a second, and she returned the embrace. I let her go before her shyness took over, giving her a slight wave and taking off to meet Mason at the cafe.

Chapter Thirteen

Every time Sassy came to refill our cups of coffee, she shook like a leaf on a tree in a hurricane. It was a wonder more of her green dust didn't settle into our drinks. Whenever Steve rang the bell for her to pick up an order, she jumped.

Mason and I ate our breakfast in relative silence. The embarrassment of how he found me at Tucker's place along with my choice not to share my concerns about my ex-fiancé with the man who'd told me everything about his former ex still burned. I couldn't think of a single thing to say.

Mason stole a piece of my bacon, and I stayed quiet. When he went after the only other strip on my plate, I let him have it.

"Oh, come on. You can't let me get away with all your bacon." He tried to give it back.

Relieved that he was joking, I stole the bacon off of his plate and crunched on it. "Have you noticed how uncomfortable Sassy is?" I asked in a low voice.

Without turning his head, he agreed. "She keeps looking over at us. I think that group of retirees over there are tired of having coffee spilled on their food."

Not as skilled at the stealthy stalking, Sassy caught me looking at her and stuck her tongue out. "Do we question her here and now?"

Mason blew on his coffee. "I didn't think this through. It's a busy time for the cafe, and we can't pull her or Steve away from their service without it getting noticed. Maybe we should finish our breakfast and convene somewhere else to make a plan for the day," the detective suggested.

"Sassy," yelled Steve from the kitchen. "You gonna pick up this order or what? Soon it'll be colder than a dead body."

The entire place came to an awkward silent standstill. "What is it with bad choices of words these days?" I uttered, buttering my last piece of toast and sorting through the basket of little jelly packets.

"Here, take the rest of my strawberry." Mason pushed the half-filled container at me.

"There you go again, finishin' my thought before I have it." It comforted me to know that whatever we were to each other, our connection hadn't been permanently severed by my bad decision.

"I told you before, I'm a detective and very observant. That's all." He ate a bite of eggs with a grin.

Plates and glasses crashed onto the floor and a couple of patrons groaned. Steve fussed at the fairy through the pass-through, and Sassy did her best to clean up the mess.

"That's it." The cook pushed the swinging door open and stomped his way until he stood in front of us at the counter, wiping his hands on his apron. "You two are messin' up the flow. You're makin' my one waitress jumpy. You got questions? Spit them out and be done."

Mason took out his notebook and pencil. "Can you tell me where you were—"

"I was at Lucky's playin' cards and winnin' money off of that idiot over there." Steve pointed at Henry, who pointed at himself, batting his eyes with dramatic innocence.

The owner of the cafe rolled his eyes at his friend. "We were there from after closin' the cafe around ten until a little after midnight. Better to leave the card table while you're up, not when you're broke."

The detective took notes. "Did you go home after that?"

Steve grunted in affirmation. "Henry escorted me home. And my wife can vouch for my arrival and me bein' there the rest of the night. Are we done?"

Mason put his notebook away. "I'll have to verify the timing and talk to your wife, but yes, I think that's it."

Steve took the towel slung over his shoulder in his hand and wiped sweat from his brow. "Sassy," he barked.

The fairy squeaked and floated over to her boss. "Yes?" Her voice trembled.

"These two are gonna ask you some questions. Y'all go out

into the side alley so these nosy nimrods don't overhear and spread lies when they flap their gums." He aimed an intentional glare at Henry, who continued his innocent act.

Sassy did her best to smile. "I don't know why they need to talk to me," she insisted.

Steve placed a hand on his hip. "Maybe it's because you were talking to the dead man about a job."

All color drained from Sassy's face, and I worried that the green would leak out of her hair. "You knew I talked to Duke?"

"I know you're overworked here after Blythe left. And maybe I haven't been a good boss, not helpin' find someone else to pick up shifts." Steve held up his hand, ticking off his list on his fingers. "You're overworked, underpaid, and a single man walked into town with a new restaurant openin'. I'd think you'd lost your marbles if you hadn't talked to him, Sass."

The fairy trembled but looked up at her boss with hope. "You're not mad at me?"

Steve straightened and patted her on the top of her green head. "I'll only be mad if it turns out you did kill him and leave me without a waitress. Go talk to them, and then come back and finish the breakfast service. Maybe after that, we can talk about givin' you a raise and findin' someone else to help."

Sassy threw her arms around the gruff man's neck. He coughed from all the green dust flying in the air, but didn't pull away. Mason slapped some money on the counter to pay for our breakfasts and asked the fairy to come outside.

Sassy followed behind me, her wide eyes full of fear. We went out the heavy metal side door into the alley and morning heat.

The fairy glanced back and forth between Mason and me, frowning. "Why does she have to be here?"

"I'm the one asking the questions," insisted Mason. "Where were you two nights ago?"

Sassy cast a mean side eye at me. "Her friend quit, leaving me all of her shifts and forcing me to close."

Mason took notes on his pad. "What time did you leave?"

"Around eleven, after I finished setting up for the morning crowd," she answered. "I went to Lucky's bar for an hour before going home."

The detective asked, "Can someone confirm the hour you arrived there?"

"I live by myself." She crossed her tiny arms. "You know, it's no wonder someone tried to attack that chef. Anyone who would help him or let him rent the space is a traitor to our town." She shot me a hateful glance.

"You're suggesting someone killed Duke to protect the cafe?" Mason led her.

Realizing her mistake, Sassy backtracked. "No, that's not what I'm saying. I know Mr. Steve wouldn't like it, and a new restaurant might take business away from him."

Mason jotted some things down. "Then you're accusing your boss of murder?"

Sassy's wings trembled and green dust wafted off of them. "You're intentionally misunderstanding me. Somebody didn't want Duke here or why would they hit him over the head?"

Unable to stay quiet any longer, I jumped in. "How did you know there were head wounds, Sass?"

"I heard someone talking about it?" Her tiny voice trembled as hard as her bottom lip, and she cracked. "All right. I admit I was there. But I swear to you, I found him lying on the floor. I didn't do anything other than enter the old diner."

"What were you doing there in the first place?" Mason pressed.

"Mr. Steve was right, I was trying to convince Duke that I could work for him when I saw him over at Lucky's. I talked to him before he went back to play cards and offered him my services to make dessert for his new business." The fairy hung her head in shame.

"You were voluntarily going to leave the cafe. Who's the traitor now, Sass?" I accused.

Large tears rolled down her cheeks. "I thought he was cute and that maybe if he worked with me and saw how good I am at baking, that he..." An uncontrolled sob interrupted her.

"You thought maybe he'd like you," I finished.

She nodded her head, her green ponytail shaking. "I wasn't going to quit the cafe. But I wanted my chance at finding a guy. They shouldn't all belong to one person." Sassy glanced at me through tear-soaked lashes.

She wiped the wet streaks under her eyes and pleaded

with the detective. "I really did head home after Lucky kicked me out of The End, but the more I thought about Duke's rejection of my proposition, the more it made me mad. I don't know what possessed me to return to Main Street, but I saw the light on at the old diner. I thought maybe if I tried one more time, Duke might reconsider."

"You entered into an empty business space some time in the middle of the night by yourself." Mason's tone sounded close to the one he used with me when I did something he didn't approve of.

Sassy grabbed his hand to stop him from writing. "I know it sounds crazy, but I swear to you, I didn't kill him. When I saw him lying on the floor, I did flit over to see if he was still breathing. I thought I heard someone else in the room so I fled."

"Why didn't you call the wardens?" I asked.

Fresh tears flowed. "Because I knew what it would look like, and I'd end up being accused of murder." She sobbed so hard I almost gave her a pity hug out of principle.

For all of the guff the little fairy gave me on a regular basis, she didn't deserve my sympathy. However, knowing Sassy as I did, it was more believable she was a victim of the circumstances of her own making.

She jumped when the side door banged open. Steve took a long gander at the three of us. "There are orders waitin'," he muttered and left.

"Can I go now, Detective?" asked Sassy.

Mason ended the interview. "Don't leave town. If you

could, will you bring us out two cups of sweet tea to go?" He took out his wallet from his back pocket.

Sassy refused payment. "Be right back."

I digested the fairy's answers. "That explains why we found her dust."

"If you believe what she says. But it doesn't totally exonerate her," finished Mason. "This case is full of too many holes and not enough solutions. I guess we have more work to do."

"We?" I checked.

The side of his mouth quirked up. "Yes, *we*. You and me."

Sassy returned with our sweet tea, and I thought of one more thing before she left.

"Hey, Sass. Did you hear any kind of scream or shriek that night?"

She pondered the question. "Yes, before I made it to Main Street. It was an odd sound that pierced the night. Is that important?"

"It is." I waved at her with genuine gratitude. "Thanks."

Alone again, Mason pulled out his pad and pencil. "Tell me why it's important."

"It somewhat clarifies her story. If she were there as the killer, she would have seen Shelby appear out of nowhere, wailing over Duke. I don't think she was present when he died. We should find Shelby and talk to her again to see what she remembers seeing when she mourned the chef."

The detective finished his notes. "We, Miss Goodwin?"

"Yes, *we*, Detective."

Chapter Fourteen

ason drove us to Zeke's family home after
lunch. I'd forgotten that the young deputy was
one of the Wilkins boys. The rest of his family
lived on a huge property right on the waterway. Zeke came
from a long line of shrimpers, and his two older brothers Eli
and Jake still ran the family business. His mother, Ms. Althea,
lived in the big house, and as a favor to the Hawthornes, had
opened it up to Duke's team while they were in town for the
wedding festivities.

When we rang the doorbell, a familiar face answered, but
not the one I was expecting. Blythe's mouth popped
open. "Oh."

My heart clenched. "How're you doing?" I asked. Talking
of walls, my best friend had erected a tall one between us.

"Good." Her short answer gave me no entry into a conversation.

"You workin' here now?" I asked.

She nodded. "I'm helpin' Ms. Althea out while she has guests." Her shoulders released a fraction of an inch. "It feels good to be useful again, and I kind of like the work. Zeke called the house already, and you can find Shelby out on the patio. I've set you up with some glasses of sweet tea, but let me know if you need anything else." She moved out of our way and beckoned us inside.

Mason whispered to me as we walked to the back of the house, "That was a little chilly, wasn't it?"

Caught between disappointment and anger at my friend's response, I grunted in affirmation. We found Shelby pacing around a wrought iron table with a tray of drinks on it. Caught up in her own thoughts, she didn't hear us approach.

"Let me take the lead this time," Mason whispered to me.

I agreed. "Be careful. She's been dealing with a controlling monster for who knows how long."

The detective pulled out one of the metal chairs, scraping it on the concrete slab. Shelby whipped around with a yelp, almost losing her balance.

"I'm sorry to surprise you, Miss Michaels," he said, taking her arm to steady her. "We came by to ask you a few more questions."

She flinched away from his touch at first before shaking her head. "I'm sorry, Detective. It's not you. I'm a bit on edge." Offering a weak smile, she took the seat.

I sat down across from her, trying my best to reassure her with a smile and distributing the glasses of tea around the small table.

"I'd really like to understand the nature of your relationship with Duke, if you could give us some more details. How long have you known him?" Mason asked.

Shelby blew out a breath. "All of my life. He was mean as a kid, too, always trying to find ways to blame me for the stuff he did. Mom never thought that I'd be the one attached to him since she was a full banshee, and most of them outlive generations."

"What happened to her?" My question interrupted Mason, and I mouthed an apology.

Shelby traced a finger following the condensation on the outside of her glass. "I was in my first year of college when I got the call. Duke's mother had passed away, leaving him without anyone else in his family. I was in the middle of a lit class when I felt the first tether binding Duke and me together right when I got a text message."

Mason wrote down some notes. "With your mother's passing, you became the banshee attached to Duke at age eighteen?"

She blinked back some tears. "I never did find out what happened to her. Duke told me she'd drowned in the bathtub. I think he wanted me to think she committed suicide or something, but she would never do that."

I took a sip of the tea, carefully formulating the question

that nagged at me. "Forgive me if this seems too abrupt, but why didn't you leave him if he was so awful?"

Shelby smirked. "I've asked myself that same question for years. Wondering if I could have paid someone to sever the link between us. Between my mom never really teaching me what it meant to be a banshee, Duke's lies, and my naivety, I set myself up in my own little prison. The only relief I had was cooking and baking."

Blythe interrupted us, setting down a tray of freshly baked strawberry muffins still warm from the oven. Done with the task, she left without saying anything or even glancing at me. The irritation from earlier stirred into anger. Even though the muffins smelled amazing, I couldn't stomach one.

Shelby reached for a muffin and savored the aroma. "It's weird not being the one doing the kitchen work. I'm not used to it."

"You haven't answered my question yet." Mason scooted his chair closer to the table. "How long were you with Duke?"

The young woman calculated in her head. "I've been tethered to him for ten years, two of those doing all the behind-the-scenes operations of his so-called catering business. You know, I tried leaving him once. Stole his keys, got in the car, and drove away.

"Mom never told me that the binding contract she signed for the two of us all those years ago would hold me forever. I got to the edge of town before the physical pain became too unbearable and I returned, seeing him waiting for me with that menacing grin he always wore." She shivered at the memory.

The whole time Shelby spoke, I couldn't help but wallow in my disappointment with Blythe and her blatant choice to ignore me. Figuring that Mason had things covered in the interrogation department, I pushed back from the table.

"Y'all excuse me, please. I need to find the restroom." I hurried inside, intending to find my friend and fuss at her until she caved.

Ms. Althea met me in the hallway. "Charli Goodwin, you're lookin' mighty fine today. You here with the detective to speak to that poor girl?" She gave me a quick hug around the neck.

"We're trying to get some more details to paint a fuller picture," I admitted.

"My boy Ezekiel told me a little bit when he brought her here and then went through the bad man's room. There are people that sometimes set your hair on end from the moment you clap eyes on them." Ms. Althea shivered. "I told Zeke it was a wonder he was still walkin' this Earth for as long as he did, the evil that he was so wrapped up in."

I didn't know what particular talents Zeke's mother possessed, but she definitely read Duke right. "Did you ever see Mr. Aikens with a black book at any time?"

She nodded. "I sure did. Was walkin' by his room and saw him produce it out of thin air. Neat little spell."

My stomach flipped with excitement. "Did Zeke find it when he searched the room?"

Ms. Althea's face fell. "My boy did a thorough job and took away a number of items to catalog at the station. He might have mentioned his disappointment in not finding that one item to me."

"Oh." So much for hoping.

"But since you're helping out with the investigation, you can take a look yourself." The deputy's mother pointed up the stairs. "At the top, it's the last room on the left."

Forgetting my desire to talk things out with Blythe, I thanked Ms. Althea and hustled to the second floor. I stood in the doorway, surveying the empty room lit by the afternoon sun shining through the windows. Anything of Duke's was long gone, and yet my gut forced me inside to take another look.

I walked around the small space with slow, deliberate steps, not touching anything. Everything had been tidied up spic and span. As much as I liked Zeke, I wondered how thorough the young deputy had been in his search? Dropping to my knees on the carpet, I lifted the pleated lace dust ruffle and peered under the bed. Not even one dust bunny tumbled underneath.

In disappointment, I sat back on my haunches thinking through everything I knew. My eyes lit on the bottom of the wooden nightstand. If I were searching for something, I would move every piece of furniture to check. And if I moved furniture in haste, chances were that I might not put it back in the same position. Yet, the stand looked like it hadn't been moved in ages.

Pushing on the wood, I moved it to the right a few inches. I didn't find a black book, but my eyes caught something round nestled into the shag of the rug. With excitement, I picked it up and held it in the palm of my hand.

The cool metal of what looked like an old coin warmed against my skin. Bigger than a quarter, the surface was dull, making it hard to distinguish any details. I flipped it over and ran my fingertip over the outline of some sort of figure.

Maybe the coin belonged to Duke? Maybe it was something long lost by one of Ms. Althea's boys. I moved the nightstand back in its place, making sure the entire bottom sat in the original grooves on the carpet. Placing the coin in my pocket, I left the room to rejoin the interrogation.

The grandfather clock in the hallway echoed, and I counted the first chimes and then the hours it marked. In a panic, I ran downstairs to find Mason escorting Shelby inside.

I pulled on his sleeve. "We've got to go. I forgot all about the second spell class, and I haven't planned anything. I'm gonna need you to drive me back to my place and then to the school as fast as your warden behind can go."

ॐ

WITHOUT DELAY, I entered the classroom a little breathless, holding onto a small bag. All heads turned in my direction. Their pleasant expressions and lack of heads buried in their spell phones gave me hope that maybe I wasn't a total dead loss as a teacher.

Heading to the desk at the front, I did my best to hide my trepidation and turned to address their eager faces. "My grandmother used to tell my brother and me that magic requires focus. And if you can't focus, you're gonna have a hard time controlling the outcome. Raise your hand if you've ever tried a spell, it didn't work, and the more you tried the worse you felt until you couldn't cast anything."

Everyone waved a hand in the air, including me. Before I could continue, the bag slung on my shoulder wiggled.

Helen pointed at it. "What's in there?"

I placed the pouch with care on top of the desk. "I forgot all about our guest professor today." A little orange head popped up, and everyone gasped.

Peaches hopped out and shook her head like a rattle, licking her paw and cleaning her whiskers. The girls squealed at her cuteness while the guys chuckled.

Glad that my last-minute idea to distract them worked, I rubbed my orange cat's head. "It happens to all of us, so when you're taking your test, don't panic and think you're the only witch in the world who feels that way. There are tricks you can learn and things you can do to help you find the best way to center yourself and work through the problem."

To punctuate the point of centering, Peaches turned three times in the middle of the desk, spread her legs, and focused on bath time. The students snickered.

"This is my pet, Peaches. Or I'm hers, since she kind of chose me. How many of you have an animal that's part of your family?"

Several hands went up. Anna waved her hand. "I'm pretty sure I have a familiar. He's a newt."

Her sister Emily snorted. "He's not the familiar."

"He could be," Anna argued. "He likes to watch when I practice spellcasting."

A young man named Connor, sitting next to Eric in the back, spoke up. "We have a black cat named Midnight. He was Mom's familiar before she met Dad. He's lived a long time, so we don't really use him for magic anymore. I guess you could say he's in retirement."

I rubbed the top of my cat's head. "You bring up a good point. Because familiars have the ability to channel our magic, it affects their life spans, and some can live a long time. But a pet doesn't have to be a familiar to help. Anna, how do you feel knowing that your newt is watching you?"

Her cousin Helen teased, "Her newt's name is Newt."

"It's Sir Isaac Newt, to be exact," corrected Anna. "And he makes me feel calm."

"Exactly. And if you can recall how that feels when you're casting, then you can draw on the power of that sense memory to help you feel the same way. Let's do a demonstration." I picked up my fur baby.

Peaches settled in my arms and demanded rubs. A steady purr vibrated against my touch, and I held her small body against my ear, listening to it.

"When I hold Peaches, she gives me a warm and fuzzy feeling, no matter how bad my day's going." I scratched under her chin and my kitty closed her eyes. "I need a volunteer for this next part."

Almost everyone stood up. I chose a quieter girl named April to hold Peaches. Like the good cat she is, my orange bundle of joy rubbed her head against April's hand, enjoying the extra attention. The girl beamed at my kitty, talking to her in a quiet voice.

"I think you've made a friend," I said to April. "Now, I want you to keep petting her, but I'm going to place a feather on the desk. See if you can lift it while focusing on how holding Peaches makes you feel."

Loving on my furry baby distracted the girl in the right away. She kept rubbing my cat between the ears, almost ignoring the feather all together.

The class applauded and she glanced up in puzzlement. The white feather floated down and landed on the desk.

I beamed at April. "Did you feel any sense that she shared your magic while holding her?"

She pondered for a second and admitted, "No. But she's just so cute and adorable that I didn't even think that hard about the spell."

"Exactly," I exclaimed. "If you can hold onto that feeling and try to use it when taking your permit test, you might be able to make it through without panicking." Taking back my cat, I addressed the rest of the class. "Line up if you want a turn with Peaches."

They scrambled to their feet, and for the next thirty minutes, my cat got all the lovin' she could possibly want.

After getting so spoiled, there was a good chance she'd start attending school on her own.

My chest filled with pride, and I marveled at my ability to pull a lesson out of my behind that wasn't that bad.

By the end of the hour, I had them performing all the spells they needed to pass the permit except one. "You get to pick an original spell to perform, and I highly suggest that you work with what you got. I'll give you an example. My gift is finding things. During my test, I had the proctor hide an object while I left the room, and when I came back, I found it for them."

Helen frowned and blurted out, "What if we don't know what we're good at?"

Grabbing some blank paper from a nearby bookshelf, I passed it out. "Try not to focus so much on the negative. Give some thoughts to what you can do and write it down on the paper."

I gave them time to scribble down some ideas and then let each of them share with the class, adding in my suggestions or encouraging another student to add their thoughts as we went around the room.

When I arrived in front of Eric, I stared him down. "I don't see anything written on your paper, but I could have sworn I saw you writing. Care to show me?"

He shook his head and tried to crumple the papers.

I stopped him. "Here, I'll write down one of my ideas." Using the pencil, I scratched something on the paper and marveled at it. "So where did it go, Eric?"

The taller Mosely boy pulled a second sheet from under the first full of writing.

Impressed, I whistled. "Now that's clever. When did you come up with it?"

"I don't know," Eric said, his cheeks getting a bit pink. He slumped in his chair.

I motioned for the rest of the class to gather around. "Show them."

With all eyes on him, Eric straightened in his seat and wrote something on one paper. *My name is Eric* appeared in his handwriting on the other.

"Cool," exclaimed Connor. "It's like that map in the third movie where it's blank but then you can see where everybody is if you know how to make it appear."

Patting Eric's shoulder, I hoped they young man recognized his talent. "I don't think you need to search for anything else. You've got your personal spell right there. It's one heck of an enchantment." I returned to the front of the class. "We have a couple more chances to review before the end of the course. We'll go through some practice runs together so you'll know what to expect."

Most of the students stayed behind to ask questions or to give Peaches more love. They thanked me and walked out excited.

Before he left the room, I handed Eric a stack of blank paper to take with him and let him know how impressed I really was. His ears turned bright red, and he gave me a genuine smile, waving as he left to join his friends.

I located my kitty chasing a spider into the corner of the room and picked her up. "Come on, Professor Peaches. Let's go home, and I'll give you all the kitty treats you want in payment for your work today."

Refusing to jump back into the bag I brought her in, she trotted in front of me, leading me out of the classroom like she was the one in charge. Since I followed behind her, perhaps she was right.

Chapter Fifteen

Pleased but exhausted after the class, I lay down for a mid-afternoon nap. I woke up groggier than when I first fell asleep.

My spell phone rang as I brushed my teeth. "Hello?" I answered with a mouth full of paste.

Lavender's happy voice chirped, "If you don't have anything planned before dinner, can you come to my place? I think Alison Kate has some good news she wants to share."

I squealed and spit toothpaste flecks all over the mirror. "Did Lee pop the question?"

"You'll have to come over and find out for yourself. Get here as soon as you can." She hung up the phone and I rushed to pull myself together.

The entire bike ride over, my heart skittered with happiness for my two friends. Unlike Mason and Logan, it took Lee too long to clue in on Alison Kate's affections for him. It took a disaster of a singles mingle event thrown by a failed cupid to get them over their shyness. Thoughts of big, poofy, flouncy hideous bridesmaids dresses danced in my head all the way to the house.

I parked my bike and ran inside, not waiting to knock on the door. "Here comes the bride," I sang off tune.

The angry expression on Blythe's face stopped me cold. "What's she doing here?"

"I'm pretty sure this is an ambush," she said, crossing her arms.

Alison Kate entered the dining room from the kitchen with a platter full of baked goods. "It's not an ambush, it's an intervention for two of our closest friends. It's a friend-tervention."

"No one needs to intervene on my behalf," I protested. I'm not the one with the problem."

Blythe leaned forward. "And I am?"

I unleashed all my frustration and let it pour out. "You're the one who won't talk to me. I could barely get two words out of you at Ms. Althea's. Frosted fairy wings, I didn't even know you were working there. You've barely talked to me for months."

"You're the one who treated me like everything had changed," she accused. "I'm the one who had her head messed with. Do you know what it's like to have no control of your own thoughts? Or not know whether the thought in your head is yours or was planted there by someone else? It's no picnic with fried chicken."

"I know," I yelled back. "I was there, unless you can't remember. I'm the one who took on the vampire who did all that to you. I risked everything to make sure you were safe."

Blythe's voice cracked. "You don't think I know that? You could have died for me, and I would have to live with that. You wouldn't have been in that situation if I'd been strong enough to fight Damien myself."

She clasped her hands over her mouth, but a sob escaped. Blythe was the strongest girl I knew, and I could count on one hand the amount of times I'd seen her cry. But she needed the release, and the whole room erupted in tears.

I rushed to her side. "Is that why you stayed away from me? Because you blame yourself for what I chose to do on my own?"

She nodded, still blubbering. "How am I supposed to face you when he almost took you away from us?" She collapsed her head on the table.

I threw my arms around her. "First of all, you have to give yourself a break. What Damien did broke the law and the moral code of decency of any being. I'm sure Lady Eveline has told you as much."

"She did," answered Blythe, the wood surface muffling her answer.

"And I know it couldn't have been easy being a pawn in his game. But you know better than most that nobody tells me what I can or cannot do. I would put my life on the line for you again in a heartbeat. For any of you," I said to the other girls.

Alison Kate hugged my middle and Lavender embraced Blythe from the other side.

"Hey, there's no room for me in this dogpile," complained Lily.

We laughed through our tears, and Blythe waited for us to peel off of her. Standing, she faced me, holding my hands. "I'm sorry."

I squeezed her back. "Me, too. I've missed you, B." We embraced again, and it turned into a massive group hug of tears, laughter, and snotty noses.

After we became too dehydrated to produce any more tears, we broke away. Lavender passed around plates, and we dug into the goodies.

I licked frosting from my fingers. "Ali Kat, I suppose this means you don't have an actual announcement."

She blushed. "I can tell you that Lee signed his deal and after I told him what's been going on with the kids in town, he is completely on board with making real wands work and brooms fly. But that's about it."

I chucked a muffin at her head. "Don't ever do that again unless it's for real," I declared. "I should eat all the honeysuckle buns to teach you a lesson."

The entire platter of sugary treats couldn't come close to how sweet it was to have my girls back. I laughed and joked with them, relieved to have harmony return.

It took us twenty extra minutes to say goodbye because of

all the extra cuddles. I hooked my arm through Alison Kate's and pulled her to the side. "Have the wardens given you any more trouble?"

"Not since that first night. Why? Should I be worried?" she asked with wide eyes.

I sighed. "The stealing of your spell did give you a potential motive. But I don't think Big Willie really believes you killed Duke. The list of people with possible motives is long but the evidence is lean. Did you give them a solid alibi?"

My sweet friend blushed. "I did, but it involved Lee. We spent the night on the phone. Sayin' things to each other." The rosy red in her cheeks told me enough of the story.

I squeezed her to me. "I think that'll be good enough. I just hope that we can figure things out." Silently, I finished my thought to myself.

We needed to solve the case as fast as possible or Tucker risked having another engagement ruined.

MATT MET me at the door of Nana's house. Peaches jumped out of my bicycle basket and skidded between my brother's legs to find her friend Loki inside. The worried glance Matt shot at me crushed my hopes for a fun and yummy dinner.

"What's goin' on?" I asked.

He held the screen door open. "Get in here."

My grandmother's house always welcomed me. For years, it had served as the soft place to land as well as a home for me and my brother, especially with the deaths of our parents. However, the air felt sicker and weighted down with trouble.

Noises from the kitchen clued me in to Nana's cooking. "Is she fixin' dinner or is it stress?"

"I think a little of both," my brother replied. He tugged on my shirt to stop me from going to her. "I don't know what you're doing with this case, but you're creating a lot of problems. Big Willie isn't happy, and he's taking it out on me."

I escaped my brother's grip by thumping him hard with my fingers. "I'm sorry about that, but I'm not going to turn down the opportunity to help, especially since the sheriff kicked you off the case."

"But you're not a warden. You shouldn't be involved. Stay off the investigation." His robotic delivery confused me.

I narrowed my eyes at him. "Are you giving me orders?" I challenged.

Matt shook his head. "No, fulfilling my duty that I was charged with from my boss. Now if he asks you if I told you that, you can speak the truth. Personally, I want you to stay on top of things. If Mason's willin' to bring you in, then you go. There's something bigger than a simple murder case going on."

Nana called out from the kitchen, "Y'all come in here and sit your behinds down."

Normally, when she had the two of us over for a meal, she went all out and set her formal dining room table, using the fancy dishes and real silverware. Tonight, she scooped the food on our plates without ceremony and insisted we eat at the small table in the kitchen. Sweat broke out on my brow from the heat of the oven, but I knew better than to say anything.

"Dig in," our grandmother instructed.

"Aren't you going to eat, Nana?" I asked.

She pointed at the cast iron skillet on the front burner. "I'm gonna fry up some catfish, so I can't leave the stove." She got out a pie tin and poured yellow cornmeal in it, and then cracked some eggs in a bowl and beat them to dredge the fish.

Matt got up from his chair and made her stop. He kept his hands on her shoulders and directed her to her usual spot, not giving her a choice and forcing her to sit. Pushing his plate of food in front of her, he handed her his fork. Without saying a word, he fixed a new plate for himself and joined us. The silence in the room stretched while we stared at the cooling meal.

I broke the tension with my frustration. "Is somebody gonna tell me what's going on?"

Nana blew out a breath. "I don't think the two of you need to be burdened. Why don't we—"

"If you don't tell us, then who are you going to tell?" Matt cut her off.

"You know how you always say that our problems never go away if we volunteer to carry them around on our backs? It's time to unload, and we can take it, Nana." I reached out and squeezed her hand three times.

Our grandmother looked between Matt and me. "We've got a definite dilemma," she offered.

"*We* as in the three of us?" clarified my brother.

"Yes," stalled my grandmother, "there are some issues that involve our family. But I mean *we* as in the collective *we*. All of Honeysuckle."

I pushed my plate away and settled into the back of my chair, crossing my arms and waiting. "What went on at the meeting you attended?"

Nana shook her head. "Everything was going fine, boring as usual. We all reported basic town business, and nothing seemed out of the ordinary. The magical communities of Southeast America are pretty well-organized. So when it happened, I was caught off guard."

Matt scooted his chair closer. "Explain."

Our grandmother spoke more like the high seat on the town council than our kin. "The council from Charleston proposed that Honeysuckle is close enough to their district that we should be absorbed into their overall governance. Meaning, they were making a play to take over."

Anger and surprise swirled inside my chest. "Can they do that?"

Nana took a swallow of tea and continued. "It's not a question of whether or not they can. The proposal was made. The issue is that the burden falls on me and our town council to prove that we deserve to stay separate from any magical district. That we can govern ourselves without being overseen by outsiders.

"When the world seemed smaller and we were more isolated, nobody cared that we existed on our own. It's not the first time that the idea has been brought up, but I normally have a sense that it's coming and can talk to people behind the scenes prior to it becoming a formal item on the agenda."

"If somebody has tried this before and failed, what makes it a problem this time?" asked Matt.

Nana frowned. "We keep to ourselves here, and don't force people to stay although most choose to remain in Honeysuckle on their own. But I've never worried about important information making its way outside of our small community."

"What kind of info?" I asked.

She slumped into the back of her chair. "The Charleston council members who made the proposal had access to some of our town's charter. Old legal mumbo jumbo, but words that, if interpreted in the right way, could leave a wide opening to being taken over. They left the area authority with enough questions as to why we couldn't stay a sanctuary town but have the seat of authority be moved to Charleston?"

Matt almost growled. "In other words, they want to remove you from power."

Nana nodded. "It seems that way."

I stuck my chin in the air. "You're a stubborn and strong Goodwin woman. I know you can fight this."

Our grandmother slammed her fist on the table, and Matt and I jumped. "It's not the battle that worries me. It's the fact that we have a leak. A mole. Someone powerful is working with those in Charleston. And I can't fight what I don't know."

I swallowed hard. "How can we help?"

Nana grabbed a hand from both Matt and me. "Promise me you won't do anything. Right now, the only advantage I have is that whoever it is doesn't know that I'm on the hunt. You have to act like you know nothing."

"But Nana," I protested, "If there's something to find—"

"You don't do anything." Nana stopped me short. "At least not until I ask you to. I'm serious, Charlotte Vivian and Matthew Duane Goodwin. I appreciate you wanting to help, and I may need you. But for now, just be my source of comfort."

My brother shot a look at me to stop me from saying anything else. "We can do that. But please don't shut us out. If you get into a bind, you have to let us help. We're not little kids anymore, and Charli's right. If...no, *when* you're ready to find what you need, you will use her talents. I'm not askin'."

His spell phone vibrated in his pocket and he pulled it out in frustration. "Can I pack up some food to take to TJ?"

After the news our grandmother had shared with us, I couldn't find it in me to tease him about being a whipped man to a pregnant woman. Glad to have a task to do, Nana busied herself, putting food in containers and wrapping up cornbread in tinfoil. My brother took the food from her and managed to kiss me on the top of my head before hustling out.

"Eat your food, Birdy, it's gettin' cold," instructed my grandmother.

I picked up my fork and pushed the collards swimming in vinegar around on the plate. "I can see how upsetting all this must have been, but it doesn't explain why you were gone so long."

Nana poured us more sweet tea. "After the ambush, I went down to talk to my friend who lives near the Angel Oak on Johns Island. I wanted to know how her community managed to stay out of the reach of the political powers in Charleston."

"You mean the sea island Gullah culture, right? They're not part of Charleston's district?" I asked.

"Not for lack of tryin'. My friend didn't have a whole lot of words of comfort, but she did promise that she might contact the local root doctor to give me all the help she could."

I remembered Nana taking Matt and me down to the sea islands near Charleston. I could understand those who practiced hoodoo in their own lives had issues with the power grabs of those who thought themselves better than others.

Doing a little calculation in my head, I asked, "How much time did you spend on the island?"

Nana avoided my gaze. "I stopped off at another place on my way back. Can I get you more tea?"

I stared at my full glass. "Why are you stallin'? Who did you stop off to talk to?"

She tilted her head. "You sure you wanna know?"

"Try me," I challenged.

With a sigh, Nana gave in. "Since I was traveling so close to their house, I thought it couldn't hurt if I checked in on Dina, Enya, and Frida Gray."

I wrinkled my nose. "Aw, Nana, the Gray sisters? They are so gross. They share an eye and a tooth between the three of them. And they're older than dirt. Their entire place smells like a garbage dump. Why did you need to talk to them? Could they help you with the problem in Charleston?"

"They had no advice about the power grab. But that's not why I was there. I hope you can forgive me when I tell you what I asked them." Nana took her seat again.

"I can never be that mad at you. Now, spill it," I demanded.

"I asked them about your family. And your future." Nana refused to answer my inquisitive glare. "I know you haven't said anything since that night with the vampire when he burned the papers that could have told you where and who you came from. I thought that maybe I could find answers for you."

I closed my eyes. "Please tell me you didn't pay those weird sisters a dime. You've told me again and again never to seek out fortunetellers."

"I know, I know," Nana admitted. "And under normal circumstances, I would follow my own advice." She leaned forward and cupped my chin. "But, Sweet Bird, I would do anything to help you grow, no matter what. And if you need to know where you come from, then I will move mountains. I will cast a net far and wide. And yes, I will talk to the Gray sisters.

My heart ached from the swell of love rising in my chest. Despite everything she was going through, my grandmother was willing to do what she could to take care of me like she always had.

I took her hand away from my face and held it between mine. "I know where I come from. You're my family. It's why I haven't said anything. I think I was afraid that you would think less of me when I was disappointed that Damien burned those papers."

She squeezed my hand. "I completely understand why you would be."

The words came gushing out of me. "I haven't pursued anything else because I'm not sure knowing would make a big difference. I'm growing confident in who I am more and more. Because of the solid foundation you helped me build, I can consider opening my own business and using my talents to help others in a more official capacity. You don't have to listen to fools to help me."

"You don't want me to tell you what they said?" Nana smiled at me with adoration.

I considered the possibility of hearing words that might point me in the right direction to my biological connections in this world. When I thought all my chances were gone with the burning of the papers, I'd made my peace with it. Without knowing it, my grandmother had pulled off a newly formed scab.

I patted her hand and let her go. "I don't think so. I'm going to listen to a wise woman who told me that prophecies and omens are dangerous things. They're usually vague and we risk trying to manipulate things to make them come true and mess everything up in the process. Don't you always tell me to remember the famous Scottish play?"

Nana smiled for the first time tonight. "And the fifth movie of that witches and wizards series with the kids. The villain of it all chooses to fight that one boy with the scar because he interprets the prophecy in one way. Nobody thought that there might be another boy who could have fit the bill. The villain made a choice based on his interpretation, and my guess is it will spell his doom in the end."

Shocked and impressed at the same time, I chuckled. "Nana, I can't believe you're watching those movies."

She shrugged. "Why not? They're fun because they get some things right but what they get wrong about magic is kind of hilarious. Plus, I'm enjoying seein' our local kids take pride in their own magic again.

I rubbed the top of my head where Timmy had hit it. "Sure," I agreed.

Wanting a change in subject, we talked about the changes in Mason's and my relationship. Nana knew about the dinner and the discussion about walls and barriers.

"So Dash is out of the picture?" My grandmother had been a fan of the wolf shifter from the beginning.

"I haven't heard anything from him," I said.

She sipped on her iced tea. "The man and his animal have some battles to fight. Those are his struggles to deal with and you have your own. It may not be your destiny to wind up together. But I continue to be more impressed with the detective. Let me know if he ever makes you that chess pie."

I played with the food left on my plate. "But I don't know how to handle the personal and the professional. And what happens if Dash returns?"

Nana nodded at me. "You hold on. You're strong because you're a Goodwin woman. I suspect that's why the men gravitate to you. It's a hard burden for us to bear." She fanned herself and giggled.

I helped her clean up the kitchen and agreed to take a huge chunk of red velvet cake home with me. We stood in the evening air on the front porch, delaying our goodbyes.

"Nana, can't you tell me what to do about everything?" I whined.

My grandmother patted me on my behind. "My job is to give you wings and let you fly. But I'll tell you what my own Gran passed on to me. Whether you have the privilege to live for a century, a few decades, days, or minutes, life on this earth is finite. Live boldly and love hard. That goes for jobs, men, and everything in between."

Later, as I fell asleep, I came up with a plan to make some bold moves and take the next steps in my life.

Chapter Sixteen

I hid in the kitchen from the massive hoard of friends waiting for me in the living room. Nana chuckled while she cooked at my stove, and I pushed the swinging door open and peeked at the noisy bunch.

"I can't go out there. They're gonna think I'm crazy." I let the door go and sat down at the small table.

She stopped stirring the pot and circled her finger at the side of her head. "Birdy, this was your idea. And I'll bet they already know you're crazy."

TJ barged into the kitchen. "Charli, you need a bathroom downstairs. I can't keep waddling my behind up and down. Ooh, that smells good." My sister-in-law looked over Nana's shoulder.

Matt followed close behind, entering with a scowl. "Bird,

you better get out here. Everyone wants to know what you want them to do."

I pointed a finger at him. "Are you responsible for this? I called a handful of my friends. There's a massive crowd out there."

"Stop being so dramatic." He rolled his eyes. "I might have played phone tree to those who want to see you start your business. They love you, Birdy. Go talk to them and see how much."

"I'm stayin' in here with the food," TJ declared, stealing a cornbread muffin off the cooling rack.

Nana stopped me on my way out. "I'm proud of you for living to your fullest." She kissed my cheek and swiped my behind on my way out.

Walking toward the noise, I second-guessed myself a couple times. Was it crazy to want to start a business? I knew nothing about running one. And what if I failed? Then again, if I never tried, that would be the bigger failure.

I approached the room and spotted Mason talking to Ben off to the side of the crowded room. The detective spoke in hushed tones, but whatever he said to my advocate friend, it must have been serious. He stopped talking and smiled at me, nodding his head to encourage me to get on with things.

When the entire room of friendly faces quieted down upon my entrance, my nerves did a dance. I waved at everyone and swallowed hard. "Well, this is a few more than I expected."

Blythe beamed at me. "Hey, if you're on the fence about

opening up your business, we're here to help you make up your mind to do it."

I smiled despite the butterflies in my tummy, glad to have my best friend at my back. "I'm not making up my mind just yet, but if I'm gonna do it, I have to know what my limitations really are. And to know that, I have to push myself. And that's why y'all are here."

Lee raised his hand. "When do we get to eat the good food your grandmother's cookin'?"

Everybody laughed while Alison Kate elbowed him. I couldn't help but smile at the reunited couple and their intense cuteness together. "When we finish, so we better get on with it. If y'all were told right, you brought a couple of personal belongings with you. I'm gonna go upstairs to my bedroom, and I want y'all to find a place to hide your first object. Then I'm gonna go through my paces and see how far my talents can be pushed."

"I claim geezer privileges on this first test," Henry said, surprising me with his presence. "In about two seconds, it's gonna be too hot and humid to run around outside."

"Then why'd you come?" asked Flint.

"Because if Charli's gonna finally value herself enough to open up a business, then I'm here to cheer her on. No harm in that, is there?" The older rascal of a gentleman nodded at me and snuck a wink when nobody else was looking.

My cheeks warmed. "Thanks, Mr. Henry."

Horatio's voice boomed from the back of the room. "When would you like us to start?"

"Oh." In my embarrassment, I forgot to give the go-ahead. "I'll go upstairs now. Anywhere on the property is fair game."

With great enthusiasm, everyone began chatting with glee, probably planning what hiding place they wanted to use. Beau followed me upstairs. He and I had practiced last night so I could see if my powers still remained limited with vampires. I didn't know if I still kept a little of the extra juice of magic from the founders' tree or if I could just push myself harder, but out of the ten times we tried the exercise, I managed to find the object twice with a lot of effort.

"I'm gonna go nap," my vampire roommate told me with a yawn. "Good luck today."

I entered my bedroom and closed the door. The voices from downstairs quieted as they all hunted for a good hiding place. Left alone with my thoughts, a few doubts crept their way back in, and I sat on my bed contemplating my sanity again.

After about fifteen minutes, someone knocked lightly and cracked the door open. Mason stepped inside, and I freaked out, trying to kick some of my dirty clothes under the bed. Rushing to push him out of my room, I slammed the door behind me.

The corners of his lips quirked up at my efforts. "I think everyone's ready downstairs. And perhaps you should think about hiring Henry to help you. As much as he said he didn't want to do anything, the man herded all of us. He might make a good secretary."

I smacked the detective on his arm and walked

downstairs. My friends waited for me to choose who to start with. Lee pulled me aside and asked if he could go last, which puzzled me but I gladly obliged.

Ben volunteered to go first. I held his hand and had him picture the object. A connection to an ink pen formed quickly. "Is it in the curio cabinet in the parlor, second shelf from the top, hidden behind the collection of flasks Aunt Nora refused to accept from Tipper's will?" I asked.

My friend raised his eyebrows. "That's impressive. I thought you used to have to lead me around to find it."

I let go of his hand with a slight squeeze. "Sometimes I still have to do that, letting the thread of connection tug me forward. But for some people and some lost items, it's a little easier now. Although I may still have to do it the old-fashioned way to prove to a client that I used my talents to find whatever it is they hire me for or they might not want to pay me."

It was a little odd to have everyone watching my every move and really learning how my magic worked. But if they could understand it and me a little better, then they could also help me figure out how in the world I would set up a business.

I found most of the objects hidden either in the downstairs of the house or close by outside. When it came to my brother, the twinkle in his eyes alerted me. Taking my hand, he looked away, whistling.

"You're not concentrating," I accused.

"I know. I wanna see if I can beat you at this. Can I keep something hidden from you if I want?"

As one of the first people to help me learn about my talents, it both annoyed and amazed me that he still knew how to push me. Concentrating harder, I tried to win the game. A thin glimmering thread stretched to me, and I grabbed onto it with my will, binding it to me.

"It's somewhere outside," I declared. Tugging on Matt's hand, I walked with impatience toward the barn that housed the horses.

"I see you haven't lost your touch." The glee rolling off my brother bothered me.

Ignoring most of my friends following us, I entered the barn wary of the horses whinnying in their stalls. Aware of my brother's devious nature, it didn't amuse me when I stood in front of a steaming pile of manure. "Pixie poop."

His snicker joined the laughter of my watching friends. "No, horse poop."

"You're the idiot who hid his spell phone in the middle of a pile of crap. I'm not fishing it out." I dropped his hand and crossed my arms over my chest.

"You might," he teased. "It's not *my* spell phone." Matt slipped his own device out of his pocket and showed it to me. Choosing my name from his list of contacts, he hit Send. The phone in the manure rang and vibrated.

Without hesitation, I slugged him on his arm. "You jerk. You're gonna get it out of there and clean it until you'd let your unborn baby eat off of it." I stomped out of the barn.

"Hey, I really did try to keep it from you. Your magic is much stronger than it used to be," Matt called out.

I shot him a middle finger and made my way back to the porch. Henry sat in a rocker, sipping on a glass of sweet tea. "I told that boy not to do it, but you Goodwins have a stubborn streak that runs a mile wide."

I found items for the rest of my girls, and paid special attention when I came to Flint. If I'd had issues with vampires and fairies, I didn't know how other supernatural beings might work with my magic. Finding a connection with the gnome as well as Horatio wasn't that different. I told Flint where he hid the pink pin Goss gave him and informed Horatio that I might have to keep the copy of whatever old book he'd slipped into the bookcase full of Tipper's old collection.

My gigantic friend guffawed. "That's a first edition of *A Study In Scarlet* I found in a rare bookshop in Bloomsbury. I think you should keep it, Holmes." He leaned closer and did his best to whisper. "And I think it is a most capital idea for you to open your business. Give me the word and I shall create more cards for you to hand out."

Juniper hovered close by, her blue-green dust floating down. "I'm not sure how I can help, Charli."

"Actually, you're one of my most important test subjects. I'm a little confused with fae magic. Moss hid stuff from me, but when I went looking for Mrs. K's brooch, I found it easily at Flint and Goss' house." Too many times I wondered whether or not fairy magic blocked me. I'd just never had the motivation to find the answer.

"Oh, we fae can befuddle others with our magic." Juniper

thought hard, tapping her finger against the side of her tiny mouth. "I would imagine if Moss didn't want you to find something, she could block your magic. With the brooch, I think it could be a couple of things. One, Goss wasn't hiding it. And two, she's pregnant, and that makes her a little vulnerable right now."

"Speaking of, I'm goin' home to my missus." Flint wished me well and headed out to check on his pregnant fairy wife.

Juniper let me hold her hand, and I had her try to block me from finding her item. Touching her directly gave me a bit more juice to work with. Although the picture in my mind was fuzzy, I could see her wand but couldn't quite pick the place.

As soon as I had her concentrate on wanting to find it, the image in my head cleared. "You've placed it in the red and gold vase sitting next to the window."

Horatio confirmed its location, picking up the vase and shaking the delicate porcelain to retrieve the rattling wand.

Henry snapped the piece of paper he held in his hand and cleared his throat. "So you can charge more for finding items that require more effort and magic. You would price on a scale, but you should charge a minimum up front. Kind of like how our postal service does it."

We all gaped at him, and he sniffed. "Hey, I wasn't born old. I led a very productive life before I became the amazing old fart standin' in front of you."

Lily raised her hand. "Can we eat now?"

"Oh, I forgot the second part of this. How many of y'all brought a second thing?" I asked.

Several hands shot up so I could give my second round of instructions. "I think I have enough evidence to help me make a decision for the 'lost' portion of Lost & Found. But I've never tried my talents in reverse. What if someone brings an object in and wants to find who it belongs to? I'll go back out of the room, and those of you with a different item can place them on this table. Then I'll try and figure out who they belong to."

It didn't take long for them to be ready for me, and I studied the pile of things. I ruled out a couple of them, knowing exactly who they belonged to because of what they were.

Since I'd never tried to match an item to the person, I thought I better add a little extra oomph to the exercise. Breathing in deep and letting it out to center myself, I recited an extra special spell. "*If Lost & Found is the game to play, I need to keep my doubts at bay. Finding things is what I do, my magic talents help me through. If something lost can be found, let's try to turn this trick around. Found item to owner now restore, I task my magic to give me more.*"

A little bit of energy sparked inside me, and kick of power surged through my body. Ready to try it out, I picked up a tie pin. "At first glance, I might think this belongs to a guy because of what it is. But it could also be a sentimental piece."

I flipped the cool metal over in my fingers, searching for any kind of connection to someone in the room. With all eyes boring into me, my anxiety grew with each second that ticked by without my magic jumping to life.

The power was there for me to access, but it didn't appear to work in the opposite way. My friends shifted in their seats, their silence weighing on me until I couldn't take it anymore. "Gah, I don't think this is going to work."

"You can't give up that quickly," stated Mason, his brow furrowed. "I'm betting that when you first started getting a hang of your talents, it didn't just happen."

I looked at Matt, who nodded in agreement. "We had to practice a bunch."

"But I'm an adult now who accepts her magic. It should be easier, shouldn't it?" Old familiar doubts reared their ugly heads, telling me I couldn't do it.

Henry scoffed. "Well, of course it's not working. You're asking your powers to start from scratch. You have to do something they already know to do. Now, I've been watching you today. The first thing you do when you're trying to help someone find something is—"

"I hold onto them," I finished. "So maybe I need to touch the person it belongs to in order to match the item to them."

As awkward as it was, I held the tie pin in one hand and reached out to every person sitting in the room, starting with Mason. His warm touch felt inviting but held no zing of connection. He winked at me and urged me to the next person.

I paused when I held Henry's hand, thinking I'd felt something. Unable to make a clear decision, I moved on until

I'd touched everyone. Wanting to give up, I furrowed my brow and went with my gut instinct. Standing in front of Henry, I asked the man to stand up.

Closing my eyes, I concentrated on the tie pin and then touched Henry's hand. When I opened my eyes, I saw a glow around the item and where our skin met. "This is yours. Isn't it?" I hoped.

The older man's gruff expression broke into one of glee and he cackled. "You got it. See, there's more in you than you expected."

One by one, I matched the objects to the person, although the process took longer than I'd like. At this point, how would I translate the new skill into something I could use to make money? If someone turned something they found in to me, it might take me a year to touch every single person in town to find the original owner. It wasn't a very practical skill.

The last object, a small dark blue box, lay in the center of the table. It didn't take my magic to tell me that it most likely held a very important piece of jewelry. Confused, my eyes darted around the room. Who would use a ring for this exercise?

For a second, my stomach clenched, wondering if this was Mason's weird way of telling me he wanted more between us? I knew it couldn't belong to my brother, and I'd given the items back to my girlfriends. Lee caught my eye, his face turned bright red, tilting his head toward his girlfriend.

Relieved and hit with sudden joy, I cleared my throat and

made a show of finding the potential owner. "Who might this tiny leather box belong to?" I walked around, waving it in front of people, touching them on the shoulder.

Passing by Alison Kate twice, I flashed her a quizzical glance. I placed my fingers to my temple. "Ali Kat, I think that this box is meant for you." I stated in my most mystical voice.

My friend shook her head. "That's not mine."

Lee scooted to the edge of his seat next to her and got down on one knee. "Yes, it is. If you'll have me." He took the box from me and opened it.

Alison Kate squealed and covered her mouth, tears forming at the corners of her eyes. I backed away to let Lee have his moment, but Blythe, Lavender, Lily, and I stood at the ready.

Lee tried to speak, but his voice broke. He coughed a couple of times and attempted again. "Alison Kate, I was blind for so long to the hope and joy that was right there beside me for all those years. I don't want another one to go by without making sure that you'll be mine for the rest of our lives. Will you marry me?"

With a shriek of pure happiness, Alison Kate tackled Lee around the neck, giggling and crying at the same time. "Yes, yes, yes!"

The entire room erupted in cheers, applause, and more tears from us girls. Lee attempted to put the ring on his new fiancée's finger, but she hugged him too tight.

Ben came up to me on my left side. "He got that ring

while we were working out the contracts for the spell phones and other development deals. When he heard about the friend-tervention and how the others tricked you and Blythe with their engagement, he thought why not do it now."

I wiped a stray tear from my cheek. "I'm really happy for them." Noticing Ben's warm glances at Lily, who did her best not to look at her boyfriend in that particular moment, I wondered how long it would take the tall advocate to ask her the same question.

We watched Alison Kate pull herself together long enough to let Lee slip the ring on her finger. They stood up and welcomed the jubilant embraces from the rest of us.

"I'm declaring my experiments over. Let's get us some food," I shouted over the din of merriment.

Mason stood off to the side, leaning against the wall. He watched the scene with a little bit of sadness in his eyes. I walked over to him and placed my hand in his. "You okay?"

His thumb swiped over my skin. "I am. Just remembering how it felt."

After everything he'd shared with me, I couldn't help but recall the pictures of Mason with Jessica. "Do you wish things had been different?" I asked without looking at him.

He squeezed my hand once and paused. He did it again twice until I looked him in the eyes. "Not at all."

The rest of the world dropped away in that brief moment. We'd flirted back and forth before. This felt like...more. And for the first time, my doubts about what there was between the two of us stayed quiet.

"Mason," I breathed out. My eyes flitted to his lips, and I wanted to find out if the stubble he still kept would scratch against my skin.

Henry hacked and spluttered with dramatic intensity to interrupt us. "Your grandmother sent me to find out if y'all gonna come eat or what?"

Mason shut his eyes for a second. "Be right there." When Henry left, the detective bent his forehead against mine. "One of these days..." he trailed off.

"I know," I whispered, squeezing his hand and letting him go.

We turned to follow the elder gentleman to the kitchen to fix our plates when Mason's phone went off. He answered it, his expression darkening into a scowl. "He did? When?"

I went to fetch Matt and pulled him aside from the rest of the group. "I think there might be something going on." My brother rushed into the foyer to find Mason.

The detective held up a hand to make both of us wait. "I understand. We'll be there as soon as we can."

"What's going on?" Matt asked. "Do we need to go to the station?"

Mason shook his head. "I need to get to the station, but I have to take Charli there."

My brother moved his body in front of mine in defense. "Why?"

Mason's eyes rested on mine, all the warmth in them gone. "Because Tucker's just turned himself in for the murder of Duke Aikens, and he won't talk to anyone but her."

Chapter Seventeen

Matt drove me to the station, following behind Mason. When we got there, we found a distraught Clementine pacing at the front desk.

She rushed to me, grabbing my hands. "He doesn't want to see me at all and told me not to tell our parents. I don't know what to do." Breaking down into tears, she hugged me.

Taken off guard, I patted her back. Matt's mouth dropped open, and I mouthed my surprise to him. When Clementine sobbed, I remembered that she was family and truly embraced her.

"He wants to talk to you," my cousin managed through hiccuped breaths.

I flinched at her revelation. "I'm sorry."

She pushed away from me and pulled out a lace

handkerchief from her purse, wiping under her eyes. "No, that's a good thing. You can go in there and convince him that he's being silly. There's no way he's guilty, so he doesn't need to stay in jail."

I couldn't bring myself to tell her that her fiancé might be right. Matt offered to look after our cousin while Mason escorted me to the back of the station.

"I don't like it," he growled. "I'm coming in there with you."

I stopped walking and waited for the detective to notice my absence. He turned around and came back, frowning.

"Tucker asked to talk to me. You have to see this as an opportunity to maybe find out the truth. If you go barging in there, he might clam up." The last thing I needed was to play referee between an upset warden and a broken man.

Mason noticed another young warden watching us. He pursed his lips and motioned for me to follow him into his office. Shutting the door behind us, he leaned against the edge of his desk and crossed his arms. "It's incredibly risky, having you go in to hear his confession. What if he did hurt Duke? Then you're putting yourself directly in harm's way. Again."

Not willing to let the detective dictate my choices in life, I closed the distance and squared off with him. "And I'll be fine. You've gotta let me in there to at least try."

Mason huffed and thought about it for a second. "What if he attempts to hurt you?"

"Isn't he locked up? What could possibly happen?" I

countered. "Once he's in the cell, doesn't it negate his ability to cast spells?"

"It does." Defeated, the detective chewed on his lip.

I reached out to touch his arm. "I promise to tell you everything he tells me, but let me try to help. Besides, my gut says that something's off."

Mason placed his hand over mine. "And what exactly is your gut going to do if you're wrong?"

I slipped my hand out from under his. "I thought you trusted me and my gut? Has that changed?"

"No—"

"Then I'm going in there." Opening the door, I stomped down the hall to the room with the cell.

Mason caught up and held me back. "Okay, fine. I *do* trust you. But him...listen, I'll let you go in there, but I'm casting a surveillance spell so I can hear everything. It's either that or you don't go in." His hand extended to touch my cheek, but he stopped mid-air, remembering where we were. "Be careful in there."

He opened the door into a room with two jail cells separated by bars. Tucker lay on the rickety old cot in one of them, his arm over his eyes. When he heard us, he bolted upright.

"You've asked to speak to her so here she is. She will tell me everything you say, so keep that in mind. I'll give you fifteen minutes alone with her, and then I'll come back." Mason shot me a look of caution. Before he left, he flourished his hands by his side, casting the surveillance spell.

I waited in silence for Tucker to take the lead. He pushed himself up, the cot creaking under him. His head hung low, his disheveled hair drooping over his brow.

He rubbed the back of his neck. "Do you know why I turned myself in?"

I stepped closer to the floor-to-ceiling metal bars separating us. "Because you think you committed a crime."

He glanced at me through his hair. "But not just any crime."

Panic gripped my stomach. If Tucker continued talking, he would definitely incriminate himself. I wanted the details behind the murder, but having him confess while sitting in the jail cell at a warden's station was a very bad idea.

"You know, maybe you do want a warden in here and not me." My eyes roamed over every inch of the place, trying to figure out how Mason's surveillance spell worked.

Tucker groaned and pushed his hair back with his fingers. "I should probably have Jed Farnsworth here. That's what my dad would require. But I'm tired, Charli. Tired of trying to live up to the family name. Trying to be the man my father expects me to be. Tired of trying to live the life everyone thinks I have. Exhausted from playing the prince when I'm more of the fool."

I grasped one of the iron bars, its cold metal a sharp reminder of what stood between Tucker and freedom. "I can understand that. But what I don't get is why you voluntarily came to the station and turned yourself in for the murder."

He stood and walked over to me, placing his fingers over mine. "Because I did it. I took a man's life."

Pixie poop. If Tucker kept talking, there wasn't anything I could do to keep him from being formally arrested and rotting in a cell for the rest of his life.

Knowing Mason could hear me, I spoke up in a clear voice. "You have to trust me."

"I do," replied Tucker. His thumb brushed the back of my hand.

I pulled out of his touch. "Not quite what I meant, but good. Stay right where you are." Gathering the energy inside me, I focused it. "*Against the wishes of a friend whose listening has to come to an end. Give us space, a silent bubble, where we can talk without more trouble.*"

Power flowed through my fingers, and I willed a protective layer of magic around us, shutting the rest of the world out. It wouldn't last long between my lack of food in my stomach to fuel the spell and the likelihood that Mason might come in at any second. I hoped he'd heard what I'd said and gave me the benefit of the doubt.

"You've got to tell me what happened that night as fast as you can, Tucker. And then I'll help you decide what steps to take next, okay?"

He nodded. "I already told you that I wasn't doing okay, and there were...things that had happened in Charleston that caused me problems. One of those problems was Duke. He had this book that he recorded things in and used to blackmail others."

"He was blackmailing you," I clarified.

"Yes," Tucker confirmed. "I paid him off for a while, but was running out of money. I thought I'd be safe in Honeysuckle, but then he showed up. He pressured dad and me to hire his company to cater Clem's and my wedding events. That's why he was here for the bridal shower. At least he had someone on his team who could actually cook."

"Had you ever seen her before? That girl, Shelby." Perhaps some of what my ex told me could shed more light on her role in Duke's life.

"I don't think so, although there are big blocks of time that I can't account for." He gazed at me through the bars. "I'm pretty sure someone either spellcast something on me or slipped something in my drinks. Because what Duke had on me..."

Knowing the seconds ticked by faster and faster, I waved him off. "You can tell me the specifics later. Right now, I need to know about the night of the murder and why you think you're the reason Duke's dead."

Tucker leaned his forehead against the bars, his face framed by them. "I fought with him at Lucky's. We were playing cards, and I wanted to win back some of *my* money he'd taken from me. But he kept taunting me with my misdeeds, almost telling everyone in the room the exact details. I couldn't take it anymore, and, I'm ashamed to say, I attacked him. I haven't been back to The End yet, but I'm pretty sure I owe Lucky some money to repair his place."

Muffled shouting echoed around our bubble, and I

stepped closer to the bars until only the metal separated Tucker and me. "What happened after you fought him at the bar?"

"Lucky kicked us out. I was already drunk and woozy, so my memory is patchy at best. Duke kept verbally attacking me and I took a couple of swings at him. He must have made contact with his fist at some point because I woke up with this." Tucker pointed at the purple and green healing black eye.

The voices grew louder on the other side of the door. "A fight doesn't get a guy killed, Tuck."

"But it all goes a little blank after that. I know I followed him, but not sure where. I can remember more of his taunts and me yelling at him. And then..."

Hollis' voice shouted on the other side of door. "You will *not* arrest my son."

"Then what, Tucker?" I pushed.

He reached through the bars and grabbed my arms. "The only thing I can remember is looking down and seeing something in my hands. It was something hefty. And I remember seeing blood. It has to be his. I have to have used whatever I held to kill him." His eyes widened in desperation and fear. "I killed him."

Hollis burst into the the room, and my spell popped and fizzled. "I don't know what you think you're doin' but you will step away from my son." He pulled me out of Tucker's grip and pushed me hard enough that I stumbled.

Mason caught me. "That's enough of that, Mr.

Hawthorne. She was here at Tucker's request and I allowed it."

Hollis glared at Mason. "Then I'll have your badge when all of this is done. He will not be speaking to anybody without our advocate present, which is what should have happened in the first place. And she," he pointed at me, "has *no* business being here or having anything to do with my son or this case."

"Father, I didn't want an advocate. I asked to speak to Charli." Tucker did his best to calm his dad down.

"No," Hollis bellowed, his voice rough and cracking a little. "It's enough."

For the first time, I studied the angry father. He and his son wore the same run down expressions with furrowed brows and frowns. Dark circles rimmed Hollis' eyes. Although stubble didn't cover his chin, he tied with Tucker for his haggard appearance.

Mason placed his hand at the small of my back and escorted me out of the room. He instructed Zeke to watch Hollis and Tucker, and took me back into his office.

Once the door clicked shut, I whipped around to face Mason. "I'm more than pretty sure he didn't kill Duke."

The detective either didn't hear me or didn't care. He stalked forward, until his face hovered next to mine and my back touched the door. "What do you think you were doing?" he seethed.

"Did you hear me? Tucker didn't kill Duke. You gotta get him out of there," I insisted, placing my hands on Mason's chest to back him off.

He covered them with his. "You knew the deal was that I listened in, and then you deliberately made a choice that went against that." Pulling my hands off his chest, he stepped away and turned his back to me.

"I made a quick decision in the moment, and it paid off. Based on what Tucker told me, he couldn't have killed Duke." I softened my voice. "I wasn't trying to make you angry."

Mason's shoulders stiffened. "But you were trying to protect him. Your ex."

Realization dawned on me. "Is that what your problem is? This is some sort of man jealousy thing? You think I chose him over you?"

"No," he replied a little too fast. "I mean...yeah, maybe a little." He blew out a breath and turned to face me again. "I wanted to watch out for you and you took that option away. It made me feel...helpless."

"I asked you to trust me. Didn't you hear me? When I said it, I meant it for you, not him." Disappointment settled over me like a wet blanket.

Mason looked at the floor. "I heard you. It's why I didn't break down the door and come in there."

"But you still don't trust me. Not really. Otherwise, you'd want to hear what Tucker said and try to add that to the evidence to figure out the case."

He narrowed his eyes. "The same could be said about you. You don't trust me to listen to *my* instincts and follow the rules I create to keep you safe."

I reached for the door handle. "Then I guess we're done

here." A part of me paused, hoping his rational side would kick in and he'd stop me from leaving.

"I guess we are." Mason's cold tone sent chills down my back.

Pulling the door open, I checked to make sure I wouldn't run into either Hawthorne man on my way out. Although my stubbornness demanded that I leave without saying anything else, I couldn't help but contribute the little I'd learned to help with the case.

"Oh, and Mason?" I waited until his eyes met mine. "Tucker confirmed the fight at Lucky's bar. And then he said he thought he was holding something heavy in his hand that had blood on it. That's why he turned himself in. He thinks he hit Duke on the head and killed him. But you already know from the doc that he didn't die that way. If you put those two elements together, it means that it's most likely Tucker didn't kill Duke. There, now you know everything he told me."

Ignoring the commotion coming from Big Willie's office and shaking my head at my brother not to talk to me, I stormed out of the warden station, perhaps for the last time.

Chapter Eighteen

Mason's final words affected me more than talking to Tucker. I went home defeated, not wanting to talk to anybody. Beau bounded down the steps once he was awake and ready to take on another night of wooing, but he took one look at me and poofed into a bat, flying out of an open window.

I picked at the leftovers from Nana's cooking, but nothing tasted good. At any moment, Matt would be bounding up my porch steps to tell me how I'd screwed up at the station. If Mason dared to step foot on my property, he'd better be ready to leave in a real hurry because I was prepared to bless his heart and hex his hiney into the next county over.

The inevitable knock echoed through my house. Ready to defend myself to my brother, I opened the screen door and tramped onto the porch. Big Willie waited for me at the foot of the stairs, holding his hat in his hand.

The surprise of his presence stopped me from making my prepared speech. "Oh."

"Charli Goodwin, what did I tell you? No, don't answer that, just listen." The sasquatch rested his right foot on the bottom step and sighed. "I tolerate when you get yourself mixed up in things as long as you're being appropriately monitored."

"You knew I was working with Mason?" I asked.

"Does a unicorn crap wherever it wants to? Of course, I knew you were workin' with the detective. If it weren't for me bein' his boss, I would know because it's a small town and you aren't exactly invisible when you go questionin' suspects." He scratched his shaggy head.

I offered him a seat in a rocker and some sweet tea, but he refused both. "I guess you want me to lay low."

Big Willie scoffed. "That's the understatement of the year. You cannot be involved in the case anymore. Don't talk to anyone who might be involved. And especially stay away from anyone with the last name of Hawthorne. Or anyone about to marry someone with the last name of Hawthorne."

I hung my head, studying a cracked board on my porch and tracing it with my big toe. "Hollis was pretty mad, was he?"

"Let's just say that I'm under strict orders to arrest you if you interfere again. And as many times as I threaten you with puttin' you in our tank, this is the first time that it might happen for real." The sheriff placed his hat on his head. "Take my advice. You Goodwins already have enough trouble comin' your way from what I've heard. Best to keep your nose clean by keepin' it to yourself."

I narrowed my eyes. "What have you heard about my family?"

He held up his hands to stop me from getting upset. "Nothin' your grandmother didn't want me to know."

If Nana was bringing Big Willie into her inner circle, then chances were that he knew about the attempted Charleston takeover. The sasquatch might have let more information slip than he should have. I filed away more questions about the Hawthornes to ask Nana later.

"I don't want to cause problems, only to help solve the murder and get the right person behind bars. I told Mason I'm pretty sure it's not Tucker." When the detective's name rolled off my tongue, all kinds of emotions swirled in my stomach.

Big Willie placed one hairy hand on his hip. "I hope it isn't. We had to release him into his father's custody."

I whistled long and low. "Hollis really is throwin' around his authority."

"You can say that again," muttered the sheriff. He tipped his hat to me. "Please, for your own good, stay out of things and let us wardens handle the case." He walked through the field to the road where he'd parked his car. I listened for him to drive down the road, too many questions crowding my brain.

What exactly was going on in Honeysuckle? Between Duke's death, the Hawthorne's involvement, and the outside threat, the storm clouds of trouble were brewing overhead. If the wardens were the only ones who could bring an end to it all, then they needed to do it fast.

In such a short amount of time, my entire world went from bright beautiful colors to dull drab grays. The only thing that got me out of the house was teaching my young students. I pedaled through the back roads to the school, avoiding Main Street at all costs.

For an hour and a half over two afternoons, I forgot about everything else except making sure the kids were prepared to take their spell permit test. Watching their confidence grow in their magic acted as a balm to my emotional wounds. I helped them, and in turn, they helped me to press pause on my problems for a short period of time.

With so many distractions floating around in my head, I feared I didn't give the students my best. Despite my efforts to forget about the case, I couldn't help but think about Tucker and his confession, or whether or not he really did have more to do with Duke's death.

On the date of the last class, I passed out a practice written test that I knew all of them would ace. While they filled in bubbles with their pencils, I walked around the desks, monitoring them and letting my mind wander into dangerous territory.

What had happened with Tucker in the long run? What

was Hollis doing, using his authority to protect his son? Did Mason hear what I said about Tucker and the object he thought he held or did he ignore me because he was mad?

Obsessing over the case I wasn't supposed to be thinking about turned me into a bad teacher.

Anna caught my attention. "We're all finished. Can we check our answers?"

I managed to pull myself together and help them figure out what questions were most commonly missed and how to choose the best answer when they were completely uncertain.

We spent the rest of the time practicing the basic spells they'd have to perform. I paired them up and had one student play the assessor and the other perform the spells. That way, they could learn by seeing both sides and help each other out with better details. For a job that was supposed to be temporary, I could picture myself working with students again sometime in the near future.

Before I dismissed them, Helen raised her hand. "Miss Charli, do you have any last words of advice?"

Pushing out all thoughts about Mason and the case, I tried to recall any valuable piece of advice that Nana had given to Matt and me all of our lives. "I think it's important to remember that magic isn't something to be afraid of. It's a part of you and something you have to learn to master. But you can't control something when you're scared of it. Try to remember some of the techniques we've gone through in this course to help you relax when you're taking your test."

The students thanked me and began to pack up. One

more piece of Nana's advice popped in my head. "Oh, and don't worry about making mistakes. Casting a spell isn't always about perfection. Think of it like you're cooking. Maybe you're following a recipe and you don't have all the ingredients. Or maybe some of you have watched your own grandmothers at the stove. I'm bettin' they could improvise and change things as they needed to but the end result would still be delicious."

April spoke up with her quiet voice. "My grandma cooks with Grandpa, and they never use recipes. I love their chicken and dumplin's when they make it just for me."

I beamed at the shy girl. "My Nana makes me the creamiest mac and cheese to cheer me up. But she's practiced over the years to not need a recipe. Remember, even if you make a mistake, there's always room for you to improve or pull a spell out in the end. If you can't, then you can learn something from the experience and try again."

Hearing my grandmother's words coming out of my mouth to a younger generation felt weird and at the same time kind of wonderful.

Some of the girls hugged me as they left the class, and I received a couple of fist bumps from the guys. Eric promised not to hex me by accident. I listened to the teenagers talking and joking on the way down the halls of the school, their enthusiasm bouncing off the walls.

Walking outside with happiness in my heart, I didn't mind the afternoon heat and humidity. I wandered over to where my bike waited for me underneath the magnolia tree. Mason leaned against the low branches, waiting for me. Too many restless emotions surfaced, and I ignored his presence, picking up my bicycle and walking it away from him with the clicks of the gears.

"Charli, we need to talk," he called after me.

"I don't think that's a good idea. At least, not right now." I placed my bag in the basket on the front of the bike and straddled it.

His deep voice reverberated through me. "If you ride away from me, I'll come after you. I made a mistake and I want to talk to you about it."

One foot rested on the pedal and the other steadied me on the ground. "I think it's best if we don't see each other," I said, protecting my heart.

Mason approached with his hands held up in surrender. "I can understand why you feel that way. But if you'll give me a chance to explain some things, and then if you want me to leave you alone, I will. But please, allow me a chance."

Not more than mere minutes ago, I'd told the students that mistakes were okay and could be used to learn something. Maybe I needed to figure out that Mason I would never work on any level. But the man deserved at least some last words before I closed the proverbial door on him.

"Fine. Do you want to talk here?" Sweat beaded on my top lip.

"I was hoping I could go back to your place with you." He watched me with great care, his detective's eyes discerning every tick of my facial muscles.

I acquiesced and nodded, not saying another word. He told me he'd meet me in a few minutes, but I took a very long way home. Allowing the bicycle to access my magic, I rode as fast as I could, letting the wind blow my troubles away and losing myself in the blurs that passed by.

Chapter Nineteen

While riding around delaying my return home, a call from above and a small shadow followed beside me on the pavement. Biddy cawed out to me, soaring high and keeping me company. When I turned the bike in the direction of my house, she circled in the air, letting me know she intended to come over for a visit. Her presence might be more welcome than Mason's.

Cautious and curious at the same time, I walked my bike from the road over my yard and parked it at the side of my house.

Mason rocked in one of the chairs on my porch. "I was starting to think you'd changed your mind."

"I very nearly did." I watched Biddy float down from the sky, flapping her wings and settling on the porch railing. "I'll be right back," I said to her more than the detective.

Going inside, I fetched a cheese biscuit from yesterday's big breakfast and poured out one single glass of sweet tea for myself. I couldn't make it out of the kitchen, grumbling to myself because my manners wouldn't allow me to return outside without an offering for my guest, no matter how annoying he was or how much he'd hurt me. Choosing a much smaller glass, I poured some tea in it. There. He couldn't claim I wasn't a good hostess.

Seeing his face again tempted me to dump the iced tea over his head, but I restrained myself and handed it to him instead. He thanked me, and I sat in my rocker, tossing pieces of biscuit on the porch for Biddy to gobble. The silence stretched between us, and yet it didn't feel awkward. In some ways, even being mad at him, I didn't mind having him close. And that realization bothered me more.

"What has you all riled up?" he asked.

"I'm waiting for you to say your piece and leave." The sharpness of my tone cut me as well as him.

The ice in his glass tinkled when he finished the small amount of his drink. "Then I should get on with it. I'm really sorry."

"For what?" He needed to be specific or I planned to withhold any and all forgiveness.

"For expecting too much from you too soon," he said.

Stunned, I met his gaze. "I don't understand."

Mason watched the crow pecking for crumbs. "When I came back from up North, I had plans. One of them was to tell you about my former life and how I'd finally let go of my past because I wanted my future to be free of any hindrances."

He needed to tell me something I didn't already know. "And I told you that I appreciated your candor."

"But I think I placed too much pressure on you to do the exact same thing. I wish I could say that seeing you with Tucker the other morning at his house didn't stir up more emotions than I was willing to admit." The wood of his chair creaked with the gentle movement. "Even though I wanted us on the same page, it wasn't fair to expect you to be free of your past, too."

I stopped rocking. "I told you that Tucker and I are over. I was only helping him because I still care for him as a person. As a friend and someone about to marry my kin."

"I know." Mason shrugged. "Sometimes you can't help what goes on in here." He tapped the space over his heart. "And sometimes it doesn't agree with this." He tapped the side of his head.

Despite my annoyance, I smiled at his gestures. "That's kinda how it's been for me for the past couple of days."

The space between his eyebrows wrinkled with worry. "When Tucker asked to speak with you and you alone, I guess I got a little territorial. I don't like it when you put yourself in a position where you shouldn't be. Where you could get hurt. It happens way too often, and I wish it didn't."

I slumped back into the chair. If a relationship of any kind that I was a part of was going to survive, I needed someone who stood next to me rather than held me back, even for my own protection. I thought for a brief moment that someone might possibly be the detective. And, if I were honest with myself, not too long ago I had hoped it might be the shifter. Now, I wondered if any male could live up to my expectations?

I kept my eyes on the sun dappling through the woods at the far end of the property. "You say you wanted there to be no walls or barriers between us. Then I have to tell you, I am who I am. I'm not the kind of girl who shies away from danger. I've been this way since I was little, and you're either going to have to adjust and support me or you can watch me from afar. I'm a grown woman less likely to change. If you can't handle that, then we should shake hands and part ways." I gripped the arms of the rocker to keep my hands from trembling.

"That's actually one of the reasons I wanted to come back to your place. Hold on a second." Mason pushed out of the rocker and disappeared around the corner of my house. I heard the rustling of some bushes and he returned, holding two brooms. "I know who you are, but I also can't change who I am. I will always worry about you and will always want you not to get hurt. But that doesn't mean I want to hold you back either."

I eyed him with suspicion. "So you want to do what? Sweep with me?"

"No, I want to fly with you. I stopped by Lee's shop and borrowed these. He's spellcast them, so I thought maybe you and I could ride together." Mason shook the one in his left hand at me.

Biddy squawked a couple of times and groomed her wings to show off. The crow was built to fly. My feet were meant to stay on the ground.

"I don't think it's a good idea." The hurt in his eyes caused me to backtrack. "I mean, I appreciate the sentiment, but I don't think I can sit on top of a thin strip of wood and then expect my body to hurl itself through the air. You said you didn't want to see me hurt, but I'm pretty sure I'd end up at the doc's if I ride that."

Mason relaxed and chuckled. "I don't expect you to go whizzing through the sky. Not on your first try." His eyes twinkled with a little too much amusement.

Biddy hopped over to the edge of the porch and cocked her head, examining the two sticks with brush ends.

"Yeah, I have doubts they can fly, too, old girl," I said to the crow.

"They can," assured Mason. "Lee is one of the best mechanic spellcasters I've ever known. Some of us boys might have been testing them out since he came back. He has visions of grandeur that your group of friends will form a broom riding gang."

I raised my eyebrows. "And none of you fools have broken bones?"

He shot me a sideways glance. "I'll have you know, I was one of the top broom racers for my class at the wardens academy."

"You didn't just ride, you raced?" I tried to picture him younger and reckless enough to fly one of those cleaning tools as fast as the wind. On purpose. "No, thank you."

He held out the shorter of the two handles. "This one has been spelled as the trainer. It hovers closer to the ground and goes about as fast as a pony ride. Think of it as magical training wheels."

Taking the broom from him, I inspected every inch of it. "Doesn't look very safe. Plus, I don't think shoving a thin wooden handle like that between my legs will be especially comfy."

Mason rolled his eyes. "They work on magic. That means it'll support your weight without being uncomfortable. Come on, Charli, don't you trust—"

"Don't ask that question right now," I warned, finding myself stuck between a rock and hard place.

In no way did I want him to see me not even try, no matter how certain I was that a fall was inevitable. Call it pride or the stubbornness of being a Goodwin woman, I couldn't *not* try. And I really did want to trust him, but didn't know if my heart could take another mistake.

Dubious, I agreed. "Fine. But you've got to be patient with me. Bicycles or motorcycles—I prefer the things I ride to be planted on solid ground."

"I know." He glanced away for a brief second, a slight frown forming at the corners of his mouth. He shook off whatever bugged him and gestured for me to join him in the front yard.

I copied how he managed his broom, holding it out horizontally in front of me. "What do I need to do?"

"This first part's easy. You straddle the handle like you would your bike." He showed me with a little too much condescension.

"Okay, maybe you don't have to be that slow with the instructions." Placing the shorter handle between my legs, I waited for the next bit.

Mason struggled not to smirk. "Now you connect your magic to the broom. Hold the handle with one or both hands and stretch your will of magic to it."

Unwilling to mess things up, I concentrated and added a quick rhyme. *"This broom in my hand, my magic should fly, but please oh please, don't let me die."* A little spark of my energy connected to the implement of cleaning. The broom jerked a tiny bit underneath me.

"Looks like you're ready. The next part is going to take your absolute faith that I won't let you fall." He made sure I was watching him, and then performed a small hop. He lifted in the air, hovering with his feet dangling an inch off the ground.

How did he expect me to have faith in nothing but a sliver of wood and a little magic to keep me from falling? I lifted one foot but couldn't make myself push off with the other. My body struggled to stay on the broom. "See, it's not gonna work."

"You're not trying. Give it a little hop." He placed his feet down again and showed me how easy it was for him.

No matter how much my head understood, I couldn't get past my doubts. Biddy fluttered over from the porch, standing in front of me and hopping up and down. She opened her wings each time.

"Even your bird knows what it takes." Mason touched down and got off his broom. He offered his hand to me. "I'll hold onto you if it will help."

I was about two seconds and one more try away from giving up the broom for good. Taking a chance, I held onto him fast. Closing my eyes, I counted down. "Three, two, one, hop!"

"Open your eyes, Charli," commanded Mason.

Obeying, I snuck a peek through one eye. The world bobbed up and down a little bit, and my feet dangled a short distance from the earth. "I did it!"

Mason snorted. "You got in the air. That's step one. Now you have to master moving."

At the thought of being in motion, I lost my concentration and wobbled off balance. Placing my feet back down, I frowned. "Maybe sitting in the air is good enough?" I noticed that he still held my hand in his.

He moved his hand to my shoulder. "You can stop now. Or...you can learn to soar." Taking a step away, he allowed me to hover in the air on my own.

At first, I gripped the handle tight and my knuckles whitened. When I didn't automatically fall off, I relaxed a tiny fraction. "So how do I move?"

Mason smiled. "Let me see if I can put this in terms you

would understand. Right now, you're kind of sitting in neutral. Your magic is your gas. Your intent is your gear shift and your will is your throttle and your brakes."

Putting it in terms of riding a motorcycle did help. "So if I focus my intent to go forward and then will it to be so..." I tried it once and the broom lurched forward, surprising me. Losing my concentration, I dropped to the ground on my feet.

"Oops." Mason reached out to help me, but I waved him off.

"I just stalled it a little. Let me try again." Sticking my tongue out of my mouth, I got myself in the air again with a hop and, after a deep breath, moved the broom forward at the pace of a snail. "I'm doing it," I exclaimed.

The detective walked beside me as I teetered a bit but didn't lose my forward momentum. "If you want to turn, you lean a little in the direction you desire. Not too far."

After five minutes, I managed a sluggish circle in front of my house with Mason at my elbow the entire way. Sweat poured down my face, but I didn't care.

A wide grin beaming across my face, I landed exactly where I wanted to. "I don't think I'll be racing anytime soon, but that was pretty cool."

Biddy fluttered back to the porch railing, her squawks sounding a little too much like cackling laughter.

"Hey, you be quiet. One of these days, I'll be up there flying right alongside you," I told her, getting off the training broom and handing it back to Mason.

He took it from me and tilted his head. "Well, if you're willing to give me a chance, may I show you how cool riding one of these can be?" Switching brooms, he picked up the longer one. "If you trust me, you can fly with me."

There was that word again. *Trust.* The two of us had a few stumbling blocks over it, but I wanted to be brave and take the leap with him. Even if that meant putting my own mortality in his hands.

I swallowed hard. "Okay."

"You get on first," he instructed.

Confused, I did as I was told, straddling the handle. "You're not riding in front?"

Mason climbed on behind me, his body cradling mine. He leaned his head over my left shoulder, speaking into my ear. "Nope. You're going to lean back into me a bit and follow my lead. When I lean, you lean. Other than that, I've got you." He wrapped his arms around me, gripping the handle in front of where I grasped it.

"Oh," I gasped. The intimacy of it all erased my previous anger. Enjoying the closeness, I nestled my back into his chest.

His chuckle vibrated against me. "I'm going to extend my magic around you. This would work smoother if we could tether our energy together, but I don't expect you to do that on your first real ride."

Mingling our magic would be the ultimate demonstration of my trust in him. It could also open a door between us that might be very hard to close.

"We can try." Centering myself, I called on my energy and brought it to the surface, the thrill of the whole experience spurring me on.

Mason drew in a quick breath and coughed to cover his surprise. "I'm tethering to you now."

The tingle of his magic reached out to me. With my will, I allowed his to mingle with mine until the steady power flowed through both of us. A smart witch kept up barriers to protect herself on many levels. I let mine down a little and found he had erected nothing between us.

Images flowed into my mind of a place I didn't know. Emotions that weren't mine bloomed in my chest. It took me a second, but I figured out I was seeing Mason's childhood, feeling how he felt growing up. The ghost of Jessica's face appeared in my mind's eye, and I almost choked on the love that enveloped my heart. My own jealousy battled the foreign feeling.

My face replaced Mason's ex's, and an entirely different emotion took over. Initial frustration gave way to awe and admiration. The emotions morphed into something more personal until my heart almost burst from the strongest emotion of all.

Not ready to accept what he was showing me yet, I threw up a bit of a barrier to stop the flow from him and changed my intent. I pushed my own memories at him, showing him my own evolution from feeling like an outcast to where I was right now. Purposefully staying far away from any emotions attached to him, I opened myself wider to share with him what it was like for me when I tracked things, something that nobody else understood.

Mason placed his chin on my shoulder and sighed. "Wow."

"Very much wow." I threw up my barriers to stop sharing quite so much and cleared my throat. "Are you gonna fly me around or what?"

"Yes, ma'am." Mason straightened on the broom. "At the count of three, you're going to hop. One, two, three."

My feet had barely left the ground when the broom took off. The world whizzed by, and I held my breath, a little bit of fear eating away at my fun. Closing my eyes, I shut everything out.

"I've got you," Mason assured me. "Open your eyes and enjoy."

We glided over the field in the direction of the barn. The long grass rustled underneath us. He tested out our ability to work together, leaning right and left to bank us or do slow turns until we worked together like clockwork. We circled the barn, hearing the horses inside whinnying at our presence.

He slowed down a bit. "Have you had enough for today?"

"No way." I shook my head. "Let's take the training wheels off."

I didn't have to see him to feel his grin. "As you wish. Hold on."

The magic we shared sparked to life, and we took off faster than before, the wind whipping around me. We zipped around the open field, climbing a little higher.

My house loomed up ahead, and we didn't steer away. "Uh, Mason."

His laugh vibrated against me again, and he leaned in closer. "Trust me."

I did, although I squealed as the structure got closer. He pulled us up and over at the last second, and my scream turned into fitful giggles as we climbed into the air. My enjoyment gave him full permission, and he pushed my limits.

Fear and pleasure churned in my stomach, and I desired more. Answering my unspoken wish, Mason directed us to the edge of my property. We skimmed past trees, coming close to limbs and branches and maneuvering out of the way before getting hit. Pulling up again, we soared through the air in the afternoon sun.

I turned my head at a familiar squawk and spotted Biddy, wings flung open and wind ruffling her feathers. She matched our speed, winging her way beside us. She cocked her head once in our direction and folded her wings, diving. Mason read my mind and followed her. She led us across the field, dipping up and down and winding back and forth to try and shake us off her tail. At one hard turn, I lost my balance and squealed.

Mason tightened his body around me. "I've got you." Every particle in me believed him.

We stopped chasing the crow and slowed down, banking our descent until we approached my house. Giving him full control, I held on tight until we floated down and he landed us. Placing my feet on the ground, I tried to catch my breath.

The world standing still felt too slow. Adrenaline pumped through me, and I craved more.

Getting off the broom, I paced in front of my porch, amped up to the max. "That was incredible."

Mason held onto the long handle, staring at me with burning fire in his eyes. "Yes, it was." He stalked toward me, and I backed up until my calf met the bottom stair.

"We have to do that again." My chest heaved, and I tried to catch my breath.

He closed the distance between us, tossing the broom into the nearby bushes. "We will."

Without anywhere else to go, I stumbled backward and almost fell. Mason caught me, holding me against his body. The nearness of him fed my excitement. And, again, I craved more.

His eyes dipped to my mouth, and he cupped my cheek with his hand. "Thank you," he whispered.

Mason brushed the sensitive skin of my lips with his thumb, and chills rippled across my body. Giving into the adrenaline, the excitement of the moment, and the thrill still coursing through my veins, I reached my hand up and stroked the stubble on his cheek, inviting him closer.

Wrapping one arm around my waist tighter and moving the hand on my cheek to the back of my neck, he tilted my head up to give him better access. The heat from his mouth blew against my skin, and my heart rate quickened. I closed my eyes in anticipation.

Both of our phones rang at the same time, shattering the

heated spell between us. We stood stock still, debating what to do. Whoever was calling me would definitely get their hiney hexed later.

Mason bent his forehead against mine and let out a rueful snort. "Well, that's a bucket of iced water."

I dropped my hand, the sudden awareness of what almost happened dawning on me. Disappointment flooded every inch of me, and I almost cursed when I pulled out my phone and answered it. "This better be good."

The detective stepped away and retrieved his own phone. "Detective Clairmont here."

"Charli," called out Blythe over a loud commotion in the background. "Could you come over to the Wilkins' house?"

Mason frowned and concentrated. "What, Zeke? Say that again."

"What's that noise?" I asked my friend.

Something crashed on Blythe's side of things. "Just get over here quick as you can." She hung up.

"I'm on my way." Mason shut his phone.

"Going to the Wilkins' house?" I asked.

"Yeah. Zeke says there's a major problem there. I'm sorry we have to cut this short." He approached me again and lifted my chin with his finger, gazing at me with regret and smoldering heat. "Really sorry."

I grasped his hand and squeezed it. "Maybe another time. Right now, can I hitch a ride?"

Chapter Twenty

We pulled up in front of Zeke's family home. Ms. Althea greeted us at the door, worry creasing her brow. The young deputy stood next to her, caught between being her son and being a warden.

Ms. Althea let us in, pointing to the back side of the house. "She barged in not too long ago. The two of them are arguing on the patio. At least I got them to move out of the house and saved some of my things."

Zeke stayed with his mother, and Mason and I headed toward the shouting, stepping over a few broken pieces of china and glass. Shrill voices filled the air, and we found Shelby holding up her hands in defense while another woman on the other side of the wrought iron table circled around it like a predator.

"You think the book buys your freedom? It doesn't belong to you," shouted the stranger.

Shelby's eyes widened in fear. "I don't have it, Tara."

"I don't believe you." The other girl lunged across the table at Shelby.

"Both of you, stop where you are," demanded Mason.

Shelby stood still, but Tara growled and attacked, her fingers curling to scratch with her nails.

"With the authority of the wardens, I command you to stop." Mason extended his power and both figures froze. With a flourish of his hand, he released Shelby from the magical hold, and she scrambled away.

I approached her, keeping a wary eye on the aggressive girl. "Who is that?"

Shelby's mouth drooped with sadness. "That's my half-sister, Tara."

I remembered that name from my eavesdropping on Duke and Shelby at the Hawthorne's kitchen. "Is she a banshee, too?" I asked.

"I'm all witch, not some half-blooded piece of trash," Shelby's sister spit out. "And let me go. Now." She struggled to move.

Mason's magic held her tight. "From what I observed, you were the aggressor. I won't release you until I'm sure that you won't go after your sister again."

Tara shot a dirty glance at Shelby. "We may share half our DNA, but she's no family to me. I'm only here to collect what I'm owed. Once I get it, then I'll disappear."

Taking a good look, I noticed the two young women shared few similarities. Where Shelby's hair was straight and a light brown, Tara's dark curls with purple streaks framed her face. They both had sparkling green eyes, but the intent behind them were complete opposites. Shelby's modest outfit contrasted with Tara's tight-fitting tiny pieces of fabric that passed for clothing and strained against her curves, showing off a lot of skin.

Sensing a losing battle, the darker of the two changed tactics. Tara's face relaxed, and she focused on the detective. "You know, I'm really very nice. I'm sure we can work something out if you let me." She licked her red-stained lips with lascivious intentions. "Why don't you come a little closer, and I'll work out a deal with you." Her eyes scraped down Mason's body, locking in on a very particular spot halfway down.

"Bribing a person in law enforcement will get you arrested," warned Mason.

Tara's expressions changed to one of contempt. "That's not been my experience."

I didn't have time for her games. We needed to know why Shelby's sister made the effort to come all the way to Honeysuckle. I had a pretty good hunch what it was she wanted. "You're looking for Duke's black book, aren't you?"

Her gaze flashed to me, morphing from seductive to rage. "So you knew about it, too? Why, are you in it?"

With a click of his fingers, Mason did something to the

magical hold around Tara, making her flinch. He snapped at her, "Answer her question."

"Yes, I want the book," she admitted through her gritted teeth. "Most of what's in it belongs to me," she snarled.

"You mean, you used your ways to seduce and manipulate people into doing things worthy of being recorded," accused Shelby. She stepped forward and leaned on the table. "With the book gone, you can start fresh, get a different job, or maybe the two of us can figure out how to work together," she pleaded with her half-sister.

Tara snorted with disgust. "You seem to think that I don't like what I do. I'm happy workin' at Hex Kittens. With a body like mine, I make a good livin', and Duke's taught me a way to make even more money. I have no intentions to follow in your goody-two-shoes ways, Sis." The way she uttered that last word sounded more like a swear word than a term of endearment.

Shelby dropped her chin to her chest, and I sympathized with the girl who wanted to save someone who didn't want to be saved. Because of what the book contained, it remained dangerous until we could find it. Desperate, I formed a quick plan.

Taking Shelby by the arm, I escorted her a few feet away and spoke to her in a low voice, telling her about my talents. "With your help, I might be able to find the book and put an end to it."

Hope eased the stress in Shelby's face. "What do you need me to do?" she asked.

I held both of her hands and mine. "Concentrate on the black book. Want it with everything you've got."

"I can do that." She nodded and closed her eyes.

Using what I learned from my tracking experiments with my friends, I focused my energies. The image of the object flashed in and out of my mind. Somewhere in Honeysuckle, someone had the book in their possession.

I squeezed Shelby's hand. "Concentrate harder," I requested. Closing my eyes tight, I tried to get past Shelby's banshee side. *"Although this girl is half a fae, please let my magic have its way. Let me take a closer look and find that dangerous, important book."*

Like a flame flickering in the wind, a small connection formed and fizzled. After three more attempts, I gave up and let her go with a regretful sigh.

Tara snorted. "You two look like you're trying to hold a séance or somethin'."

Hearing her grating voice inspired me. Shelby might be half a fae, but like Tara said, she was all witch. I approached Mason. "Can you loosen your hold on her but keep her under control?"

"Why?" His eyes bore into me, questioning my motives.

"Because she wants the book more than anything else, and she isn't half-banshee." I lifted my eyebrows and waited for him to catch on.

When he did, he glared at me. "I don't like it. We don't know how powerful she is or what she might do to you."

"We're going to have to risk that if we want to find that

book. You and I both know it's the key to solving the whole case," I insisted.

The two of us approached Tara, ignoring her numerous and unimaginative insults. Mason got physically close to her, and a pang of jealousy stung me for a second.

The detective explained in clear words, "I'm going to loosen my hold, but I warn you, try anything and I won't hesitate."

"To do what?" Tara growled.

"To take you out," he promised. Looking up at me, he nodded his head in her direction. "It's your show."

Appreciating his immediate trust, I closed the distance between Tara and me. "Let her go when I touch her," I instructed.

"Keep your hands off me," insisted the half-naked woman.

Not backing down, I riled her up. "Is that what you want most? For me not to touch you or for you to find the book?"

As soon as I was sure she was thinking about the object, I grabbed hold of her hand. "Now," I called out.

With the wardens authoritative power gone, I concentrated and called on my talents. The image of the book appeared clear in my head, and I tethered the thread of connection to me, seeking out it's path as fast as I could.

Tara pushed me away, and I stumbled over one of the chairs and fell to the ground, the connection dissipating. Her muscles tightened to attack me, and Mason extended his warden power over her again.

"I know where it is," I exclaimed, scrambling up.

A wildness shadowed Tara's face. "Tell me where it is."

I narrowed my eyes at her, rubbing my sore behind. "Yeah, that's not gonna happen."

She narrowed her eyes. "If you don't, I'm sure I can make you."

"That's going to be difficult to do since you're headed to our station." Mason called out for Zeke and instructed the young deputy to take the menacing girl to the tank.

I held up my hand to stop them. "I think she needs to come with us just in case I'm wrong and I need to try again."

Tara comprehended my words and sneered. "So you're the tracker. Duke had plans for you since someone with your magical talents fetches a high price. Better watch your back," she threatened.

Mason formed another wardens' hold over her and forced her to walk ahead of him. He turned to me, "You better come with since you're the only one who knows where to go."

Shelby spoke up, a little shaken from the whole situation. "Do you need me to come?"

I shook my head. "I hate to say it, but your sister is more useful in this situation."

"Yeah," added Tara. "You've always been pretty useless."

Allowing power to spark at my fingertips, I flicked a stinging hex at her behind.

Tara jumped and shrieked. "You can't let her get away with that."

"Keep moving," barked Mason.

I followed behind them and watched Mason force her into

his car. She kicked and screamed in the backseat until Zeke took over with his wardens' magic.

"Want to share where we're going?" asked Mason, holding the car door open for me.

I paused before getting in. "If I'm right, the book is waiting for us at The Harvest Moon."

❦

WE PULLED up to the sidewalk in front of the cafe, ignoring the spectacle we created. Without holding Tara's hand again, I only had the leftover image to go on. However, I'd rather take more time to find the location than to have to touch the witch with a capital *B* again.

"If you're a very good girl, maybe I'll bring you out an iced tea," I taunted her.

She tried to say something nasty to me, but Zeke cast a quick silent spell on her.

Mason allowed me to take the lead, and I felt the burn of stares from everyone in the place. All conversation stopped as they watched us with curiosity.

Sassy floated over to us, her wings fluttering in nervous quivers. "Can I help you?" her high-pitched voice shook.

"I need to search the place, Sass." Checking with Mr. Steve through the pass-through window, I proceeded after he nodded once. With careful steps, I went behind the counter, inspecting every shelf, drawer, and cabinet. Not seeing what I pictured in my mind, I let Mason know with a shake of my head.

Braving the heat from the kitchen, I pushed through the swinging door and walked in. Steve continued to tend to the food already cooking on the griddle but gave me room to walk around him. I opened up the walk-in refrigerator, still not spotting anything matching the image in my head.

"What are you lookin' for?" the cook asked.

"I'll know it when I see it," I uttered, getting more frustrated. "Is there a place where you guys get ready before service?"

Steve pointed his spatula in the direction of the restroom. "There's a door to the left there. It's where we can keep our stuff during the day or change clothes. The girls...well, just Sassy now... have lockers to keep their girl stuff in." He reached in his pocket and pulled out a set of keys, choosing the correct one. "Here."

Taking Mason with me, I made my way to the door and unlocked it. The small space was sparse except for the lockers and a few things hanging from hooks on the wall. I opened the metal locker on the right and found it mostly empty except for a couple of aprons lying in a pile on the bottom.

"This was most likely Blythe's," I stated to Mason, who stood in the doorway, letting me play the detective.

Checking the second locker, I opened it and took a step back. An overturned cast iron skillet sat at the bottom of the storage space. Something like that in the cafe wouldn't seem unusual except a spot of dried blood marked the edge of it.

"I think I found something important." I pointed at the skillet, letting Mason take over.

With professional precision, he cast a protective layer over the evidence and levitated it until he could grasp the handle.

"That's blood, isn't it?" I asked.

He nodded. "Looks like it. I'll have to get it tested to see if it matches Duke's, but this is most likely what caused the injury on his head." He showed a few strands of hair stuck in the blood to me.

Focusing on the skillet distracted me, and it took an extra second for me to notice the object that had been hiding underneath the cast iron pot. "And there's the book." My heart beat fast, and I resisted picking it up.

Mason handed me the protected skillet and retrieved the book in the same manner. He opened the pages, sharing them with me. One glance at the writing on a couple of them, and we both understood how menacing the object really was. And just how valuable someone else might find it.

"There are a lot of entries in there," I commented. "Some of those last names are Old Charlestonian ones. I recognize their French origins."

Mason flipped through the pages faster, the tip of his finger scrolling down some of them.

I read over his shoulder and whistled. "No wonder Tucker's been a wreck. If there are any entries about him in there, he has cause to worry." My decision not to marry Tucker seemed like an even better one now, and I worried about my cousin's upcoming nuptials.

Mason frowned. "There are pages torn out." He pulled the book open wide until the spine cracked. "See the frayed edges?" He let me take a closer look.

"Whoever took them is most likely to be associated with Duke's murder." I ran my finger down the middle, feeling the ragged paper. "Is there a spell that could restore them?"

Mason blew out a slow breath. "It would take someone very powerful and very skilled to do it. Even up North, we had access to only a few who might be able to spellcast something that specific. It also depends on whether there are any lingering spells that Duke cast himself."

"In other words, we only have a part of the puzzle. The most important piece is still missing," I said.

The detective didn't have a chance to answer. Big Willie filled the doorway with his massive body. "I thought I made myself clear," he growled at me.

"Charli was the one who used her talents and found both of these." The detective showed his boss the book and skillet.

The sheriff entered the small space, crowding us and scratching his beard. "We got a call at the station, tippin' us off that they saw somethin' related to the murder here."

I looked between the two wardens. "You know this is a set up, right? There's no way Sassy committed the murder. First of all, there's this." I waved around the heavy cast iron. "Fairies are stronger than they look, but I don't think she could fling this hard enough to hurt a flea."

"She could if she used her magic," countered the sheriff.

"Maybe," I considered. "But why would she stash the

evidence in her locker at her work? And who called the station? Also, unless her name is recorded in the book, she has very little motive."

Mason turned to the last pages. "Here she is." He tapped his finger over a small entry. "Duke recorded that she was betraying her current boss, trying to leave the cafe for a job with him." He trailed off, flipping back and forth through the book. "There's some sort of code here beside all the entries with initials and colors."

I pushed past the sasquatch to examine the book over Mason's shoulder. "Maybe it's a time code?"

"Or it could indicate who would be interested in the information," suggested the detective. "No indications of money being exchanged, although I've already got a lead on Duke's financials."

"Let me see." Big Willie snatched the book from Mason, holding it close to his face and reading words out loud. He rifled through pages and stopped. "Your name is in here." His eyes lit on me.

"What?" I grabbed the book. "It doesn't say anything other than my name and location, but there are more initials and colors." Until now, I hadn't taken Duke's or Tara's threats to me seriously. My stomach dropped as I read my name again written in the dead man's scratchy handwriting.

"Honestly, the fact that you're in here might be what we need to break the code." Mason held out his hand for the book, taking it from me with a sympathetic glance. "We know why he thought you were valuable. If we can use that to figure out the code, we might be able to crack it."

"That's not our concern right now," interrupted the sheriff. He pointed at Sassy's locker. "Since you found the evidence in there, then I'm afraid we have no choice. We have to take the fairy in." He held out his hand, waiting for me to hand over the skillet.

I grasped the cast iron tighter. "You know this isn't right," I insisted.

Big Willie sighed. "I know, but you have no idea the pressure that's being put on our department right now. It's better for everything to look like it's working the way that it's supposed to. The time to fight isn't now, you got me, Charli? Big picture."

Without him saying the exact words, I understood the threat being thrown at the sasquatch. Since he hinted that Nana had shared something of the outside threat to our town with him, he understood how fragile things were, and I needed to listen to him, even if every fiber of my being protested.

"I think you better stay behind and wait for us to do our thing," instructed the sheriff. "Detective, you're with me."

"I'll be right behind you, Sheriff." Mason lingered until we were alone. "Do you know what he means by *big picture?*"

I shook my head. "I really don't know much, but I think I need to talk to my grandmother. Go look after Sassy. Someone else is behind all this, and they need to be stopped."

Mason accepted my lack of a full answer, shouting out to

the sheriff that he was on his way. He stopped at the door and glanced back at me. "I hope I can get a rain check on another ride?"

The happy memory of our time together contrasted with the worry of the moment. "I'll look forward to it," I replied with a bit of a blush.

The detective grinned and winked at me before leaving.

From the tiny room, I listened to the commotion of Sassy's arrest, wincing at her sobs and screaming protests. Slipping out the side door, I snuck around the back of the buildings on Main Street and walked in the direction of my grandmother's house.

Chapter Twenty-One

The sun beating down soaked my shirt. I would change it once I got to Nana's, but the need to find more answers drove my sweat-inducing fast pace. Matt's car pulled up beside me, and I got into the passenger seat, confused and a little worried but appreciating the air conditioning on full blast.

"Mason called me and told me where you were headed. Nana's not home," my brother said. He drove off once I buckled in.

"Where is she?" I asked.

He kept his eyes on the road. "I don't know. She left a note on the kitchen table, saying she'd be back in a few days. I think it has something to do with the pressure from Charleston."

"Things must be more serious than she let on. I think

she's talked to Big Willie about some of it. Something's off in Honeysuckle and it's more than just murder." I watched the shadow and light of the sun through the trees as we drove down the road.

We rode in silence, pondering the situation. I recognized the path to my house, not surprised that my brother escorted me back there. No doubt Big Willie had given him strict orders to make sure my behind stayed put.

Matt put his car in park and leaned back in his seat. "Sassy's a wreck already. Ben's trying to get her calmed down enough so he can work with her."

"There's no way she did it," I repeated, hoping if I said it enough, at least one warden might do something about it.

Matt cleaned a scuff off his steering wheel. "I don't think so either, but the evidence was found in her locker at her place of work. We had to bring her in."

I heard and understood his words, but the whole situation didn't sit right with me. Sure, the fairy had irritated me over the years, and our relationship was more contentious than cordial. But she didn't deserve to go to jail for a crime she didn't commit.

"Ben can get her out, right?" I asked.

Matt frowned. "That might be a problem. Big Willie got a call from someone at The Island. It sounds like they're sending someone up to retrieve her and take her there."

I didn't know much about the big supernatural jail located on a private island magically hidden off the coast. But the few tales I had heard made it sound like one of the worst places to end up. However, I thought only hardened criminals who committed the worst crimes were sent there, not diminutive fairies whose talents lay in baking a mean flaky pie crust.

I grabbed my brother's hand. "But she lives in Honeysuckle. Big Willie can't let anyone take her there. It may be an island, but it's no resort. She won't make it that long. How in the world did it get fast-tracked to that level?"

Matt shook his head. "This all has something to do with Nana's problems. Big Willie already sent word to her, wherever she is."

"At least the sheriff doesn't seem to be a part of whatever the conspiracy is." I paused, considering whether or not sharing my theory with my warden brother was a good idea. Betting on him choosing family over his job, I took a chance. "This has to do with the Hawthornes. I think maybe I was wrong about Tucker."

"But he turned himself in. Why would he do that if he was trying to get away with murder?" Matt asked.

He made a good point. I chewed on my fingernail, thinking. "People do odd things when they hit rock bottom, and Tuck's scraping the dirt right now. Maybe his dad is involved. Maybe Hollis thinks that Tucker killed Duke, so he's trying to make sure his son can't be arrested for it."

Matt considered my ideas and nodded. "I'd buy it. But you have to prove it and fast before they come take Sassy away."

"And Big Willie made it clear that I needed to stay out of it. I think he's aware that something bigger is going on," I noted.

My brother pointed at my house. "Which is why you're gonna invite me in for some iced tea and we can continue thinking through things."

We spent time on the porch, rocking and talking things out. I pushed my brother to his warden limits and then backed off so he wouldn't get in trouble for sharing information with me. I couldn't shake my concerns about the Hawthornes, especially a nagging unease about Tucker. Perhaps my personal history with him did cloud my judgment. Even if he didn't mean to kill Duke, it looked more and more like he had reason to hurt the manipulator.

"If I were working for the wardens, I might put surveillance on the Hawthornes. Make sure they didn't suddenly leave town." Sipping on my sweet tea, I rocked and observed my brother out of the corner of my eye.

Matt chuckled. "You act as if we're a big city unit. There's only so many of us. We'd run ourselves ragged if we took to watchin' Hollis' and Tucker's houses. Besides, there's only one way in or out."

"Not true, big brother. You're forgettin' the water. If they wanted to, they could leave town on a boat." The iced tea did nothing to cool down my brain from working overtime. "Although I'm not sure they'd deem the Wilkins' shrimping boats worthy, and Wayne wouldn't just abscond with them in the middle of the night on his craft."

Matt pulled out his spell phone and tapped out a text. "You make a good point. I'm letting Mason know."

I smiled, remembering the detective teaching me to ride a broom, and then taking me soaring through the air.

"What's that look for?" my brother asked.

"Nothin'," I lied.

He pushed out of his chair. "Mm-hmm. I better get goin' and report back to my boss that you're stayin' out of the way here at your house. For the rest of the day." He held out his empty glass.

"You can't put me on house arrest," I protested, accepting the cup from him. "I'm not the one who needs to be monitored."

Matt ruffled my hair and I smacked his arm away. "Birdy, just do as you're asked this once. At least for tonight, stay off the case."

"What am I supposed to do?"

He walked down the porch steps. "I don't know, go shovel poop in the barn, read a book, write a letter," he listed out.

"Nobody writes letters anymore. They use these." I waved my spell phone at him, a bright idea dawning. My fingers typed as fast as they could.

Matt turned around and walked backwards, mocking me. "You're smart. You'll figure somethin' out." His phone pinged and he answered it, receiving my zapping *hext*. "Ouch! You brat!" he shouted, waving his middle finger in the air as he walked through the field toward his car.

BEAU FOUND me bored to tears, laying upside down in one of the big decorative chairs in the living room with my behind and legs stretched on the back of the chair and my head dangling off the front of it. I tried to comprehend the notes that Henry had left me to go over after my grand experiments with my magic.

"Are you tryin' to turn into a bat?" my roommate asked me.

I righted myself in the seat, a little dizzy from the blood rushing to my feet. "No. Reading Henry's notes. He's given me a list of suggestions on how I could charge people if I opened a business." I waved the wrinkled paper at the vampire.

"I saw it. I think he has some good ideas you could use." Beau primped in front of the decorative mirror on the wall.

I caught a whiff of a strong scent and wrinkled my nose. "What is that stench?"

He grinned, showing off his fangs. "Do you like it? Cordelia bought it for me."

"What did you do, bathe in it?" I held my nose. "You might want to wash some of it off."

"No way. Tonight's the social dance at the retirement home, and I want my cologne to act as catnip to the ladies. If I had a nickel for every girl who looks my way tonight, I might come home a rich man." He wiggled his eyebrows at me, and I couldn't be mad at my crazy lady-killer roommate. As long as he didn't actually kill anyone.

His comment about a nickel jogged my memory. "Frosted fairy wings, I completely forgot!"

"Forgot what?" Beau called out as I ran upstairs.

Digging around my dirty clothes, I found the pair of pants I was wearing when Mason and I first went to the Wilkins' house. "Please still be there," I begged, rummaging through the pockets.

Cool metal pressed against my fingers, and I pulled out the coin I'd found underneath the bedside table in the room Duke stayed in.

"Hey, Beau, do you know anything about old coins?" I asked, trotting down the stairs and doing my best not to cover my nose and offend him.

He shrugged. "A little. Why? Did you find something of value in one of Tipper's hidden stashes?"

I debated telling him where I found the coin, but held back the truth to keep him from being too involved in my theories. "I just found it and put it in my pocket. I kind of forgot it was there until just now. What do you think it is?" I handed him the brown metal.

"Let's take a closer look." Beau brought it over to a desk and clicked on the lamp. Holding the coin between his fingers, he examined it. "Where did you find this?"

"On the floor somewhere. I noticed it sitting there." It wasn't a complete fib, so I didn't need to feel guilty. "Should I fetch some vinegar or something to clean it with so we can see it better?"

My roommate gasped and cradled the small piece. "No.

Never ever try to clean an old coin with anything other than running water, otherwise you risk damaging it with scratches or pitting the metal. Also, this isn't actually a coin." He held it up for me to see but wouldn't let me hold it.

"Looks like one to me. It's round, about the color of a penny, and a little bigger than a quarter." I reached out to take it, but Beau moved it away.

"I know it looks like a coin, but it's actually a token. An elephant token to be exact, given out to promote the new Carolinas. They were made in the late seventeenth century in London. You can kind of see the outline of the animal here." He circled the figure on the metal with his finger without touching it. "On the back, an actual elephant token had words stamped on it that said something to the effect of preserving the Carolinas. In mint condition, one of those might fetch close to fifty thousand dollars."

I attempted to look over Beau's shoulder. "But that can't be mint condition. The elephant isn't that recognizable unless you hold it up under good lighting."

"True. But this token is worth far more. It's practically priceless." The vampire cupped it in his hand like something precious.

Taking advantage of his state of awe, I snatched the token from him and held it up in front of my face. "Why?"

With a sigh, Beau didn't fight me. "Turn it over and read the words stamped on this one."

Following his instructions, I did my best to read the worn letters. "*Non ducor, duco.* That's gotta be Latin."

"It is," confirmed my roommate. "It translates as, *I am not led, I lead*. There was a group of witches who didn't like being in hiding and acting like they were equal to or even less than regular mortals. They used the tokens as a way to mark their membership in an exclusive group that had intentions of taking over the world. Hiding in plain sight, using an object that was minted and given out to many to signify their cause. It's said that whoever possesses it has special powers."

I swear the metal buzzed against my skin, or my brain made that up based on my roommate's words. "Like what? Will holding it make me invisible?"

"I can still see you, so no." Beau tweaked my nose to prove his point. "Perhaps it allowed them to communicate with each other. Or maybe it acted as a talisman of luck. Who knows for sure? Like I said, it's a priceless treasure. Now, I've got to go or I'll be late for the dance."

Before he left, I asked him another question. "Why priceless?"

He stopped at the door and huffed with impatience. "Because you're holding one of the very few that's been discovered. Those who possessed them either lost the tokens or passed them down through their families. Tipper was on the lookout for one, but never found it. Trust you to be the one who did. Night, Charli. Don't wait up for me," he sang out.

"And don't be bringing anyone back here or I'll hex your hiney," I warbled off key. Bless his heart, he better not bring a date back here. If I wasn't gettin' any, nobody in *my* house was gettin' any.

I needed to tell Mason about the token. Surely, letting him know about it wasn't sticking my nose into the actual case. For all I knew, the thing had been under that bedside table for years and had nothing to do with Duke. On the other hand, if it did have something to do with the dead man, it could be a clue to his killer.

While I wrestled with my choice to tell or not, my text alert rang. Checking it, my heart raced at the message's urgency.

"*911. Sweet Tooths. Now.*"

Chapter Twenty-Two

Although my bicycle ran on magic, I kind of wished I had a broom to fly. I couldn't get to Main Street fast enough, and when I arrived, I left my bike in the middle of the sidewalk and crashed into the bakery.

"I'm here," I called out, breathless. "What's going on?"

Lee handed me a red velvet cupcake. "You'll have to excuse my fiancée." He beamed when he called Alison Kate that. "She got a little melodramatic when they took on the job."

Sprinkle flew into the room. "I thought I told somebody to lock that door. Now we have more people in here," the tiny ex-toothfairy complained, zipping back into the kitchen.

"I asked them to come," explained Alison Kate in a loud voice, her hair pulled back in a hasty messy bun and a little flour dashed on her cheek. She kissed Lee on his lips and wiped her hands on the apron tied around her waist. "Sorry for the emergency message. I just panicked as soon as she hired us. We don't have much time, and I want to do somethin' really special for her."

"For who? Somebody catch me up," I demanded, collapsing into a nearby chair and taking a big bite of red velvet.

The bells on the door jingled as Ben held it open for his girlfriend Lily and her cousin Lavender. The two girls chattered with excitement. I held up my hand to stop them and pointed at Lavender to speak first.

"You will never guess what just happened," she gushed.

Lily elbowed her cousin. "Of course she won't, so I better tell the news."

Lavender pouted. "I wanted to say it."

I rolled my eyes. "Okay, will somebody spill the beans already? Ali Kat, who are you tryin' to do something special for?"

My exuberant friend vibrated where she stood. "Clementine came in here not that long ago with her mother in tow. I guess they've decided to move up the wedding and want us to bake their cake for the reception."

Lavender burst with her news, "And she wants Mimsies' Whimsies to provide the flowers for the whole thing."

Alison Kate clapped her hands and jumped up and down. "And she told me that the cake is whatever I choose, she just wants it tasty and pretty. I could do a simple lemon one with a raspberry filling. Or maybe a vanilla one with a lemon curd. Or should I do something more delicate and floral, like a green tea and honeysuckle combination? I will spellcast the crap out of some buttercream frosting. There'll be blooming flowers and buzzing bees and butterflies fluttering."

Lily tugged on her cousin's arm. "Do we have any peonies? They would look really lovely, although they might be a tad heavy. Clementine's bouquet should be something delicate to go with her personality."

Lavender picked up the thought, "Or maybe we can work in some blooming honeysuckles trailing down from the bouquet."

Alison Kate raised her hand. "Ooh, ooh, then I will carry that theme through with the cake. Maybe I'll put some honeysuckle syrup in the cake filling and the frosting. There's so much to do and so little time," she cried out.

The boys backed away from the excitement and crowded around me. Ben grabbed ahold of my shoulders, acting like he was afraid. "I think if we stand here long enough, they're going to decorate us with flowers and frosting."

"I got this." Putting two fingers to my lips, I blew out a shrill whistle. "Listen up. Standing around and talking about getting things done won't work. What do you need us to do?"

"Oh, we've got this," exclaimed Lily, pulling her boyfriend off of me. "We just had to gush about the whole thing since it's weird that Clementine's gonna marry Tucker so quickly."

Sprinkle zipped into the room again and scolded us all in his high-pitched voice. "Y'all are disrupting things. Alison Kate, are you gonna stand around all night talking to your friends and your sweetheart or are you gonna get back here in the kitchen and help us out?"

My friend gave Lee a quick kiss on the cheek. "You may have to prop me up with a broom or something tomorrow, 'cause tonight's gonna take it all out of me. But I'm gonna help make the most amazing cake." She kissed him one more time and hurried off to help her bosses.

"Come on, Ben. You're comin' back to the flower shop with us to help pick out what we'll use for their wedding." Lily gazed at her boyfriend with enough intensity, I wondered if he picked up on the clear wish shining in her eyes.

"So I guess nobody needs me after all?" I asked a now empty room. Something the girls said hit me all at once. I ran out of the bakery. "Hey, Lily. Did you say *you're* picking out the flowers?"

My friend stopped in the middle of the road. "Yeah. I asked Clementine if she had a preference or wanted to go through our selection, but she told us she wanted things to be beautiful and trusted our choices."

"That's strange," I commented. "It's the biggest day for her, and she doesn't care what kind of flowers or cake she'll be having?"

Lavender shrugged. "Maybe she's happy having a wedding after everything Tucker's been through. She said all she wanted was to marry him." She waved at me and joined her cousin and Ben on their way back to their grandmother's floral shop.

Confused, I wandered across the street to the Harvest Moon, hoping to catch Henry there to ask him about his notes. When I reached for the door, Aunt Nora pushed it open, almost running into me.

"Oh, Charlotte. I didn't see you." She sniffed once, and her lips curled down like they always did when we encountered each other. "Clementine, darlin', we need to get you home so you can get your beauty rest for tomorrow."

"Coming, Mother," my cousin called out from inside.

Placing the fakest smile on her lips, Aunt Nora's eyes burned into me. "You'll understand if we don't extend an invitation to you."

Clementine joined her mom. "Actually, Mother, I wanted to have a minute to talk to cousin Charlotte, if you please."

Aunt Nora pursed her lips. "I see no reason why—"

"Please," interrupted Clementine with insistence. "I'll meet you back at your place." She waited for my aunt to leave a significant distance between us. "Good, now that she's gone, I can ask you something that she wouldn't exactly approve of."

"And what's that?" Curiosity bubbled in my brain, and I held back the tiny squeal that tried to push its way out.

Clementine took my hand in hers. "I wanted to ask if you'd act as my maid of honor tomorrow at my wedding."

If a herd of unicorns ridden by elves ran me over like supernatural roadkill, I couldn't be more taken by surprise. "I... you... your mother..." My mouth struggled to form real words. I cleared my throat. "Are you sure that's a good idea, Clem?"

She squeezed my hand. "Well, since we're doing the wedding so soon, my bridesmaids won't have a chance to get here in time, and I want someone to stand with me. You're my cousin, and it would honor me if you would be the one. I'd like this to be the first step of many in mending fences between our families."

A pixie might be able to fly into my gaping mouth. I closed it and swallowed hard, trying to picture myself standing next to my cousin during her wedding. Aunt Nora would be furious, although the opportunity to give her a bit of trouble didn't discount the choice. Clarice might spit nails, but at least I'd be able to watch Hollis and Tucker with my own eyes during the wedding, making sure they didn't disappear if my gut instincts ended up being right.

"If you think it will be okay, I'd be happy to act as your bridesmaid," I accepted. "Thank you for asking me."

"Maid of Honor," Clementine corrected with a smile.

"Um, is there something specific you'd want me to wear?" I didn't possess many dresses that Clarice or Aunt Nora would find appropriate for such a special occasion.

My cousin let go of my hand with a giggle. "Oh, anything that's nice will do. Again, I know this is all so sudden."

"If you want, I can check with Lily and Lavender to see

what color flowers they're putting together and try to match that," I offered. "Or you can go with me?"

Clementine checked the time on her watch. "Mother won't like the idea of me hanging around you for too long." The left corner of her mouth curled up. "Maybe a few more minutes wouldn't hurt her."

I smiled despite myself, liking this new Clementine. Offering her the crook of my arm, she linked hers through it, and we went to Mimsies' Whimsies where she picked out some delicate peach and pink flowers to be mixed in with cream honeysuckles on the vine. It made me happy for her now that she got to choose something she liked for her big day with my help. It also tickled me when my cousin smiled freely and joked a little with my friends.

We parted ways outside on Main Street with a quick embrace. Although she was not a natural hugger, I would work on making her more comfortable doing it from here on out. Wishing her luck, I headed to Mom's old store that Ms. Patty Lou still ran.

I knocked on the locked glass door and my mother's best friend popped her head around the corner from one of the rows with knitting supplies on it. With a friendly smile and twinkling eyes, Ms. Patty unlocked the door and let me in.

"Help," I implored, following her inside.

"What can I do for you?" she asked.

Explaining the situation, I stressed over not having any good dresses for Clementine's sudden wedding. Since my mother's best friend was the best seamstress and witch with a needle, I hoped she could help me find a solution and fast.

"You know, in the back I have a few dresses that might work. Why don't you follow me and we'll see," Ms. Patty Lou suggested.

I tried on three different dresses, one the color of a ripe peach, one dark navy blue, and one a blush pink. The peach one would match Clementine's flowers well, but the color didn't do much for my complexion. The navy blue one seemed a bit too casual for such an elegant occasion. But the pink one could go either way. With a pair of sandals and my hair down, it could be a good flowing summer dress. But with my hair up, some pearls and gloves, and a special crystal-encrusted sash that Ms. Patty found, it would make a fine choice for a bridesmaid's dress.

"Let me make a few adjustments," she said, using her magical talents to tailor the dress to my form, shortening the length and building out the bust a little. "There, that should do it. And you know that when you put it on for the wedding, the zipper will go up on its own."

"Thank you so much," I gushed. "With Nana not in town, I didn't know what I was going to do."

"Well, it's a nice thing you're doing for your cousin. Although you may well outshine the bride in that dress." Ms. Patty Lou helped me out of it and let me change back into my regular clothes. I met her out in the store and waited while she slipped it into a bag for me to carry home.

In my haste, I had forgotten that this was the first time I'd stepped foot in Mom's old shop. Now that I stood inside it, memories flooded back in, and I heard the echo of her laughter. My heart squeezed, a little sad and a little nostalgic, missing her with every fiber of my being.

"I miss her, too. But I think she'd be real proud of the woman you've become," Ms. Patty said in a low, sincere voice. "And I hear that you're thinking of opening a business for your talents nearby?"

I lowered my head so she couldn't see the tears in my eyes. "I'm considering it."

"Good." She handed me the garment bag. "If your mom were here, she'd be your biggest cheerleader. When you open up, you have to let me stand in her place." Ms Patty Lou brushed a tear off my cheek.

"I would like that." Sniffing, I cleared my throat. "I just wish she was with me now."

My mom's best friend handed me a lace handkerchief she no doubt embroidered herself. "She's always with you. And tomorrow, she'll be wrapped all around you. That dress is one of the last one's she had me make for her. I think it's appropriate that you'll wear it for your cousin's wedding. Your mom would love you two bringing peace between the families after all these years."

I hugged Ms. Patty Lou and thanked her for her help. She welcomed me back to the store anytime. Once outside, I waved at her through the store window. Thinking about the old saying that time heals all wounds, I disagreed. Time allowed us to change and adjust. I would never get over the loss of Mom and Dad, but having to live without them made me who I was today.

And that was a girl who could open her own business, stand with her cousin on her wedding day despite who she was marrying, and solve a murder mystery. I just hoped I didn't have to do the last two together.

Chapter Twenty-Three

A loud clap of thunder and a flash of lightning woke me up in the morning. Rain on a wedding day wasn't the worst thing to happen since there were some who believed it was a good luck sign, symbolizing a renewal of life on that special day. But dark storm clouds and whipping gusts of wind wouldn't be a good omen for my cousin's wedding.

It took a couple of quick spell phone texts to confirm the event was still on according to a very busy Alison Kate and the two cousins still putting together last-minute floral arrangements.

My dress hung from a hook on the back of my bedroom door, and I stared at it, questioning my own sanity for ever agreeing to be in Clementine's wedding. What was Tucker going to do when he had to recite his vows with his ex standing right behind his betrothed? And I could muster up some courage to go through with it, but having to deal with the icy glares from Aunt Nora and Clarice at the same time might freeze me into a block of ice.

I missed Nana and wanted her reassurances and comfort. Calling Matt in the hopes of some good news, I walked downstairs to get some breakfast.

"Nope, she's still gone," my brother said. "And it looks like we're not goin' either. TJ can't find a dress to wear that doesn't make her look like a—"

"Don't you say a beached whale, you jerk," my sister-in-law called out from the background. "*I* can say that about me. *You* can't."

"I swear I wasn't goin' to, honey," Matt shouted. "Birdy, I think you might be on your own today. I'm really sorry." He hung up the phone before I could get another word in.

Toast and coffee were all my stomach could handle for breakfast. I munched on the half-burnt bread with a thin layer of butter and a slather of homemade strawberry preserves outside on the porch, watching the dark clouds swirling above. With all of its blustering, the weather hadn't broken into torrential rain yet. I could appreciate the beauty in the storm as much as the fearful power of it, too.

Beau appeared at the edge of the property and walked toward the house. He joined me in one of the rockers.

"Didn't want to fly home?" I asked him.

He fixed the few strands of hair still decorating the top of his bald head with his fingers. "Not in this wind and weather.

I didn't want to chance getting struck by lightning. What are you doin' outside?"

I scoffed. "Contemplating my sanity." Thunder rolled in the distance, and I told my roommate about Clementine's request.

"Why in the world did you say yes?" The vampire gawked at me.

I leaned back in the chair. "Because she surprised me by wanting me to do it in the first place. Also, maybe the two of us can get along, and that's something my mom would want for our two families." She would be proud of me if I could bridge the icy gap with Nora's daughter.

With a crack of lightning and another rumble of thunder, the sky opened up and rain poured down. Beau and I ducked inside and shut the storm out.

"I get the feelin' there's more to your decision that you're not sayin'. I'm here if you wanna talk, but if you don't, I can respect that. If you need anything, you just let me know," my roommate offered

Sighing, I placed a hand on my hip. "What I need is for Nana to be here or my friend who knows how to do hair to be available and not be bakin' a wedding cake."

Beau raised his hand. "I can fix your hair."

"No way. Can you?" I gaped at him.

He grinned, and his fangs popped out over his bottom lip. "Sure. You don't date a bunch of women and not learn how to fix their hair after you help them muss it."

I held up my hand to stop him from giving me any details. "Can you do a decent up do?"

"Let's take a look at your outfit and see what style might look best." He bowed before me with a dramatic grand gesture, and let me run upstairs in front of him.

I put on the dress, and he had me go into the bathroom so he could play with my hair. We settled on a low bun with loose tendrils framing my face. Beau told me to wake him up from his nap when I was getting ready, and he would fix it up for real. Impressed, I gave him a quick hug and kiss on the cheek. He moseyed to his room with a faint blush pinking up his vampire pallor.

When the time came to get ready in the afternoon, my roommate impressed me with his hairstyling skills. "You could ask Ms. Reva for a job at the salon," I complimented.

Beau chuckled, sticking another pin in to hold the bun. "I prefer to use my abilities in a more personal manner. But I think this might do the trick." Handing me a mirror, he asked me to check his work.

"It's gorgeous, but I fear that the wind and rain will ruin it." Loud thunder echoed my sentiment.

Beau popped off the top of a can of industrial hairspray. "Not when I get done with it."

I emerged from the toxic fog, sure that my hair might stay where it was for days, even if I took out all the pins. Matt had promised he'd pick me up and take me to the Hawthorne house, so I hurried to finish getting ready. After clasping

Mom's string of pearls around my neck, I reached for the gloves to complete the look and paused.

When I told Beau about why I'd said yes to Clementine's request, I had been about ninety percent honest. But the last ten percent nagged at me. I wanted to see Tucker and Hollis up close. To look them in the eyes and examine if either of them were guilty of the crime I thought they were. At the same time, I didn't want to make a huge scene, or an even bigger one than there would be with me being in the bridal party.

Making a final decision, I found the elephant token on my bedside table and held it in my left palm carefully, slipping the glove on over my hand so that it hid the round piece of metal. I'd rather have it with me and be prepared than to need it and not have it.

I heard the knock on the door over the noise of the storm and grabbed a lace shawl to wear over my shoulders, although it would be a poor shield from the messy weather. My fancy heels clacked on the wood of the stairs as I hurried down to answer another knock.

Opening the door, I found Mason dressed up in a well-fitted suit and dark tie, all traces of his facial hair gone. He reminded me of a very famous British spy from the movies, but here in Honeysuckle, he was just *Double Oh My*, shaking my insides and stirring up some heated thoughts.

His eyes roamed over my entire body in languid pleasure. "You look beautiful," he uttered.

"So do you. I mean, you look handsome. Although I kind

of miss your scruff." The wind blew some rain underneath my porch ceiling, and I tugged on the detective to come inside.

Mason ran a hand over his smooth skin. "Yeah, between the wedding and Big Willie fussing at me to look more professional, it was time."

"Never mind the irony of a sasquatch asking you to shave," I added with a chuckle. "So you're taking me to the wedding?"

His eyes took another gander at me, lingering on my low neckline. "Your brother called me, but to be honest, it'll be my pleasure." Realizing where he was staring, he cleared his throat, red rising in his cheeks.

"How are we gonna get to your car without getting soaked?" I asked. "It took effort to look like this."

The detective stepped closer to me, fingering one of my loose tendrils of hair. "You'd look gorgeous dry or wet."

My eyes fell to his lips as he formed the words, and I swallowed hard. The grandfather clock chimed the hour and broke the spell of whatever pleasant tension blossomed between us.

"All good detectives have to have at least a level three weather spellcasting ability to keep crime scenes dry," he explained. "I can keep the two of us from getting our clothes ruined." He walked me to the door.

A gust of wind caught the wood when I opened it, and it blew back with great force. Standing on the porch, I doubted either of our abilities to make it to the car without at least our feet getting muddy.

"I've already cast a spell on my pants and shoes just in

case," Mason answered my unspoken thought. "If you won't think it's too caveman-ish, I can carry you to the car to keep your feet clean."

Wanting him to expend as little magical effort as possible, I agreed, a bit embarrassed to play the role of damsel in distress. I threw my arms around his neck, and he bent down and lifted me with care and ease into his arms.

Mason smelled like soap and a subtle spicy scent. He no longer looked like a bad boy version of himself, but I actually preferred his well-kept appearance. I snuggled in a little more than I needed to and leaned into him for support.

"Here comes the spell," he prepared me. A thin veil wrapped around us and expanded out a little ways.

Mason walked off the porch, and the wind and rain beat against the barrier but didn't reach us. We made it to his car on the road, and he placed me on my feet with gentle strength. I slipped into the passenger's side and waited for him to get in the car before thanking him.

We drove in comfortable silence, and I rubbed the spot where the token rested in my left palm with my right-hand thumb. Since I hadn't decided what to do with it yet, I didn't know whether or not to tell the detective about it. My inner debate lasted long enough until I remembered what the two of us were trying to work on. No walls.

"I have a confession to make," Mason blurted, beating my own admission by a mere second.

Grateful and hesitant at the same time, I waited my turn. "Okay."

"Your brother didn't call me to come pick you up. I volunteered to do it because I needed an excuse to be at the wedding." He watched me out of the corner of his eye while avoiding a large puddle of water in the road.

"So you're forcing me to take you as my date? Why?" I asked.

"Because I think there's a good chance the killer will be there, and they'll use the cover of the event to try and leave Honeysuckle." Mason slowed the car down and stopped at an intersection, turning to face me. "You know who I'm talking about, don't you?"

"Well, it's not Sassy, like I said." Pulling the fingers of my left-hand glove loose, I slipped it off and showed the detective the token. "I'm pretty sure that the person who gave this to Duke is either involved or committed the murder."

Putting on his hazard lights, Mason threw his car into park. He opened his palm for the token, and I let him examine it closer, explaining the information Beau had told me.

"So what was your plan? To somehow connect the object to either Tucker or Hollis? And what if they had figured out what you were doing?" He held onto the item instead of giving it back.

Truthfully, I hadn't gotten very far in my plan other than taking the token to the wedding and trying to find an opportunity to use my newfound skills in connecting it to the groom or his father.

"I don't know," I admitted. "But what could they do to me in the middle of a wedding?"

"And you would be willing to risk ruining your cousin's day?" Mason pressed.

I snatched the token back from him. "Why are you using me as a cover to go if you aren't intending to do something yourself?"

He blew out a breath. "You're right."

Stunned at his admission, I touched his arm. "We should work together on this. You're holding something back."

The rain pattered on the roof of the car and the windshield wipers sloshed back and forth. Mason ran his fingers through his hair, mussing it in that perfectly disheveled way. "We've got financial records of Duke's. It took me a while to have some people I know track down his accounts, and I'm betting we haven't found them all. The man was into some really bad stuff."

"How bad?" I pushed.

"Remember how you thought Damien might have ties to a supernatural underground? If what we're uncovering is correct, Duke definitely was a part of it. We're just not sure how deep his connections went." Looking at the time on the car radio, Mason pulled back onto the road and headed to the Hawthorne house.

"How do you know all this?" I watched drops of rain dance across the surface of the passenger door window.

"We figured out some of the code in his book from Sassy's entry and..."

"From mine?" I finished. "How much was I worth to him?"

Mason's expression darkened. "I don't think we should talk about that now."

"Hey, no walls was your idea. Don't hold back now," I insisted.

"If you insist on knowing, then I will tell you. But I think you may wish that I didn't." He turned down the road to our destination.

Mason wasn't asking me to trust him, only to consider my options carefully. The choice was mine, and curiosity forced my decision. "Tell me."

Disappointment flooded his eyes, but he held to his word. "Sassy's entry had codes that, as best as we can figure out and because Tara likes to run her mouth, meant she was to be treated as a commodity to be sold to the highest bidder."

"Sweet honeysuckle iced tea. He wanted to sell her?" It took me a second to remember my own entry in the book. "Me, too?" I asked in a broken voice.

Mason's jaw tensed. "I told you that you wouldn't want to know." He drove up to the front of the house, letting the car idle. "Before you go in there, you should understand why I'm here with you. Duke was an information broker. He bought and sold specific knowledge through what he found out himself or what he was given by others he controlled or manipulated."

"And he was killed for that," I said, spotting a very unhappy Aunt Nora glaring at me from the window inside.

Mason put a hand on my knee. "No, you don't understand.

Someone gave him *you*. They told him about you and your talents as payment to him."

Now I understood. My stomach turned, and I dropped the token on the floor of the car. "And you think the person who gave him the information about me is in there." I pointed at the front door.

Mason unlatched his seatbelt and rummaged on the floor mat, retrieving the token. I expected him to confiscate it, but he held it out for me. The rain stopped falling, and the clouds parted enough to let a little light through, piercing the dreary darkness.

I opened my left hand, and he placed the token in my palm, curling my fingers around it and holding my hand between both of his. "Whatever happens today, be careful. Whoever it is, they have to know that their ruse to frame Sassy won't work for much longer and that their time is running out. A desperate person can react horribly."

Giving it some thought, I came up with a new plan. "If all of this involves any of the people you and I suspect, then we need to keep them within sight at all times. Also, let's not give away our suspicions and act as normal as we can."

"In other words, do our best not to ruin the wedding," Mason said. "So I'm here as your date and not a detective?" He opened his door and came around to my side to help me out.

After readjusting the token and slipping the glove back on, I took his offered hand and slid out of his car. "Yes, you're my date." Using that term didn't make me want to run for the hills, and it surprised me how much I kind of liked it. I slipped my arm through his and let him escort me to the house.

Aunt Nora threw open the front door and came out onto the stoop. "You're late."

I leaned into Mason and spoke in a low voice, "Or you could just arrest everyone, starting with her."

"Tempting," he replied with a quiet chuckle.

My aunt's frosty glare didn't scare me. "Sorry, Aunt Nora. Bad weather."

"I have to say, I almost wished you wouldn't show up. But Clementine is waiting for you upstairs. Detective Clairmont, guests are expected to wait in the tent out back. Even the ones who weren't technically invited." She sniffed and attempted to close the door on him.

I caught it and held it open, rolling my eyes and waiting for her to give up and go check on her daughter. When she was out of earshot, I spoke quickly to Mason. "I'll be fine here. You go to where the ceremony will be and keep an eye out for the groom and his father."

"Yes, ma'am." The detective straightened and saluted me. Relaxing with a smile, he fixed the lace shawl around my shoulders and took my left hand in his. He tapped the token resting in my left palm under the glove. "Stay out of trouble."

"I will." With a wave, I answered my aunt's impatient call from upstairs and closed the door.

How much could go wrong with me being the groom's ex acting as the bride's maid of honor and searching for a killer?

Chapter Twenty-Four

The inclement weather delayed the start of the ceremony, allowing more of Honeysuckle's people to show up. I stood in the back of the room out of the way, watching Aunt Nora reposition the veil on Clementine's head for the third time.

"Stop fussin', Mother. It looks fine." My cousin pushed her mom's hands away, staring at her reflection in the mirror and smoothing out the lace.

"I wanted everything to be perfect for your special day, but you're the one who wanted to push it to today rather than wait." My aunt walked over to the window. "At least it looks like the rain's stopped for the moment."

"Rain or shine, I don't want to wait another minute to marry Tucker." Clementine applied another layer of gloss to her lips and pursed them together.

I admired her determination and appreciated this new version of my cousin, willing to stand up to her overbearing mother. Smiling quietly to myself, I stifled a chuckle.

"You can wipe that grin off your face, missy. I still think my daughter's crazy for asking you to be a part of all this." Aunt Nora sneered at me. "Although it would be poetic for you to have to stand there and witness my daughter marrying the man you couldn't."

"Enough, Mother," insisted Clementine, standing up. "We talked about this last night. You will do your best to be civil to your sister's daughter from here on out. I'm sorry, Charli."

Not wanting to be the cause of a fight between mother and daughter today, I tried not to say too much. "It's fine."

The photographer came in to take a few pre-wedding pictures. My aunt pasted a happier countenance on her face and cuddled up to her daughter.

"How about one with the bride and her maid of honor?" the innocent photographer asked.

"You don't need one with her," spit out Aunt Nora, her lips frowning again.

Clementine pointed at the door. "Why don't you go ahead to the tent and get ready for the ceremony since you'll be performing it. We'll take a few photos together and then get ready to make our entrance."

Aunt Nora attempted to protest but stopped when Clementine didn't back down. She huffed her way to the door, stopping long enough to shoot me an icy glare. "I would be able to enjoy my daughter's day if your grandmother hadn't up and left so she could perform her duties."

"Consider this an opportunity to take part in a more intimate and personal way, Aunt Nora," I suggested, doing my best to keep my tone light and indifferent.

Stomping her high-heeled shoes on the hardwood floor, she clacked her way downstairs, leaving Clementine to take a couple of photos with me.

"Thank you for doing this, Charli," my cousin said in a quiet voice. "Today will be full of new beginnings." She gave me a side hug, careful not to mess up her beautiful cream lace gown that was more fitted and modern than I would have expected for her.

"I'll go and see if they're ready for you," I offered. Once downstairs, I decided to take a shortcut through the kitchen to check and almost collided with Shelby. "What are you doing here?"

"Hey, Charli. The bride asked me to cater her wedding before I left. Since it's so last minute, I recruited some help." She pointed at Mr. Steve, who stirred some pots on the stove.

"I guess the bride and groom found a way to involve all of Honeysuckle after all." I carefully navigated my way through the cooking chaos and to the back door.

At some point, the Hawthornes had added a temporary covered walkway from the house to the canopy. Soft music floated through the air, and Clarice stood at the entry to the tent, looking up at the house. When she spotted me, she scowled but waved at me, tapping her wrist to indicate it was time.

I held Clementine's train to keep it from getting dirty until we arrived in the bigger structure, trying not to drop my designated bouquet in the process. When we got to the entryway, I fanned it out behind her and took my place to walk in first.

Someone pulled the white fabric aside to let me see in, and I gasped, spotting my grandmother standing at the front waiting for us. All of my nerves about the day evaporated, and I struggled to stop myself from running down the aisle to hug her.

"What is she doing here?" murmured Clementine.

I turned in excitement to celebrate Nana's return and found the bride standing with her father, scowling. "Now your mother can enjoy your wedding the way she wanted to."

Suddenly aware of my presence again, my cousin shook off her concern. "Of course, you're right." She nodded her head for me to proceed.

I waved at Uncle Percy, the kind and quiet ghost of a man, and made my way down the aisle. The slight murmur of surprise from the attendees made me self-conscious. Although I had come to terms with being my cousin's maid of honor, they hadn't expected me to attend the wedding of my ex at all. No doubt tongues would wag long and hard after the ceremony. My feet slowed, and I felt like I was walking through deep mud.

My grandmother's bright smile and twinkling eyes helped

give me courage, but I needed more reassurance. Searching the sea of faces for a friendlier one, my eyes lit on Mason sitting toward the front row. He gazed at me like I was the only one in the room, his mouth open a little and his eyes watching me with admiration.

I gripped the bouquet of flowers tighter and grinned just for him, finding it easier to walk to my designated place. It took a second for the fog of relief to clear to notice the rest of my friends sitting next to him, smiling up at me. I turned to face Nana, trying to convey my utter happiness at her presence. The music changed, and Clementine entered, becoming the focus of attention.

With all eyes on my cousin, I took the opportunity to observe the groom's side. Tucker watched his bride walking down the aisle with absolute devotion. His father stood behind him, acting as his best man. Hollis glanced my way with concern, but when I caught him, he turned his attention back to Clementine.

Nana performed the handfasting ceremony with great authority. I did my best to focus on the back of my cousin's head and ignore anyone watching me for my reactions instead of the couple. When Nana came to the part to spellbind them together, the couple turned their backs on their guests to face my grandmother.

Tucker's eyes flashed to mine for a brief second, and I tried to read the emotions in them. I hoped he didn't regret his decision to choose my cousin, and deep down made a wish that in the long run, he wasn't really responsible for Duke's death so that the two could live a happy life together. I felt the token in my left hand press against my bouquet while I held Clementine's in my right.

With the focus on the couple, I observed Hollis with more care. The dark circles under his eyes were almost black. His haggard face hardly conveyed any happiness for his son. The once proud man appeared fragile and close to breaking. His shoulders drooped in relief when Nana finished spellcasting the binding, bringing the ceremony to an end.

"Ladies and gentlemen, I present to you Mr. and Mrs. Hollis Tucker Hawthorne, the fourth," my grandmother pronounced in a loud voice.

Everyone in the tent applauded, and Tucker and Clementine held onto each other with pure joy. They kissed each other harder than I thought Aunt Nora would deem appropriate, but their immediate passion inspired my own whoop of enthusiasm.

Nana held up her hands in the air. "And now, the wedding party will return to the house while the rest of you help to prepare this space for the reception." She nodded at Mason, who acknowledged her directive.

Clarice and Aunt Nora rushed to the front, and Tucker and Clementine turned to my grandmother in surprise.

"That's not the plan," hissed my aunt.

Nana didn't back down. "It is now, and I would suggest y'all look like nothing's wrong if you don't want folks gawkin' at you. Let's go."

Clementine took her larger bouquet from me, her eyes no

longer shining bright. She and her new husband did their best to smile and accept the congratulations of others while they made their way to the back of the tent followed close behind by their mothers.

Tucker's father stopped Nana. "Vivi, I don't know what you think you're doing—"

"No, Hollis, you're the one who started all this. It's time to finish it." My grandmother narrowed her eyes at the man and gestured for him to move forward. "After you."

Hollis' eyes darted around the room, no doubt looking for a quick exit. The presence of Zeke and Mason alerted him to the futility of trying to escape. With hunched shoulders, he marched to the back entrance, the younger of the two wardens following him.

"What's goin' on, Nana?" I asked my grandmother, allowing her to lead us out.

"There are many moving parts to a larger game that is coming to its end here and now. Detective." She touched Mason on the arm as she passed him.

He put his arm around my shoulder, holding me close and looking like he really was my date. "Your grandmother showed up at the right time."

"She has a special knack for knowing when she's needed. Although she has a lot of explaining to do," I complained.

Once we were outside of the tent, Mason slowed down. "Listen, I have an idea that might be really crazy but I think it will help in the long run. Your presence tends to upset everyone in the wedding party except your cousin."

"Actually, something's gotten under her skin ever since she saw Nana was here. I think there's more to today than she's let on so far," I said.

Clementine's surprise at my grandmother's presence and the change in plans at the end of the ceremony could be chalked up to normal wedding day jitters and wanting things to be perfect. But I couldn't shake the idea that maybe there was more hiding underneath her surface than a newfound ability to stand on her own two feet.

We arrived at the back door to the kitchen, and Mason pulled me to the side and out of the way of a server. "I think you should take the lead when we get in there. Your prior involvement with the Hawthornes might be enough to throw them off balance."

"But I'm not sure which one is the guilty party. Is it Hollis? Tucker?" The only thing I had to go on was my gut instinct and the token.

Mason placed both hands on my shoulders. "This isn't your first time facing murder suspects. Talk it all through like you do, and I'll bet you'll figure it out. I'll be there to jump in when I need to as will your grandmother. You can do this, Charli."

I nodded, not quite sure I believed him.

He tipped my chin up to face him. "We can do this together."

The two of us avoided the commotion in the kitchen, and walked through to the parlor. Tucker and Clementine sat in the middle of the settee, holding onto each other. Clarice occupied a nearby chair as did my quiet uncle, but Aunt Nora paced in front of the newlyweds, scowling. Hollis stared out the window with his back to the rest. Shelby stood off to the side apart from the wedding group, her wide eyes watching everyone else.

"Good, you're here," Nana said. "Now we can talk freely."

"I don't feel so free. What's this all about?" demanded Aunt Nora.

Mason whispered in my grandmother's ear, and she smiled. With a tip of her head, she gave me the floor.

I cleared my throat with a cough. "It's about murder, Aunt Nora."

She scoffed with dramatic emphasis. "Not this again. They arrested the one responsible for the chef's death. That green-haired fairy."

"No, the wardens took in the person set up to look like they killed Duke." I noticed Shelby wince when I mentioned his name. "A little planted evidence helped, but it wasn't meant to be a permanent solution." My words sounded more assured than I felt.

"Since when did you become a member of the local wardens?" asked Clarice. "How are you involved?"

I recalled seeing my name written in Duke's book. Mason had warned me that someone in the room had given him my name and information about my talents as payment. All doubts and hesitation vanished with the sudden rush of anger.

"Everything about this case has revolved around what Duke actually did for a living." I tipped my head to Shelby.

"He wasn't a chef, he was a thief. One that stole precious information and used it to his benefit."

Tucker stiffened next to his new bride. She placed a protective arm around him and whispered something in his ear, causing him to relax a bit and lean on her for support.

"So you've discovered a possible motive for why someone might kill him. Great. What does that have to do with any of us?" Clarice pushed.

With careful eyes, I examined her face, looking for any ounce of deception. Her sincere annoyance and concern told me she had no idea how deep in trouble her son had been. Hollis glanced at his wife, but said nothing.

"There were names written in this book that Duke used to extort people to gain what he wanted. Money. Power. More useful data. He had a formidable weapon in all the information he gathered to provide him the life he desired and to ruin the lives of others." I took a step closer to the newlyweds, looking down on them. "You were trying to tell me how you were listed in there, weren't you, Tucker?"

Aunt Nora tried to block my way. "I don't know what nonsense you're talking about with this book, but you should leave these two alone. I knew it would end in disaster if you were involved in the wedding."

"Let her talk, Leonora," insisted Nana.

My uncle got up and put his arms around my aunt, pulling her away. Her ignorance to Duke's collection of information ruled her out from being the one who'd given him my name. It seemed that someone managed to keep the two mothers in the dark, but the sudden shadow of concern over my cousin's face alerted me. Instead of reacting with stunned surprise, Clementine clung to her new husband with fearful protectiveness.

"Tucker, I think you need to finally explain the whole truth. Tell me, what did Duke have on you?" I implored.

The new groom looked up at me, fear and apprehension clouding his eyes. "I...I..."

"Don't say a word, Tucker," interrupted his father. Hollis turned away from the window. "Unless you have concrete proof of connection between my son and the deceased, I suggest that you stop this harassment now. But you don't, do you?"

He didn't ask the question if we had the evidence. The way he said it made it sound like he knew that the wardens didn't have any proof.

Mason spoke up. "It's not so much what the book had in it but what specifically was taken out of it. What's missing."

Hollis met the detective's gaze with a slight grin. "Exactly."

Tired of the game, I loosened the fingers on my right-hand glove and yanked the delicate fabric off. "You want proof? Here." Getting down on my knees in front of Tucker, I took his hand in mine.

Voices around me erupted in protest, but I shut them out. The exhausted groom didn't pull out of my grasp, and his eyes almost pleaded with me to get things over with.

Gathering my energy, I cast a spell to focus my magic.

"Something precious once was lost as payment at too high a cost. My theory and truth together bind, the rightful owner help me find."

Unpracticed, I concentrated the spell on the token still sitting in the palm of my left hand and waited for the thread of connection to form between Tucker and me. Nothing. I repeated the focusing spell again in a whisper, squeezing his hand in mine. No zing, no energy, and no connection to the token manifested.

"What do you think you are doin', missy?" Aunt Nora yanked my arm hard enough that I fell backwards.

Ignoring her ranting voice, I squeezed Tucker's hand and spoke in a low voice directed at him. "You've been trying to tell me all along. You were angry with Duke. He had something on you and kept using it as a weapon."

Clementine scooted forward, trying to listen in. Feeling bad for her, I kept my suspicions of what the dead man had on Tucker and pinpointed on the results of the blackmail.

"You paid him off, but he wanted more, didn't he?" I pressed.

The new groom nodded. "He wouldn't leave me be. Even threatened those near me." He kissed the back of his bride's hand. "It was my responsibility. I couldn't let him hurt anyone else but me."

"You tried to play poker with him," I led him. "You're a good card player, or at least you are when you're not stumbling drunk. And maybe you could have won enough hands to get him to back off if he weren't a cheat and a liar. Someone who didn't live up to the bargains he made."

Tucker lost his composure, and he crumpled in his seat. "He was never going to stop or leave me alone."

"So you followed him outside of Lucky's and into the old diner." I leaned closer. "You had to make him understand, didn't you? And instead of agreeing to back off, he promised you more pain."

Tucker squeezed his eyes shut. "I don't know. I don't remember."

His lack of memory wasn't enough to back me off. Not when I was pretty sure he had sold me out to Duke. "The two of you had already gotten physical that night. You needed to find a way to take care of him. Make sure he didn't keep coming back again and again, demanding more from you."

Tucker opened his eyes wide, a wild desperation reflecting in them. "I paid him. He was supposed to back off. What was I supposed to do?"

Grasping his arm, I yanked him to me, almost pulling him off the settee. "And what did you do when money wasn't enough? Did you pay him with information?"

Tucker gasped, realizing I knew his big betrayal. "I'm sorry, Charli. I am so sorry." The tears fell and he sobbed hard. Clementine clasped him to her, letting him fall apart in her arms.

"That's enough," insisted Hollis, moving closer to his son.

Mason crouched down next to me. "You okay?"

I didn't have an immediate answer to his question. To think that my former fiancé may have used me to protect himself was one thing. To have it confirmed shook me to my core. Once upon a time, he was the one I had chosen to be with. Tucker's treachery cut deeper than I expected, and it took me a moment to gather my wits.

Letting his question go unanswered, Mason stood up and offered me his hand. I took it, rising and moving away so I didn't have to look at the couple. It took several deep breaths and a few reassuring words from Nana for me to keep it together.

Hollis attempted to comfort his son, but Tucker shrugged off his touch. Clearing his throat, he addressed Mason. "What is the point of all of this? You have the guilty party in custody. Why are you accosting my son?"

"Because he's the one who swung the cast iron skillet, Mr. Hawthorne," I explained. "Before you arrived at the warden station, Tucker tried to tell me what he remembered. He's been trying to live with the idea that he took someone's life and not been too successful at it. His lack of memory is a blessing and a curse to him. Only you have the ability to set him free."

Hollis' eyes darted around the room. "I don't know what you mean."

I plucked each finger of my left glove. "Tucker wasn't the only one affected by Duke. You were involved, too, although you tried to keep that a secret. In a desperate attempt to get him to back off, you gave the man something of high value. Something priceless." With a slow yank, I pulled off the glove and showed him the token.

A bright blush rose in Hollis' face, pinking his pale complexion. "I don't know what that is."

I pointed at his son. "Then Detective Clairmont should consider that Tucker acted on his own and arrest him now for the murder of Duke Aikens. At least then your son will have a definitive answer. Did he or did he not kill the man?"

"You can't arrest him." Hollis stood in front of his son.

Mason glanced back at me. Technically, I didn't think he had enough to make an arrest stick, but we needed to flush out the truth. If it took a little lie, then maybe the ends justified the means.

"Why not?" I challenged. "Tucker remembers holding something heavy in his hand, and he told me as much when he talked to me at the station."

Hollis shook his head. "That's inadmissible."

I took a step closer to him. "I think he remembers more than he says. Like how he hit Duke over the head with the skillet. And that Sassy came to the old diner, interrupting him. How else would he know to put the evidence in her locker at the cafe?"

"Maybe I did do it, Father." Tucker held onto Clementine but looked to his dad for help.

"Keep your mouth shut, son."

One more slow step closed the gap between Hollis and me. "Or maybe Tucker had help. Perhaps the two of you planned all this together. After all, a disgraced son brings dishonor to your entire family." I sneered at him.

"Don't you dare. I love my son. I would do anything for him." Hollis raised his hand to strike me.

Anticipating his reaction, I caught his wrist and held on. My spell with the token worked, and an immediate connection of energy thrummed through my arm and into my core.

Excited that my talents worked and to have confirmation, I let Mason know. "It belongs to him."

"Dad?" questioned Tucker.

Hollis yanked his wrist away from me. He glanced at his son with great angst in his eyes. "I'm sorry. I should have told you."

"Told us what?" insisted Mason.

Standing up straighter in front of all of us, the head of one of the founding families and a member of the town council put on the mantle of pride and spoke. "I will tell you everything, but if I do, there will be no charges leveled against my son." He looked to my grandmother for assurance.

"You are in no position to bargain, Hollis," she reminded him.

The father turned to Mason and put out his wrists. "I'm the one. I killed Duke. Take me, but leave my son alone."

Chapter Twenty-Five

Mason asked for Hollis to explain himself, directing him to sit down in the nearby chair.

The husk of a man collapsed into it. He pointed at me. "Your talents have developed nicely. I didn't know that you could link an object to its rightful owner."

Hollis didn't need to know it was a recent development. "Well, I can."

"Hold the token up," he requested, waiting for me to comply. "The back of it says *Non ducor, duco*. It translates as *I am not led, I lead*. In this matter, I am taking the lead."

"I don't understand." Tucker sat on the edge of the settee.

Hollis held up his hand to stop his son from saying anything else. "You got a lot of things right with very little to go on. I underestimated you, Detective."

"It wasn't all me." Mason flashed me a quick glance.

Comprehending our connection, Hollis nodded. "Of course. Even when you're pressured not to be involved, you couldn't help it." He nodded at the newlyweds. "I guess when it involves people you care about, you'll do just about anything."

Mason took out his notebook and pencil. "And what did you do?"

Hollis sighed. "Tucker hid his troubles from me for a while, but when money started disappearing from his personal account, I did some digging. Our bank backed his development business, so I had access to the old H&S Holdings account in Charleston."

It took me a second to realize the initials of the account stood for Hawthorne and Sharpe.

"You knew?" Tucker asked. "Why didn't you tell me?"

"Because I thought, like you, that I could work things out with Duke. At first, he seemed placated when I offered him more money. But then he wanted more from me, enough that it would get noticed by others." Hollis stopped, taking a moment to think about his next statement.

Nana pulled up an old wooden seat next to him. "So you traded information about our town. Something that would be valuable to Duke in many ways. Something he could sell to interested parties."

Hollis pursed his lips together and nodded. "I didn't mean for it to cause problems. What would anyone want with our small town anyway?"

"You are a founding family member. You know our history,

Hollis." Nana grasped his hand. "We wield great protective magic here and harbor many supernatural beings. Some who may be considered valuable." She reached out her hand to me and I grasped it, assuring her I was still here and not going anywhere.

"I know," whispered Hollis. "I didn't mean for it to go as far as it did."

Nana released his hand. "But you aren't completely innocent in all this. They offered you something for your cooperation, didn't they?"

The pitiful man hung his head. "I think you already know the answer to that."

"I can understand you wanting to protect your son, but to sell out your town, and for what? A flimsy promise of power once Charleston took over? Hollis," Nana stood and moved away, too upset to continue.

"You tried to destroy Honeysuckle?" asked Tucker in a low voice.

"I'm not proud of that part of this, son," admitted Hollis. "But I did try to buy my way out. Traded something of great worth and tried to get it all back."

I held up the token. "With this."

He nodded. "It's been passed down for generations. It should have gone to Tucker on his wedding day." Hollis swallowed. "Today."

"But you gave it to Duke to get him to stop everything. When did you know it wouldn't work?" I asked.

"When he showed up in town," Hollis said. "He liked

Honeysuckle. Confirmed that you lived here. Thought he might find other valuable...others like you that might be worth something. So he demanded I set him up with the restaurant as a legitimate front."

Mason's jaw ticked with tension. "Did it ever occur to you to tell the wardens? If you had let someone know, we might have been able to help you."

Tucker spoke up for his father. "Duke had a way of making it clear that if any legal authority was notified, bad things would happen." He looked down at his fingers entwined with Clementine's. "After a few things I'd witnessed, I believed him."

Needing to keep the conversation flowing, I pushed with another question. "What about the night of the murder? Am I right that you saw Tucker hit Duke over the head?"

Hollis nodded. "I went out that night to find Tucker. I knew he'd been getting worse and worse. I was going to bring him back to the house here and dry him out and try to make a plan to get us out of the mess. But I heard him arguing with Duke and followed them to the old diner. Things escalated quickly, and I watched Tucker swing that heavy cast iron skillet and hit Duke over the head.

"I managed to get Tucker out of there. He was so drunk, he didn't remember me helping him out the door. I checked on Duke, not knowing what I was thinking." Hollis stared into the distance. "When he opened his eyes and I knew he wasn't dead, at first I was relieved because Tucker didn't kill him. But then he laughed at me. Laughed at our family. Our town. Said we were insignificant, and that he would destroy us all and enjoy it."

The weight of what was coming next hung in the air. I held my breath in anticipation, and the silence pressed in on us.

"It was an act of defense. Instinctual. I didn't even think about it. One moment, he was laughing at me and the next, I took away his air. It was a simple spell that required nothing but my will," Hollis confessed.

I had mistaken his poor appearance as concern for his son. The talk I'd had with the spell class came back to me, and I realized I was witnessing a clear example of the consequences of our spells, our actions, and our choices. Tucker's father may have had reasons, but he chose to take another person's life with magic, and he had been paying for that ever since.

Tucker got up from his seat. "I can't hear anymore of this." He helped Clementine stand and looked back at his father. "You should have talked to me."

"I know," admitted Hollis. "I'm sorry."

A tear ran down Tucker's cheek. "Me, too." He turned his back on his father and left the room.

I checked with Mason, who shook his head. "He won't go far."

Someone pounded on the front door, and Nana went to answer it. After a quick conversation in the foyer that I couldn't quite understand, Big Willie followed my grandmother into the parlor.

"I guess there's a lot goin' on today, what with a weddin'

and an arrest." The sasquatch took off his hat and scratched his head. "Y'all remember Deputy Inspector Pine from the W.O.W."

The deputy had been one of the officials sent to Honeysuckle after I took down Damien. I remembered I preferred his boss over him, but it didn't surprise me that the bigger organization was getting involved.

"Miss Charli, it's good to see you doing so well," he directed at me, surveying the room. "I'm here to take Hollis Hawthorne in."

Mason frowned. "On what grounds? He should be held here in Honeysuckle. I haven't even made the formal arrest."

"Good," said Deputy Inspector Pine. "Less paperwork to deal with. Hollis Hawthorne, I arrest you under the authority of the World Organization of Wardens. You will be taken to one of our facilities where you will be prosecuted for your crimes."

"*Aspetta*, Deputy," a high-pitched voice with a lilting accent called out. Agent Giacinta appeared behind Big Willie. "You are not the only one who wishes to discuss his dealings with the deceased. I was sent here to investigate, and my agency takes precedence over yours." Her wings quivered, and a lilac-colored dust floated down.

Mason approached his boss. "Sheriff, the murder happened in Honeysuckle. Surely, we aren't going to ship him off to wherever they wish to take him."

"It's out of my hands, Detective." Big Willie held up his

fur-covered mitts. "They'll have to fight it out amongst themselves, but Hollis will be leaving Honeysuckle."

"When?" I asked.

"Immediately," answered Deputy Inspector Pine.

Agent Giacinta crossed her arms. "With me. I also will need to speak to his son as well."

"I'm taking custody of him," countered the inspector.

"Hold on," I said, stopping the two from arguing. "How important is it for anyone to leave right this second?"

"I am not sure of what you are meaning, Charli," said Agent Giacinta.

Against my better judgment, I couldn't help feeling sorry for Hollis. His actions were deplorable, but in the long run, everything he'd done was to protect his family. And eventually, he tried to protect our town. I asked for everyone to wait a second and went and fetched the rest of the family members from the kitchen.

They filed in, and Clarice went to her husband's side. Tucker must have told her what had happened. He and Clementine stood together, holding onto each other.

"This is his son's wedding day," I explained. "If we can ensure that he won't go anywhere, perhaps we can allow the entire wedding party a chance to celebrate the day, even for a short while. It won't change the outcome."

Deputy Inspector Pine frowned. "I've already made arrangements—"

"I see no problem giving them a small amount of time to celebrate together," offered Agent Giacinta, holding up her chin in defiance of the inspector. "But no one will be able to leave the premises."

"We can assist you in that," said Big Willie. "My people can watch the perimeter for you."

"What will everyone say?" asked Clarice.

Aunt Nora stayed unusually quiet but nodded her agreement with her new in-law.

Nana joined in. "They will think that after whatever happened in here, y'all came back down and finished the celebration. You can eat the food, cut the cake, and maybe get in one dance. What happens tomorrow can't be helped, but we can assist you in salvaging the rest of today. And that's the best you're goin' to get from the entire situation."

Clementine took a step forward, still holding onto Tucker. "I have something to say. I'm very sorry for everything that has happened, but I would like to have my father-in-law with us for as long as possible. What he did, he did so Tucker and I could have a future."

"The bride has made her decision," I said, nodding my approval at my cousin. "Y'all can head back down, and I'll inform the cook to start sending food to be served."

Nana ushered the group out the door and Big Willie spoke to Mason and Zeke, making plans with the inspector and the fairy agent.

Before she left, Agent Giacinta fluttered over and kissed me on both cheeks. "It is so good to see you again, Charli. I wish it were under better circumstances."

"Me, too." I flashed her a quick smile. "Will you be arresting Tucker as well?"

She shook her head. "From what I understand of the situation, any of his actions can be taken care of with the local authorities. However, he can add to the information that we have been extracting from the unpleasant woman already in warden custody here."

"Tara?" I asked.

"*Sì*, she is not so nice." The fairy screwed up her pretty face. "I will need to interview her half-sister and Tucker to get a better picture of the underground dealings of this Duke Aikens. And then Mr. Hawthorne will need to answer for his crime. My agency will have to work with the inspector's to determine his outcome." She kissed me on both cheeks again and flew away.

Mason waited behind the others. He pulled me aside. "You surprised me, sticking up for the newlyweds. Especially after you confirmed Tucker was the one who sold you out."

I would not get over my ex's betrayal anytime soon. However, I couldn't help feeling pity for him, even though his actions had backed him into the corner he'd found himself in. Responsibility and accountability. I had tried to teach that to the students in such a short time, but I guessed it was a lesson we had to keep learning throughout our lives.

"I think he'll pay a pretty steep price for his actions," I said. "But things will definitely be different between us from here on out."

The entire political power structure in Honeysuckle

Hollow would be blown to pieces in one fell swoop. With Hollis being taken away, the vacancy for his seat on the council should go to the next in line—Tucker. Assuming that he didn't get arrested as well, he would take on a seat of power way earlier than anticipated. And my cousin would have great influence over two of the council members. Her children would be eligible for either council seat in the future.

"Frosted fairy wings," I exclaimed, putting all the pieces together.

"What?" asked Mason.

I shook my head, not wanting to give more credence to the questions bubbling to the surface. "Nothing."

The two of us went through the kitchen and talked briefly with Shelby. The half-banshee couldn't hide her relief that the case was over. She didn't mind having to talk to the agent about Duke, and hoped it meant that she could start living her life for herself.

On our way down to the tent, Mason stopped me before I walked in. "I guess I'm on duty now."

"As a warden or as my date?" I teased.

He bumped me with his hip. "If I have my way, both. If I can, I'll try to sneak in a dance with you." He winked at me and walked over to talk to Zeke.

No more storm clouds filled the sky. Bright reds and pinks painted the leftover wisps against the darkening backdrop. At the end of a disrupting tempest came such beauty. I wondered if Honeysuckle would recover from tonight's outcome while I watched Tucker and Clementine bond together, stronger than ever in front of everyone. Hollis held onto Clarice, watching his son with love and regret.

Unable to join in and act like nothing had happened, I stayed on the periphery of the tent. Nana joined me, putting her arms around me. "I'm proud of you, Birdy."

"I didn't do anything other than ruin their day," I replied.

"Their days haven't been good for a while. Look at their faces," my grandmother directed.

I did as I was told, and found the young couple focused on each other, pure joy lighting them up.

"See? The not knowing was eating them both up. Now that they know, they can move on." She joined in the clapping when everyone tapped their crystal glasses to get the couple to kiss.

I leaned in closer to her. "Have you thought about what their moving on will mean to the town council and the balance of power?"

"One step at a time, child. That's a problem for tomorrow. Tonight, try to enjoy what you helped make happen." She squeezed my hand and left me standing at the back.

I knew she meant for me to appreciate that Tucker and Clementine might have a few moments of happiness before the worst happened. But my own enjoyment would be marred by the knowledge that I was instrumental in bringing out the truth.

In all of the fuss, I'd forgotten that I still held the token tight in my left hand. Opening up my fingers, I flipped it over and over in my hand. "*I am not led, I lead*," I said out loud.

I made a quick decision to hold onto this one piece of evidence to hand over to Mason. Maybe we could ensure that it would get passed on to Tucker, and in doing so, maybe he would make better choices than his father on what type of leader he might want to be. Out of the chaos, maybe the future could hold more promise.

Epilogue

I fought my way through pink balloons, pink streamers, pink banners, and pink glitter falling out of the air at Sweet Tooths. Gossamer managed to cover every single surface in the immediate area with her signature color.

My diminutive friend had given birth to two healthy babies, one girl with a cute button nose like her father and a boy who had the beginning nubs of wings on his back. It was hard to tell them apart since Goss dressed them in the same color she loved. I cooed appropriately over the tiny pair, too afraid I might break them if I touched them.

TJ waddled up to me, holding a pink cup with bright rosy liquid in it. She rubbed her belly and sipped. "Tell me how she turned the sweet tea pink? When our baby gets here, I might just send her over to Goss."

I kissed my sister-in-law's cheek. "I'll bet our fairy friend will bestow upon you gifts galore for Junior."

TJ bumped me with her expanded rump. "I'm making no promises with the name. We were thinking maybe something having to do with sunshine in honor of your mom."

Sadness and happiness swirled in my heart. "That sounds like a beautiful idea. But this little one will always be Junior to me." I patted TJ's tummy.

Mason smiled from across the room, and my sister-in-law clinked her paper cup against mine. "I think you may have to save the Junior for yourself someday."

I hotfooted my way out of that conversation. The detective and I were nowhere near even having a discussion of what we might be to each other. For now, we spent most of our time talking and getting to know each other without walls being erected on either side. We made a great team, but mixing personal with business might not work, and I wasn't ready to choose between the two with him.

Nana brought me a slice of red velvet cake. "And this one won't blow up," she joked.

I gave her my best imitation of her own glaring stare. "I told you, it wasn't me. Although I'm sure Aunt Nora and Clarice will blame me for it anyway. Those two may never forgive me despite how much I tried to save the wedding reception."

"And yet, you seem to have made some headway with your cousin. Rayline would have liked that. So would your father." Nana rubbed my back.

"I know. Although…" I trailed off, not wanting to ruin the overall good mood with my lingering suspicions.

"If you're having thoughts that perhaps the little lady knew more than she let on, you're not the only one," confirmed my grandmother.

I breathed out a sigh of relief. "I don't want to think ill of her, not after we've finally made some sort of progress."

Nana took a bite of my cake. "You work on your relationship. Leave the worrying and watching to me."

"You're gonna have a huge struggle on your hands to keep the high seat on the council. The scales of power will definitely tip their way," I warned.

My grandmother pinched my cheek and smoothed out the worry lines between my eyebrows. "Tonight's celebration is too special for you to be this concerned. Try to enjoy it."

"I will," I promised. Before she walked away, I grasped her arm. "Okay, it's killin' me. What did the Gray sisters tell you about me?"

She stopped chewing. "You sure you want to know?"

"Yes. No." I thought about it. "Yes, with everything that's happening tonight, I think I do want to know."

Nana shrugged. "Okay. This is what they said. You were going to have to suffer a storm, a fire, and darkness. If you made it through all that, then you would find your heart's desire."

I stared at her. "That's it? That could mean anything. And did they mean a literal storm, because we just had one."

Nana tweaked my nose. "I don't know, Birdy. That's the

thing about prophecies and premonitions. They can mean practically anything."

"You shouldn't have gone to them," I scolded.

She furrowed her brow. "They have their purpose."

Nana hadn't filled me in completely about what she'd done when she was gone from Honeysuckle. I got the feeling she had gathered a few very powerful acquaintances together to figure things out, but she kept what happened to herself. For now, I trusted her decision. But I had absolutely no faith in the weird sisters' prediction. It gave me the willies, and I wished I hadn't asked about it.

My friends gathered around me, joking and talking in their loud fashion. The normalcy of the chaos comforted me, and I listened with grateful ears.

Lee held up his spell phone. "Y'all, check this out." He stuck out his tongue and typed something in with his thumbs.

Ben's phone buzzed, and he flipped it open. The device sizzled, and a pimple popped out on the end of the advocate's nose. "Holy unicorn horn!"

"Ha," snorted Lee. "That'll get you back for the prank wars you ran back in the day. That Mosely kid taught me how to send a hex through texting. Someday, I'm gonna hire him. We're already putting this through development and seeing if it's something we can market. He told me they call it *hexting*."

"I think I'm done with spells and magic for a while," I declared. "So you better not be *hexting* me anytime soon."

"You can't be finished with magic all together," protested

Blythe. "I heard you made one heck of a teacher for the spell permit course."

I saw a few of my students laughing together and smiled. They caught me looking at them and waved back. Helen rummaged in her purse and pulled out her permit, pointing to it and mouthing a thank you.

"Yeah, I'll admit it was kind of fun, although I don't know how many of their parents were happy I used prank spells to teach them." Every single one of the kids had passed their test, so maybe their parents could give me a break.

"I think you might have a future as a teacher," suggested Alison Kate.

"If she has the time," Lily said. "She's gonna be pretty busy from here on out."

I blushed under all the attention being thrown at me. My girlfriends gave me hugs and uttered reassurances.

Completely unaware, Lee pushed his way into our small group. "Ooh, hey. Have y'all heard that we've got a celebrity movin' to Honeysuckle?"

"Who?" asked Lavender.

Lee beamed at all of us. "The Mud Dobber has bought a house here."

I looked around at my friends, and all of us shook our heads at each other. "Who is this Mud person?"

Lee pushed his glasses up his nose and rolled his eyes. "Billy Ray Dobber. The Mud Dobber. Come on, you've never heard of him? He's only one of the most legendary broom racers there's ever been. And he's retiring right here in our small town."

"Okay. Cool." I tried to fake enthusiasm.

Lee sighed. "Fine. I'll be the excited one. I'm working on perfecting more brooms and their flying power. Maybe I can spellcast one he'd like to ride."

"As if you aren't already busy enough with your new business and your upcoming wedding, whenever that will be," I teased.

Alison Kate kissed him on the cheek. "I like it when he gets all inspired. He usually comes home to me and—"

"Say no more," I stopped her. "I think I get the picture."

"Did you like flying on a broom?" Lee asked.

"It was okay." My personal struggle to stay afloat on the trainer didn't bode well for my abilities to go very fast. "It's gonna take some practice."

"I think you should stick to riding with someone who's experienced," Mason uttered from behind me.

I leaned my body into his in acknowledgment. "That might be fun from time to time. But I think solo, I'll stick to two wheels on the ground."

"That reminds me." Lee snapped his fingers together. "I finally heard from Dash. He said he should be headin' back soon and has found all the parts needed to fix up Ol' Joe." My friend yelped in pain when Alison Kate stepped on his foot.

Mason's body stiffened at the mention of the wolf shifter. So much change in such a little time would mean that Dash would be returning to a completely different playing field, and

I was no longer sure I wanted to be a player on it. I liked a man who stayed and didn't run away. Who stood beside me to weather the storm.

Henry interrupted our conversation, and I almost kissed the older man in gratitude. "Y'all stop your jawin' and come out here already. It's time." He beckoned everyone outside onto the sidewalk.

I made my way to the front of the crowd and stood next to my brother. "Are you still sure this is a good idea?" I asked.

"I wouldn't be giving you the discount of free rent if I didn't believe in you, Birdy." He ruffled my hair.

I slapped his hand away. "Don't call me that."

Nana joined us. "You two behave."

"Well, get on with it," grumbled Henry, winking at me.

My grandmother pushed me out in front, and I turned to face everyone. "I guess I should have prepared something to say." I swallowed hard. "Never in my wildest dreams did I think something like this was possible. But because all of you believed in me, I get to do something really special right now."

I looked out at all the faces, waiting for me to take the lead. Turning back around, I faced my future. With a wave of my hand and a flourish of my fingers, the big red bow hanging on the front window of the store unfurled and fell to the ground. Gold letters were etched on the glass. Painted sunflowers flanked the name of the business, *Lost & Found*, and underneath in smaller gold letters, it read:

Charli Goodwin
Tracking Services

"I guess I'm officially open for business," I declared, and a loud cheer erupted from my friends.

I got passed from person to person, receiving hugs and offers of congratulations. In all the world, I didn't think anyone else was so rich in support as I was in that moment.

"Yeah, yeah, hugs later. First, get in there, boss." Henry directed me to walk inside.

The elder gentleman and I talked about his ideas of how the business might be structured and run. He really did have a good head for it all, and it didn't take me long to realize I needed him. Henry surprised me when he negotiated his position as my assistant with absolutely no pay until my business was in the black.

I walked into the small space, which had been painted a seafoam green. Ms. Patty Lou had donated a couple of her personal watercolor paintings to hang on the walls. A desk that Henry would use sat right up front, and I had one a little further in the back. It would take me a while to figure everything out, but taking chances was better than being afraid.

Everyone crowded in and out of the small space, oohing and ahhing over my huge achievement. Henry did a good job making sure nobody touched anything they shouldn't and shooing them away when they spent too much time. After a while, he pushed everyone out, leaving me inside with Nana, Matt, and TJ.

My grandmother handed me a wrapped present. "Here. This is from all of us."

Excited and embarrassed, I set it down on my desk and ripped open the paper. Pulling the box lid off, I gasped at its content.

"It's my favorite picture," I uttered. Pulling out the beautiful frame, I held it up with absolute admiration.

Mom and Dad sat on Nana's porch with Matt and I sitting on the step in front of them. Someone must have said something silly, because all four of us were laughing with abandonment. Nana had captured that moment, and a faded version of the picture hung in her house.

"You know they're here with us right now," my grandmother said, wiping a tear from my cheek.

"I know," I whispered. I held out my hand to my brother, and when he took it, I squeezed three times.

"Me, too, Birdy." He squeezed me back.

"Ooh, I think Junior wants to get in on the action." TJ clutched her belly.

I touched her stomach and rubbed a circle over the moving mass three times. "Love you, too, kiddo." One of her tiny limbs stretched and pressed against my hand. "I swear, my niece just high-fived me."

Henry opened the door. "If y'all are done being all sentimental and stuff, Steve's invited everyone over to the

Harvest Moon. He says he made those barbecue thingies you liked so much since that Shelby gave him the recipe. You better get a move on or I'm gonna eat them all," he threatened.

We followed him outside. Nana shook her head at the crotchety old guy. "You sure he's the right choice for your assistant?"

"He'll be fine," I assured her. "The worst that could happen is that he literally drags people in to bring me business."

"And he might do that," Matt said, pointing at the man pushing Ben into the cafe.

Mason waited off to the side, leaning against the brick of the building, and I told my family to save me a couple of the barbecue bites. Walking up to him, my stomach flipped when he smiled at me.

"I didn't want to take you away from them," he said.

"And yet you're standin' out here instead of with everyone else," I noticed. "Why?"

He nodded his head at my logo on the window. "You're putting yourself out there. Do you think that's safe?"

I'd already spent hours and nights of contemplation about whether or not to put my information on the window for anyone to see. Damien had scared me into thinking someone might come after me. Knowing Duke had the information and having no clue what had been done with it was also daunting.

"I'm tired of being afraid. I'm not gonna hide who I am or run away from it. This is me, embracing everything about me, and it feels fantastic." I opened my arms wide. "If someone's gonna come after me, then I'll fight them off."

"They'll have to go through me first," growled Mason, stepping closer.

I placed my hand on his chest. "Thank you for that. And thank you for standing with me."

He took one of my hands in his and lifted it to his mouth. Resting his lips on my skin, he gave me a quick kiss. His eyes lifted to mine. "Always."

I swallowed hard, not sure what should happen next. The laughter and voices from across the street called out to us. "We should go."

He offered me his arm, but I told him to go without me. I needed to turn off the lights inside the office. Inside *my* office. Dipping his head once, he winked and sauntered across to the cafe.

I walked into the room and took a long gander at the space. It might be small in size, but my future inside of it would be limitless if I allowed it to be. I picked up the picture of my family and gazed at it. The little girl in the photo hadn't gone through everything I had yet. She had no idea how lucky she was that she'd found a family that loved her hard. I would honor that little girl and my family by living to the absolute fullest.

Flipping off the lights and locking the door, I walked toward the sound of those who would help me do both.

DEAR READER -

Thanks so much for reading *Sweet Tea & Spells*. If you enjoyed the book (as much as I did writing it), I hope you'll consider leaving a review!

NEWSLETTER ONLY - If you want to be notified when the next story is released and to get access to exclusive content, sign up for my newsletter! https://www.subscribepage.com/t4v5z6

NEWSLETTER & FREE PREQUEL - to gain exclusive access to the prequel *Chess Pie & Choices*, go here! https://dl.bookfunnel.com/opbg5ghpyb

Southern Charms Cozy Mystery Series

Magic & Mystery are only part of the Southern Charms of Honeysuckle Hollow...

Suggested reading order:

Chess Pie & Choices: A Southern Charms Cozy Prequel

(*Available exclusively to Newsletter Subscribers*)

Charli Goodwin is engaged to Tucker Hawthorne, the admired "prince" of Honeysuckle Hollow. Underneath the perfect surface of their union boils an ocean of doubt. If he's such a catch, then why does she feel like she's on the hook?

When Charli's magical talents are put to the test to find something valuable to Tucker's family, she's set on a path that will test her love and show her where her true *happy ever after* may be.

Moonshine & Magic: A Southern Charms Cozy Mystery Book 1

Charli Goodwin doesn't expect her homecoming to go without a hitch—after all, she skipped town, leaving her fiancé and family without a clue as to where she was going or why. Now that she's ready to return home, she plans to lay low and sip some of her Nana's sweet tea while the town gossips come out to play.

Unfortunately, on her first night back, Charli discovers the body of her crazy great uncle (hey, everyone has one). She suddenly finds herself at the center of a mystery that threatens the very foundations of Honeysuckle Hollow and the safety of every paranormal citizen in it—starting with Charlie herself.

With the clock ticking, will Charli's special magical talents be enough to save not only the town but her own life?

Lemonade & Love Potions (a short formerly included in the anthology Hexes & Ohs)

Charli Goodwin can't help herself when it comes to helping out her friends, especially a failed cupid trying to earn his way back into the matchmaking ranks. A singles mingle in her small Southern town should be the perfect event, but trouble with a capital T shows up when someone attempts to boost the odds of love in their favor.

Sweet honeysuckle iced tea, it's gonna take more than lemonade and a little magic to help Charli find out what's wrong, solve the mystery, and save Honeysuckle Hollow from disaster again.

Fried Chicken & Fangs: A Southern Charms Cozy Mystery Book 2

An upcoming election shakes up Honeysuckle. When an outspoken resident who opposes the changes to the magical small Southern town turns up dead, it's up to Charli Goodwin and her special talents to get on the case...except her valuable magic doesn't seem to be working.

What starts as a simple search uncovers a darker layer of manipulation and sabotage. Will Charli be able to figure out who is pulling the strings before the foundations of the town are destroyed?

Sweet Tea & Spells: A Southern Charms Cozy Mystery Book 3

With her ex-fiancé's wedding to her cousin on the horizon, Charli Goodwin has to be on her best behavior. But when an outsider infiltrates Honeysuckle, another murder threatens to ruin more than just the future of the upcoming nuptials.

At the same time, wolf shifter Dash Channing is gone and a changed Detective Mason Clairmont makes a new declaration. Will Charli be able to cast her personal feelings aside to break all the rules and help capture the real killer or will more trouble be heading to the small supernatural Southern town?

Barbecue & Brooms: A Southern Charms Cozy Mystery Book 4 (Coming Soon)

Acknowledgments

There are many people I need to thank for helping me get this book out there:

To my reader group, the Southern Charmers - Thank you for being so enthusiastic and wanting more Southern Charms. You've kept me going, knowing you were hungry for the next installment. Your dedication and support helped me write every word.

To my editor, April - This Southern Girl appreciates your Southern expertise, your dedication to making my story the best it can be, and your absolute faith in my writing. Book 3 wouldn't be here without you.

To Melanie Summers - Without your willingness to pick up the phone and talk me through, I wouldn't have a story to write. Thank you for being my friend and my plotting buddy!

To my cheerleading squad of fellow writers - I don't know

what I would do without you pushing me for more words. Many drinks will be bought for you at the Tiki Bar this year in payment!

To my family - You may find your names sprinkled throughout the stories, but it's your love in my life that weaves its way into the words. Thank you.

To my husband - This book will be extra special because of all the support you gave me in writing it. Even when the movers tried to pack me up to send me across the world, you helped me find a space to keep working. Thank you for your belief in me.

About the Author

Bella Falls grew up on the magic of sweet tea, barbecue, and hot and humid Southern days. She met her husband at college over an argument of how to properly pronounce the word *pecan* (for the record, it should be *pea-cawn,* and they taste amazing in a pie). Although she's had the privilege of living all over the States and the world, her heart still beats to the rhythm of the cicadas on a hot summer's evening.

Now, she's taken her love of the South and woven it into a world where magic and mystery aren't the only Charms.

bellafallsbooks.com
contact@bellafallsbooks.com

facebook.com/bellafallsbooks

twitter.com/bellafallsbooks

instagram.com/bellafallsbooks

amazon.com/author/bellafalls

Made in the USA
Lexington, KY
07 September 2018